TO BE THE BEST
Book Two: Rematch

By H. L. Hertel

HH Castle-Mac Publishing
St Louis Park, MN

ISBN: 978-0-9826684-0-5

Published by HH Castle-Mac Publishing, St Louis Park, MN

Dedication

This book is dedicated to my wife, Lisa. She is my one constant best friend and my soul's perfect mate (not to mention, awfully darn cute). She will always be my one true love.

Acknowledgements

I am forever grateful to all of the people and organizations who have contributed to making the *To Be The Best* series a success. I am only saddened by the list being too vast to properly thank everyone.

This second installment in the series has come together thanks to hundreds of hours of work by many people including my two state-champion nephews who took the time to be cover models for their uncle's book. Their parents, Heidi and Brian, not only allowed the boys to be on the cover but also gave me the first "wrestling family" feedback as test readers which led to some strategic alterations.

My test reader corps was incredible as Dr. Darci kept me in line as to medical procedures and terminology, Coach Jeff provided a high school teacher / coach's perspective, Jordan spoke for male high school readers, Dan represented junior high teachers, Bill acted as super-editor, and Kathleen and Mel contributed to the believability and helped me soften the wording.

I also appreciate Janis's suggestion of the title, "Rematch," and Ingram Book Company for ensuring that the book is available wherever readers may look for it.

A long overdue "Thank You" goes out to Mrs. Carney for ensuring that I could write well beginning in Junior High and also for supporting my writing as an adult.

Finally, I have been wonderfully blessed by Lillian, who has given up an incredible amount of Daddy-Daughter time so that I could promote *To Be The Best*, and Lisa who continues to be my greatest partner as she has given feedback before any other test readers get to see it and acted as a "Final Gate" before the completed work reaches the general public.

Thank you all!

Introduction

It was the first read-through of pieces of this book and I paced, waiting for some kind of reaction. Would she like it? Would she hate it?

The love of my life had been such a strong supporter of the first book that I was very curious to get her take on the plot as the characters found themselves having to cope with very different circumstances. I stole an occasional glance at her pretty face but didn't get any hint other than a look of firm concentration. Finally, she looked up. "Wow, this is dark" was her first comment.

Her first impression about sums up the tone set for the second installment of the *To Be The Best* series. The first novel dealt the characters several challenges but, by and large, the high schoolers all came from homes that remind me of my own growing up – stable with two loving parents. With that firmly in place, I turned to the background story of the assistant coach to create a home life that is the antithesis of my own.

Based very loosely on an account from one of my fraternity brothers, Sean MacCallister's background grew mainly from a single comment. When asked why he would choose to go to college half-way across the nation from his home, this particular brother replied, "I chose the school that was farthest away from my father." It's odd how this single phrase could end up developing one of my favorite characters in the series.

The darker aspects make the target audience for this book slightly older than that of the original. The language choices in the prologue would not have been acceptable for book one but, when I tried to tone them down too much, the character seemed inauthentic. Hopefully this won't offend anyone.

Whether you like your books "dark" or prefer something a little more uplifting, I've tried to provide a solid mix in this novel and hope that the twists and turns are enough to keep you guessing as to what will happen next as the boys from Riverside continue their quest to be the best.

Prologue

One final heave. There was nothing left. His dinner, lunch, breakfast, and seemingly everything else he had consumed in the past week were now in the toilet. His stomach hurt and he was jittery, but he felt a bit better.

He reached for the toilet paper, tore off a small piece that someone else may have touched with dirty hands, and threw it into the stool as well. He then tore off a larger piece, wiped the vomit from his lips, threw it into the toilet and flushed.

At least this hospital bathroom was clean. He would hate to think about spending his time kneeling in filth. He left the stall and went to the sink.

"What have you gotten yourself into this time, MacCallister?" he asked the face he saw in the mirror. "What were you thinking?"

As he splashed some water on his face, he momentarily thought about how cold and brisk it felt. Very nice. Then his thoughts returned to the situation at hand. He was going to be a father soon, perhaps within half an hour. But was he really? Veronica had cheated on him once before that he knew of. Was this baby really his? He supposed there was some way that they could test to find out. But, that was a chore for some other day.

Reasonably, it was a chore for a day when he had more money. He didn't know how he was going to pay for food or rent. How was he supposed to pay for some stupid test? He'd have to leave Green Bay, that was for sure. "There goes two years of college, down the drain."

At this point, going back to his little hometown and working in the lumberyard seemed like his best option. "Best option?" Try, "only option." The thought of working for Old Man Schwartz wasn't appealing but it was a lot better than starving. He was a smart guy, he'd find a way to go back to school eventually and then they would be all right.

It had to be all right. He was going to be a father and he would not let his son or daughter go without. As long as Veronica would work with him, they would be a team capable of handling any situation.

The thought of that team made him smile. Having been raised without a father, he knew that his kids would have a leg up. "War took my dad but my kid won't have to go without one," he promised himself. Not only would he be there, but he would be a good dad, hugs in times of celebration and a swift swat when the kid got out of line. That's how he was raised and he turned out all right. Didn't he?

His hand shook a bit as he reached for the door handle. He had been really nervous and irritable for several months now. Or had it been over a year? No time to think about that now. He would be back to feeling like himself in no time, as soon as he finished this transition and was used to being a dad.

Maybe a drink would calm his nerves? He had never been much of a drinker. Mom said that alcoholism ran in his family and he should avoid the stuff. One drink couldn't hurt, could it? Besides, this was something to celebrate. He would allow himself to have one celebratory drink. That would calm him. Wouldn't being calm make everything better?

As he entered the hallway, he thought of what he still had to do. Call their parents after the baby was born. That was a must. He would have to tell them whether it was a boy or a girl. Veronica liked the name Shawna for a girl. He really hated that name but knew that she would end up getting her way if she bore him a daughter. If it were a boy, they would shorten the name. However, he would change the spelling to S-e-a-n. He hoped for a boy. Their family would be Don, Sean, and Veronica. It had a nice ring to it.

He heard a baby crying in the delivery room. His ears perked up and he became tense. The nurse came out.

"Mister MacCallister?" she asked.

All Don could do was nod.

"Would you like to meet your son?"

With tears in his eyes, the young man went to meet Sean. "Sean MacCallister," he thought, that would be his son.

* * *

He drove home with mixed feelings. He was frustrated, very frustrated with this new plastic card. He was supposed to be able to put it in the machine at the bank and get money. All he had to remember was to type in the security code and it was supposed to give him access to his savings account. He knew the code; it was the year his son was born. Was that thirteen years ago already?

It was all right. Hal had let him run a tab this evening. Good old Hal. Don felt happy enough when Hal came through for him that he put a couple extra drinks on the tab for Steve and his scruffy friend. What was Steve's friend's name? Well, it didn't matter. Having had seven shots over the course of happy hour, the man's name could have been the same as Don's own and it wouldn't make a bit of difference.

Seven shots in two hours. Was that a lot? Probably for most people but Don MacCallister could hold his liquor. Besides, it was a night to celebrate. He had turned in his resignation as office manager at that godforsaken lumberyard. After thirteen long years, not counting the time he had worked there in high school, Don would be free of that place and free of the watchful eye of Old Man Schwartz.

Not only that, but he would be free of this town. Between him and Veronica, they had been able to save over $8,000. That, along with the money they were to receive for selling their little shack house would be more than enough to get them started in Milwaukee. The economy wasn't booming but surely there was a good job waiting for a hard-working office manager in the big city. He had a few leads and Veronica would easily be able to get a job waiting tables like she did in their little one-horse town. There were lots of restaurants in the city. He was sure that the patrons would tip much better there than they did at the Club House.

The kids were excited about the possibility of moving too. They were both very bright, just like their old man. For a moment, Don got sad. He had hit Sean hard last night, much harder than he had intended to. He would have to apologize for that. He didn't want to hurt his boy. He just wanted to get the message across that drinking was not appropriate for thirteen-year-olds. He wished he hadn't been drunk when Sean had gotten home last night, but he was and that was not a good time for him to deal with problems. He would watch his temper from now on, but he could not be held accountable for people making him angry when he had been drinking.

Maybe he had eight shots at Hal's tonight. Could it have been eight? It didn't matter. He was feeling good. This was better than he had felt in years. For the first time since before Sean was born, he didn't feel especially jittery. Why did he have to feel so rotten ALL the time? It didn't make sense. Luckily, he was on his way home. Nothing was going to ruin his mood tonight.

Of course, if one of Amy's little boyfriends was over, that might ruin his mood. Well, maybe not. He would just send the little dink home. She was too young to have a boyfriend anyway.

Could it have been nine shots? Surely not. Well, maybe it could have been. There were eleven drinks on the tab, right? One for Steve and one for Steve's friend. What was his name? That would be nine for Don. Was that a lot? Maybe he had bought two shots for Steve? Or maybe Steve's friend had ordered a second one when Don was in the restroom. Scruffy bastard! Don was in the filthy restroom doing his business and that guy was charging drinks to his tab.

Wait a minute. Hal wouldn't let that happen, would he? He had always been good to Don. It is a true friend who lets you charge your drinks when the damn bank machine won't work.

"NOT SUFFICIENT FUNDS, MY ASS!!!" Don yelled out loud. He had over $8,000 in that account. Withdrawing twenty bucks was a mere pittance to him today.

Once he got his big city job, maybe he could buy pads and get Sean into hockey. The boy was a pretty good skater when he was little. He had gotten Veronica's size, poor thing, so he would never be much of a football player like his old man. He was a scrapper, though. With the way he skates, he could play for the Badgers, even if he doesn't weigh two hundred and ten pounds when he graduates, like his old man did.

As he pulled into his driveway, Don had a brief moment of panic. What if he couldn't find a job in Milwaukee? What if the eight thousand wasn't enough to get them started? He parked the car and sat for a minute and a half, slowly letting his breathing stabilize.

"It's going to be ok," he said out loud. "In fact," he thought, "it's going to be great!"

What will make it even greater was his friend in the kitchen cabinet. There was still some left, right? Left … right, he snickered to himself. Left … right, that was funny. Anyway, there had to be some Johnny Walker left. He couldn't have drunk that all last night, could he? Of course not. He would have remembered seeing the bottle when he woke up in his recliner this morning.

His thoughts drifted again as he walked to the door. He had been two hundred and ten pounds when he graduated. Gaining thirty more by age thirty-three wasn't such a bad track record. When a person considered that he spent fifty to sixty hours each week behind a desk, gaining thirty pounds in fifteen years didn't seem like much at all. Especially when one considers that he had driven back and forth to Appleton every weekend for four years to finish his degree, not that anyone appreciated him for it.

How big was Sean? Maybe one hundred pounds? Maybe, but Don would bet that his boy wasn't even that big … which made it especially important that the kid stay away from booze. A thimble-full of the good stuff would knock a kid that size on his ass.

He unlocked the door and entered. It was a great day and it was great to be home for one of the last times in his little shack.

Why didn't it smell like food? Don looked at his watch. 8:00 wasn't so late, it should still smell like dinner, especially as hungry as he was.

He walked into the kitchen and saw his kids. Amy was crying. She ran past him and up the stairs as soon as Don arrived.

"What did you do to her?!!!!" The words came out louder than he expected. Sean braced himself as if he expected to be hit.

What was with the boy? His eyes looked puffy as well.

"Nothing," Sean replied. His hand was trembling and he was holding an envelope.

"What do you have there?" Don was getting impatient. He was hungry and had already had enough frustrations for one day.

The boy held out the envelope with his trembling hand. Don quickly snatched it away. The envelope wasn't sealed. He had a feeling that the kids, and probably Veronica had already seen what was inside. He pulled out the piece of paper and read it.

Don,

By the time you get this note, I will be far away. Do not try to find me as I will not be in the country. I am not coming back.

I tried for too long to be your wife and a good mother but I need to do what is right for me. Divorce papers that I signed in front of a notary today will arrive within the week. I don't want any alimony but have taken the money from our savings account. You can have everything else, including the house. The buyers withdrew their offer last week but I did not want you to know until I was gone.

Do not try to find me. I don't want to be your wife any more. I don't want to be a mother. I just want to find who I once was and be her again. You never even knew the real me. You just knew the shell of the person who was willing to stay with you for far too long.

Goodbye,
Veronica

Don trembled as he crushed the letter in his hand. Sean was crying, apparently not for the first time that night.

"What does it mean, Dad?"

Don was so far beyond angry that he couldn't comprehend the question, much less think of an answer. The money was gone, he was stuck with the shack that he had worked to sell for so long, his wife – the tramp she was – was not only gone but she was no longer his wife. His panic reflex set-in again. His chest was heaving and he started breathing heavily. He needed a drink. He went to the cupboard but his bottle was gone.

"WHERE IS IT?!!!!"

Once again, his voice was much louder than expected.

His boy, if this truly was his son, was standing in the corner. Tears were rolling down his cheeks. He had drunk it, hadn't he?

"Where is what?" the boy asked, still sobbing.

"WHERE IS MY BOTTLE? YOU DRANK IT, DIDN'T YOU, YOU LITTLE BASTARD?!!!"

"I didn't …"

"DON'T LIE TO ME!!!! DID YOUR SISTER HAVE SOME TOO? YOU COULDN'T HAVE DRANK IT ON YOUR OWN, YOU SCRAWNY LITTLE PRICK!!!"

That proved it. This wasn't even his kid. How could a man his size be father to a runt like this. Sean was NOT his son. He was HER son and the son of some other guy she had been with.

"Dad, I didn't …"

How dare he call him "Dad." Don lunged at the boy who quickly ran into the living room.

"AMY, LOCK YOUR DOOR!!!" the boy yelled.

Don MacCallister removed his belt and chased the boy up the stairs, failing to notice the empty bottle of Johnny Walker which sat beside his favorite recliner.

Chapter 1

One final heave. Sean felt weak and more than a little dizzy as he steadied himself in the bathroom stall. Two primary thoughts crossed his mind: He needed a ride home and he needed to be coherent enough once he got there to slice up the ten-pound turkey breast sitting in the fraternity refrigerator. He had promised the cook that he would do so and he wasn't a man who broke his promises.

"What are you doing to yourself, MacCallister?" he whispered, knowing full well that the time he was spending in the men's room at Whitey's was a direct result of this evening's activities. Evening's activities? He would not let himself admit that the lines had blurred and his drinking binge had truly begun mid-afternoon.

Sean flushed the toilet and sat down, fully clothed. "It's a good thing Whitey's can pull in customers based on the atmosphere in its three bars," the young man thought. "They could never win customers based on restroom cleanliness."

He mumbled some Jimmy Buffett lyrics under his breath. The master of the parrot heads had sung about being drunk for over two weeks and hitting rock bottom. Given Sean's recent track record, two weeks didn't seem like much of a stretch. He pondered whether he should be ashamed of living his life in such a wayward fashion or inspired that he could be following in the footsteps of a very successful musician and businessman.

He closed his eyes and let himself relax for a moment. How could he have slid so far? A year ago at this time, he had been sober for over four months. This year, he felt a sense of pride whenever he made it through an entire day.

"Last year was different," he told himself. In many regards, the statement was true. Since his concussion delivered by Kevin Lakes eight months earlier, Sean had certainly not been the same person. While his personality had remained somewhat stable, his thinking capacity had changed completely. He couldn't concentrate. His once photographic memory had been replaced by one needing to review his text books three to four times in order to thoroughly grasp a concept.

His grades had suffered as well. Even with the extra effort, he often earned B's which he had once considered a disgrace. He was on his way to his first C in one of his Engineering classes before he decided to drop it. He was ashamed of that move as it ruined his chances of graduating a semester early.

Even worse than his strained mental capacity was his pattern of recurring migraines. They were more frequent now. He didn't mind so much when he got the nausea first. At least that gave him time to prepare. The worst ones were those that split his brain out of nowhere like a shaft of lightning and sent him to the floor.

That was the kind he'd had this morning. Fortunately, Kelly had been there for him, like always. His faithful roommate had put a blanket over Sean's head and given him a pillow so that he could ride-out the pain without the added stimulation of light and sound.

What would he do without his best friend? Then again, even that relationship had seen signs of strain. Kelly had insulted him last week, mentioning that Sean had better watch his drinking before he became like his dad. It had been all that Sean could do to keep himself from hitting the big guy. "I'm NOTHING like my dad!" Sean had informed him angrily. And besides, who was Kelly to lecture Sean about drinking? A year earlier, the big man was doing all he could to get Sean to fall off the wagon. The young man got mad just thinking about it.

Yet, despite the occasional heated arguments, Kelly was still the one person Sean fully trusted. The two had been roommates so long that some guys around the fraternity joked that they were legally married via common-law in some states. Financially, they were both in dire straits and received daily calls from collection agencies. Their only transportation was Sean's decrepit Galaxie 500, while their only window to the entertainment world came through Kelly's TV. If they hadn't been living in a fraternity, surrounded by friends who knew they would make good on promises to pay back-rent, both would likely be sleeping in the street.

There was a bond there, beyond just the need both had for someone to shoulder part of their financial burden. Kelly was always Sean's main confidant and "go to" person and vice versa.

He stood up but quickly sat down again. He needed to feel better soon. He had a job to go to tomorrow.

Sean smiled as he thought about his job. He would be coaching wrestling again at Riverside High School. He looked forward to the physical activity and even more so to the wrestlers themselves.

In particular, he thought about Nick Castle. "My protégé," he thought. The boy had begun to realize his potential half-way through last year's season. Sean was sure that Nick could take the next step and place at state this year, maybe even win a state title. Why not? Who would stop him? Heck, the boy was probably studying wrestling videos right now, if not actually running or working out.

Who indeed? In addition to technique and attitude, Nick would now have a head coach who actually cared. Sean had applied for the position when Coach Granger resigned during the summer. While he was frustrated when he did not get the call, this frustration was short lived when he discovered that Cole Tyler, the former assistant coach for the University had accepted.

Cole had saved Sean's life eight months earlier. The least Sean could do was feel happy for him in his new role, even if it did mean that Sean had to go without the medical benefits provided to the head coach but not to assistants. Since his concussion, his debt from medical care had skyrocketed, accumulating to the point that he no longer dared go near the clinic.

Again, Sean got to his feet, this time, more slowly. He steadied himself against the stall wall and opened the door. Cautiously, he walked to the sink.

He leaned on the basin and looked in the mirror. He didn't even have the same face as a year ago. A deep scar ran down his left cheek. His hair had gotten shaggy and he hadn't shaved in three days. As he splashed water on his cheeks and eyes he took a moment to savor the cool refreshment.

"It will be better tomorrow," he thought. "Everything will be better tomorrow."

He wiped his face with his shirt and staggered out to find his friends. They would get him home. Slicing the turkey would be up to him.

Chapter 2

With your head up like that, you're asking to be thrown."

Coach Granger's gravelly voice was still echoing in Nick's ears when he realized he was airborne and his stomach lurched … followed by the thud … followed by the excruciating pain which spread like a gas-fed fire almost up to his knee.

Lying in a crumpled heap on the mat he had pleaded, looking Coach MacCallister in the eye, "Don't make me throw this match."

The memory jarred him awake.

"That was then …" he told himself, already out of bed and two steps across his room, headed for his tape and ankle brace, yet unable to shake the horrible scene from his mind. He was taped, dressed, and ready within minutes, "… this is now."

The state title was out there and it wasn't going to get any closer while Nick lay in bed. He left the room and headed down the steps with his coach's words still resonating through him, "You're not throwing it, kid. You're saving yourself for the future."

"Darn right!" the boy said aloud, throwing on his jacket and leaving for his paper route and morning run.

The next phase of Nick's future began today. In less than ten hours, he would return to the mat for the season's first practice. Every ounce of his body was ready.

Chapter 3

Cole Tyler rolled over in bed again. Was it time to get up yet? The alarm clock showed 5:17. He gently slipped out from beneath the covers, taking care not to wake the woman who lay beside him.

It wasn't the time that he had planned to wake up. Then again, neither was 1:00, 2:45, or 4:00, but his mind was racing and pulled him to consciousness again and again. Now, for the fourth time in the last several hours, he repeated the ritual of turning off his alarm clock and quietly crossing the floor on two re-built knees.

Donning his robe, he opened the bedroom door and stepped into the hall. He paused for a moment to look back at his bed. She hadn't stirred. "She must be awake," he thought. His many trips to the kitchen were sure to spawn an argument later in the day. "Ugh," he lamented.

He returned to the kitchen table to continue working through his other problems.

Cole was not the type to take an assignment lightly and he had two large boxes on the table to prove it. Each was filled with newspaper clippings, tournament programs, match footage and various other memorabilia from his university recruiting trips the prior year.

Riverside had placed in the bottom quartile at the prior year's state tournament. School administration repeatedly reminded Cole that the team's best hope for a championship had died the night of the conference tournament and that another standout had been injured in the same tournament but Cole considered this a cop-out. He needed a team that would produce results, not scenarios of how things should have been better.

"An excuse is like a butt, everyone has one," was a favorite saying of his. He studied the styles of some of history's great coaches … Vince Lombardi, Herb Brooks … these men didn't clamor for the love of their players on day one. They led their teams, won their respect and the results followed.

He again, as in past hours, pulled out the roster that he had compiled from one-on-one interviews with all of the boys who had signed up for the team. He had subsequently modified where certain individuals would fall in the line-up but, even then, he did not like what he saw. He had ten wrestlers with substantial varsity experience, which meant that a minimum of four of his fourteen positions would be held by newcomers.

Of those ten experienced wrestlers, the nine who had wrestled the prior season had a combined winning percentage of 51%. "Ugh," he thought again. The scenario got worse as he looked at the paper. The three wrestlers with the best prior records were all lumped together. Kevin Hermanns was their only returning wrestler to have placed at state. He was currently slotted at 152 pounds where he had a solid shot at placing third but little to no chance of placing higher.

Occupying the neighboring weight classes were the two Castle brothers. Nick, who had shown some promise late in the past season, was currently slotted at 145. While the boy had drive and had developed some tools, Cole was disappointed at his lack of ability to motivate his teammates. If the team was going to be a success, it had to have leaders to motivate the masses. From what he could tell, Nick and Kevin had held the title of "leader" over the off-season but had failed to find anyone to follow them. He would need to find ways to push some buttons and light a fire under those two.

The final entry on Cole's list was the one that intrigued the coach the most. Ron Castle's return to the line-up was one of the reasons that Cole had even considered this job. After an amazing sophomore year and missing his junior year due to injury, Cole wondered exactly what the boy could accomplish in his senior season. The 140-pound weight class in which he was currently slotted had some solid competitors, but it did not hold returning champions like the two at 152 or Travis Spegidos at 135. The bigger question in Cole's mind was whether or not the boy could wrestle at all. After nearly a year as a paraplegic, Ron had shown that he could walk and later run. These basic physical acts were only a portion of those he would need in active competition.

This team's initial lack of clear championship contenders would not keep him from making them great. He would bring in football players, track stars and any other athlete he could find to add depth to the roster. These characters would beef-up his non-existent junior varsity program and provide competition for his varsity. They would also add a lot of extra work to his plate.

Cole rubbed his eyebrows as he gently shook his head. As if it were not enough that his team was in disarray, he had been handed a coaching staff that may need more guidance than the wrestlers themselves.

One assistant coach was a newcomer, Randolf Kreitzer. As far as Cole could tell, the man had no interest in the position beyond the fact that it put him in a better position politically. He was the assistant principal at the school and, from what Cole had heard, had been passed over for several principal positions. Titles had never impressed Cole so, while it was frustrating that the man knew little about wrestling or coaching, it was downright disturbing that this man was Cole's assistant as well as his boss; not a situation that Cole would have readily sought out.

The only real benefit the he could see to having the man around was in possibly leveraging Kreitzer's political clout to update the team's gear and equipment after several years of under-investment.

His second coach, Sean MacCallister, had a year of coaching experience under his belt but could prove to be a detriment as well. Cole's history with the man had been limited but intense. In addition to a few conversations in which Sean had tried to get him to look at Riverside wrestlers for scholarships, Cole had broken up two fights that Sean had gotten into, the second of which had seen Cole send a man to the hospital. This incident and the related assault charges had cost Cole his assistant coach position at the University.

Whether MacCallister was a bad egg or just had bad luck remained to be seen. Cole's only recent contact with the man had been an outing at a bar in which he saw the man completely inebriated mid-afternoon. The main point in the assistant coach's favor was the support and admiration he had from the team as evidenced by multiple glowing comments from the wrestlers. Yet, if MacCallister was going to be the "Good Cop" to Cole's "Bad Cop," he wouldn't do so as a drunk.

He put his tablet back in the box alongside the practice routine for the next two weeks.

More than anything else, he wanted to create wrestlers who would make something of themselves and create results by working hard. The results were the question mark right now as he knew that his mere presence would ensure the hard work.

"Oh yes," Cole thought, "they will work hard."

Chapter 4

He was running again, moving swiftly across the frost-covered grass on the banks of the coulee. His heart pounded and his breath shown white in the crisp early-morning November air.

It had been a good run. Unlike most days, he let himself move at a moderate, even pace. He didn't have to give his all to stay ahead of his usual running partner who was quickly turning into his nemesis. He had given him the slip this morning so that he could save some of his endurance. He would need to do so as today was the first day of practice. There was an un-written rule that the year's first practice would be heavy on conditioning to weed out those who were not serious about the season. Such a group would never include him. Wrestling meant everything to the boy. He would save some of his breath accordingly, ignoring the usual ringing in his ears of his brother pushing him to move, "faster."

As he lengthened his stride, his mind drifted to a place where he was already wrestling. His thoughts fell back to the matches of his last season. As scenes flashed by, he felt the adrenaline rush of victory and the bite of defeat. The one defeat that burned particularly bitter was that of his last match. He had that match won, and it was stolen from him. That match …

He shook his head. That match no longer meant anything. He would prepare for THIS season and he would not look back. He visualized himself stepping onto the mat and doing what he needed to do to win. "Technique first," he told himself, "endurance second, and strength third." If he could out-wrestle his opponents, which was usually the case, he would not have to rely on out-lasting them. Strength was always important but was only his focus as a last resort.

He wondered about his new coach. The last time he stepped off a mat, he had Coach Granger barking in his ear. "Granger was an idiot," he told himself. He never listened to the man, nor would he listen to this new coach. He would wrestle his matches without the interference of others. Nobody knew how to make him win as well as he did. Technique … endurance … strength.

A blur of fur raced into his peripheral vision and jarred him back to his run. A brief moment of panic caused him to break into a sweat. There was Chewie, now five yards in front of him. He knew that Nick would not be far behind. Ron picked up his pace. He was not far from turning the corner onto 17th Avenue. When he did so, he would turn his head slightly to see how far back Nick, his usual running partner, was. He had less than a mile until he reached home. This would not be the day that his brother would pass him.

* * *

Fifty yards behind Ron, Nick was furious at himself. How could he have let the dog go? He had known that Ron would try to get out of running with him this morning. Nick had been getting too close in recent days.

He had hoped that surprise would be his ally and that this was the day he would overtake Ron. He was constantly amazed by the fact that his older brother, while officially rehabilitating, could always find another gear when competing with Nick.

That sibling competition had shown itself almost as soon as Ron had regained the use of his legs. The boy went from taking a few wobbly steps in February to walking without aide by early April. Countless hours of rehab and his relentless determination had driven him to clumsily run his first mile in early June and never look back.

As Nick increased his pace, he focused on his ankle. It should be well protected under the pre-wrap, tape and brace, yet the boy worried that it would only take one wrong step on the slippery grass to turn his ankle and re-aggravate his injury. This was the injury that had let his brother surpass him. After breaking it eight months earlier in the conference tournament, he had tried to stand on it and finish his match. That had been a bad idea. The additional weight had caused bone and nerve damage. It had taken him until late July to get back to 100%, enabling him to attend only the final wrestling camp of the summer. He then re-injured it the first week of cross-country practice in September, at which point Ron's health had surpassed his own and left Nick once again playing catch up.

Despite the current danger of re-injury, Nick now increased his speed. He had to. Especially on this morning, of all mornings, when he was about to overtake his brother and make history in the Castle household.

The thought of this afternoon's practice crossed his mind. Should he be saving energy? His brother would argue, "yes," but Nick disagreed. Even with a brisk run this morning, he would have more than enough stamina for whatever the coaches would dish out. He was certainly not one who should worry about being cut when so many of his teammates would be arriving in sub-optimal condition.

The thought of this angered Nick. He had taken pride in his position of summer captain. He had arranged nearly a dozen events to help his teammates get into the shape they would need to be in to excel during the season. He led by example, being the first to show up each time. Even though he was recovering from an injury, he still led the first event, a four-mile run and finished with the leaders of the pack. Sadly, by the fifth event, which contained swimming and weight lifting, Nick, Ron and Kevin Hermanns were the only ones to attend.

"At least we'll be strong through the middle," Nick thought. He knew that his brother had his sights on the 140-pound weight class. This worked well with Nick, whose 144-pound pre-season weight would make it comfortable for him to weigh in at 145. Completing the heart of their line-up, Nick did not envy Kevin Hermanns. The boy was strong and had placed third in the state at 145 the previous year but he was weighing close to 155 these days. He would be stuck in the 152-pound class, along with two returning state champions. It was a difficult place for anyone with a dream of earning a state title.

He looked forward to today's practice. Not only did it mean the beginning of a new season, one in which he could become a state champion, but it also meant being re-united with Coach MacCallister. Nick wanted to make his assistant coach proud. This man was the only person to believe in him early in the prior season. He was also responsible for making Nick believe in himself. The man could do no wrong and Nick was set on proving that this coach's confidence in him was well placed.

Nick poured on the speed as he and his brother neared their house. Still ten yards back, he knew that his slightly-longer legs would give him an advantage in this home stretch, although it did not appear that Ron was willing to relinquish his lead.

* * *

And so the brothers raced, Nick focusing on the back of his brother's head as he picked up even more speed, Ron begrudgingly breaking into an all-out sprint to fend off his younger brother's longer stride.

As they turned into their yard, Ron's advantage had shrunk to a mere five yards. His eyes watered in the cold November breeze as he pushed himself a bit harder, past the point that his doctor would have recommended. Then again, his doctor had admitted that he could not figure out Ron's body. It had been a miracle that Ron even had the ability to walk again, much less run at the level that he was. Yes, Ron truly believed that he was indestructible and unbeatable. He was focused on proving this again today.

The air stung Nick's face and burned his lungs as he pushed himself a bit more. He could now reach out and touch his brother if he wanted. But this was not what he wanted. He wanted to pass him and beat him to the finish line, which was, as always, the front porch.

Chewie yapped happily a few yards ahead. Many years ago, he had learned that when his masters were running, he needed to stay out of their way. Being stepped on once as a puppy had taught him this lesson. He bounded forward ahead of the boys as they closed in on their destination.

Two bodies hurdled the front cement porch, nearly in unison at break-neck speeds. Nick's foot touched the finish line an instant after that of his older brother. Each did his best to slow his momentum but inevitably slammed into the side of the house and door, the jarring of which cracked the frame of the screen door.

Completely spent, the two boys ventured onto the lawn to catch their breath, a moment before their father emerged from the house shouting.

"I saw that, you two. One slip on this ice is all it's going to take to put you both back on crutches. Do you realize how dangerous this can be?"

As the man pointed to the thin layer of ice covering the front step, he knew his lecture would fall on deaf ears. He loved his boys, with all of their faults, not the least of which was the fierce competitiveness they had somehow developed.

"Dad," Ron started. It took him a few breaths before he could finish. "I ... couldn't ... let that ... little kid ... beat ... me." He shrugged his shoulders as if to say, "How would that look" in lieu of being able to get the words out.

"Well, we cannot afford any more back operations, son. And that 'little kid' is bigger than you these days." As Nick smiled, his father gave him a stern look, "and should be old enough to know that one wrong slip could turn that ankle again and cost him the entire season."

Nick avoided his father's gaze as he paced the yard with his hands on his head before deciding to bump his chest into his brother. "I … had … you."

Ron smiled back at him. "Apparently … not."

Chewie jumped up at both of the boys, yapping as he did.

"That dog has more sense than either of you. By the way, you will both be paying for a new screen door, as you seem to have broken this one. Breakfast is in two minutes."

Mr. Castle returned to the house and left his boys to chain, feed and water the dog. Nick took great joy in this task, wrestling Chewie to the ground as the dog nipped playfully at him. The boy responded by putting his own face right up to the dog's muzzle and giving him a big kiss on the nose.

"No girl is ever going to kiss you if she sees you do that," Ron jabbed as he broke the thin sheet of ice on the dog's water dish with the toe of his shoe.

Nick paused for a minute. As a junior who had been too shy to ever ask anyone out, he pondered a snappy comeback but came up empty. Instead, he opted to change the subject.

"I think we're ready for the season," Nick commented as he grabbed the pooch by the collar and fastened his chain.

"I think we're ready for a Granger season," Ron replied, reflecting back to their most recent coach. "But I just don't know how to gauge this Coach Tyler. I heard that he was a training fanatic at the university. I just don't know how that translates to high school."

"It probably translates to you, Hermanns and me being the only members of the team to survive today's practice," his younger brother sounded off.

"You may be right," Ron nodded as he held the screen door open for his brother. "You may be right."

Chapter 5

Sean heard the click and pulled the pillow tighter against his head. In a moment, the Gear Daddies *Statue of Jesus* would help him ease into the day ... a day he was reluctant to face.

His alarm clock now read 8:30 which meant he must have gotten nearly five hours of sleep last night. Vast experience had taught him that, if he dragged his hung-over butt out of bed right now, he would have just enough time to throw on clothes and a baseball cap, grab a breakfast he could eat while walking across campus, and have about a minute to spare as he entered his Polymer Engineering class.

Burping into his pillow, Sean soon admitted to himself that today would be like too many other days this semester when he had skipped the step of grabbing breakfast for the road. Nothing was likely to stay down this morning.

"Are you going to get up and turn that off?" Kelly's voice asked from the bunk below as the song neared the end of the first verse.

Sean knew that it was rude to let the music run, even if he was having trouble finding the motivation to get up. He reached over and tapped the snooze button.

"You just hit snooze, didn't you. You're going to wake me up again in another nine minutes."

Sean cursed under his breath as his stomach made a gurgling sound. He wasn't in the mood for arguing this morning. In fact, he wasn't in the mood for much of anything other than sleeping this one off. Reluctantly, he forced his arm out of bed a second time and turned the alarm completely off.

The clock now read 8:33. While he was often late, Sean hadn't completely missed a class in two years. Certainly he had gone feeling worse than this. Still, he had to find motivation to get up. Even thinking about getting into a vertical position made his stomach lurch.

"I ran into Mandi's friend Ginger last night ..." Kelly broke the silence.

Sean's mind wandered for a moment and his stomach did a double flip as the young man anticipated his roommate's next comment having to do with Mandi. Sean didn't want to hear any updates on her. Most of his friends blamed her for the incident nearly nine months earlier that gave him his first concussion. That night set in motion his return to the bottle and his life's downward spiral. He didn't want to hear her name. He just wanted to forget about her.

"... Ted Graham is coming back to campus for the spring semester."

The mention of Mandi's other man raised Sean's ire to the point that he snapped, "Shut up" at his best friend before rolling out of bed and trying to cross the room to where the couches were located. His head spun and he felt weak, collapsing on the couch. Ted was the first person that Sean wanted to punch and the last person he wanted to hear about. His anger flared, suddenly hoping that the man did return to campus so that Sean could give him a well-deserved beating.

"You got yourself into this situation," he scolded himself, "you get yourself out. Get your worthless raggedy butt to class and learn something so that you can fix your life."

Sean really needed something to go right today. The creditors kept calling and would likely continue to do so until the phone company disconnected his and Kelly's phone due to its own delinquent bills. He wanted to quit drinking again, he just didn't have the will power or support to do so ... or at least that was his excuse this week.

Polymer Engineering was at 9:00, Engineering Measurements was at 10:30, and then he would have a break before Project Management at 2:00 and coaching wrestling at 3:45. The afternoon would certainly be more pleasant than the morning. Maybe he could even take a nap during his break to help him feel human again?

Pulling on his clothes, cap, jacket and sunglasses, Sean stumbled out the door of his room. He'd fill a water bottle on his way out of the house and he prayed that the brisk November air would help revive him as he made his way across campus to yet again be late for class.

Chapter 6

Nick let his mind wander as he worked through the accounting problem. He was getting pretty good at matching the debits to the credits although it was still not quite settling in why liabilities were referred to as credits. Liabilities were supposed to be bad but, when Nick's bank gave him a credit, it was a good thing. It was nearly lunch time and his mind quickly grew weary of sorting out the debits / credits mess as it wandered over to its usual subject … Sandi Davis.

Sandi and Nick had paired up on several occasions in French class toward the end of their sophomore year. She was undeniably the girl of his dreams – incredibly sweet and unassuming, not to mention painfully pretty. He always told himself that if sophomores could have gone to prom, he would have found a way to ask Sandi even though he was sure that, if she said "no," it would be the end of him. They had talked regularly that spring, even sometimes outside of class but had largely lost touch when she had moved to France for the summer.

He wished he had her in a class this year, assuring himself that, if he had a place to see her and something in common for a conversation starter, it would spur his ability to talk to her. He never would have enrolled in French II had he known that Sandi's summer abroad experience would propel her straight to French III for her junior year. He was far too shy to call her and even fumbled for words when he passed her in the hall though he was encouraged by how patient she was with him during each bumpy conversation.

Oscar was the only one who knew how much Nick liked the girl. The smaller grappler lived down the street from Sandi in one of the newer developments in town, and Nick had asked him enough questions about her that his interest was obvious. Despite Oscar's obnoxious manner, as far as Nick knew, he had never told Sandi or anyone else about Nick's feelings. It was one bond that kept the boys' often-tense friendship afloat as Nick longed for the day when he could force himself to ask Sandi out so that Oscar would no longer be able to potentially hold it over his head.

Having Oscar as his closest ally made Nick long for a friend like Dino Benz. Benzy would have been the perfect confidant for this situation, always displaying a combination of genuine empathy and tough love. A year earlier, the big guy had never put up with Nick feeling sorry for himself and it made Nick a stronger individual. The older wrestler's tragic death had been the most painful event Nick had ever experienced. Occasional aftershocks still reverberated through Nick nearly nine months later.

As the bell rang, ending the period, the youth's mind was filled with thoughts of how to grow a relationship with Sandi, find a best friend like Dino, and obtain a double-lunch to fuel him through today's first practice.

Chapter 7

Ron sat at the table at the end of Riverside's "commons" area. It was his rightful spot, surrounded by the school's royalty.

Across the table from him was the quarterback of the football team, playfully hamming it up with the homecoming queen while her boyfriend was off getting lunches for all three. The student body president and assorted others adorned the table and there sat Ron, a member of this group seemingly by divine right. There was no question when the elder Castle walked into the room which crowd he would choose to join.

In a school year broken into four nine-week periods, Ron had chosen to continue working from home with private tutors the first nine weeks to give him more flexibility and time to devote to his rehabilitation. Returning for the second nine weeks allowed him to begin school just prior to the start of wrestling season. Everybody at this table had already mentioned how eager they were to see him back on the mat. The boy was anxious to give them a show.

"Ladies and gentlemen, how are you this fine day?"

Ron didn't have to look to see who was behind him. Assistant Principal Kreitzer, the wrestling team's newest assistant coach, was always stopping over to hobnob with the school's social elite. It struck Ron as a bit sad that this man was thirty-something and still trying to live in his high school glory days, like an aging prom king who never got past that need for being included with the cool kids at school.

Something about the man's phony demeanor rubbed Ron the wrong way. Looking around the table, he noted that the group gave the man a mixed reaction as some basked in his attention while others seemed to consider him a nuisance.

Looking from face to face, the realization struck him that, while he had been welcomed back with open arms, very few of the members of this high society had bothered contacting him the past year-and-a-half during his recovery. As he listened to their tales of special year-book photo sessions to recognize their contributions and scholarships to reward their accomplishments, for the first time, he felt slightly out of place.

For all of his success on the mat his sophomore year, triumphs that certainly overshadowed anything that anyone in this crew had done to that point, he was now in an unusual position of having to play "catch up." Among this largely superficial group of friends, he was the only one that had yet to distinguish himself in a way that would leave a lasting heritage in the halls at Riverside.

As he continued to absorb the shallow banter, the thought gnawed at him until he made himself a silent promise, the same one he had been making since elementary school. He would secure his legacy; going through life as "almost a state champion" was just not good enough.

Chapter 8

Nick sprinted with everything he had. His chest was pounding and the sweat shot like a million tiny geysers from his pores. Reaching the end of the gym, he tagged some sophomore named Freddie who looked like he was about ready to hurl but dutifully started running to the far end of the gym from where Nick had come.

It was the three-person sprint relay, designed to get the team in shape. It was appearing to do just that for the ones who survived. Had Nick been able to choose his team, he would have grabbed Ron and Hermanns. He suspected that the three of them had better endurance than anyone else in the room, which was probably exactly why Coach Tyler had separated them from the beginning.

Nick clasped his fingers behind his neck, stood up straight and expanded his lungs as he watched Freddie losing ground to several of their teammates. There were nine teams in all with Coach MacCallister having to fill in as the third man on the ninth team.

The boy smiled as he watched his coach trying to keep up. It had been fun catching up with him briefly before practice.

"You look like you've been hitting the weights," had been MacCallister's first comment.

Nick had been glad that someone had noticed and wasn't surprised that Coach MacCallister had been the one. The lean wrestler had worked hard during the offseason to add some bulk to his slender frame, resulting in nearly ten pounds of added mass.

He had also taken the opportunity to introduce his favorite coach to Ron, even though his older brother quickly gravitated away from them toward Kevin Hermanns who welcomed Ron back as "the legend" while labeling Nick as "the legend-in-training." It was the role Nick seemed destined to never outgrow.

Nick was half surprised that the school hadn't held a parade to welcome his brother back. All he had heard since the first day of the school year were excited questions: "When is Ron coming back?" and "Is he going to wrestle this year?" Despite Nick's own role as summer captain, he still felt like the inferior Castle brother now that Ron was returning to re-claim his throne.

Time for pleasantries with Coach MacCallister had been cut short as Coach Tyler had emerged from the adjacent weight room, light gray tee shirt clinging to his muscular physique in several dark sweat spots, clear signs of having just pushed himself in a workout. The head coach had instructed the boys to take a knee and went headlong into an impromptu speech.

"I will tolerate no foolishness," the man had begun, getting straight to the point. "Your actions, whether you're in this room or not, wearing a Riverside uniform or not, reflect on this team. As such, in all situations, you will act as gentlemen."

The man was so powerful in his tone that Nick believed he had seen fear in the eyes of many of his teammates.

"When you are at practice or on the mat representing this team, you will give 100%," Tyler continued. "If you don't, one of these other wrestlers will give 100% in your place. You participate as an individual but you are a component of a team. Each of you varsity guys will have thirteen other varsity guys and a whole lot of JV guys depending on you each second you're wrestling. DO NOT let them down."

Nick found it odd that the coach had then pulled Derek O'Shea and Oscar forward to lead the team in running twenty laps around the wrestling room … usually the duty of the summer captains as they transitioned into the season as team captains.

Nick had been amazed at the man's intensity. This new coach had led the live wrestling drills and seemed to be everywhere at once, giving a live technique demonstration to one pair of grapplers while yelling instructions to another, always keeping his whistle handy to change up the drill.

The live wrestling had been the most relaxing part of the practice and painfully short lived as Coach Tyler quickly moved the team into conditioning – foot fires with sprawling, running sprints while carrying teammates, jumping rope, all the while being pushed to go faster and faster under the direct supervision of the new head coach.

Now, as the end of the first practice drew near, Nick wondered what kind of a team would emerge. As Clifford Vassec lumbered toward him, Nick held out his hand to accept the tag, jolting forward in one last-ditch effort to gain some ground as he made his way across the gym for the twentieth time during this drill. He knew that his dad's emotions would have been mixed had he been there as Nick sprinted like a champion instead of yielding in the end, leaping into the far wall of the gym to gain the fraction of a second's advantage that it took to surpass a runner from one other team.

"Bring it in," Tyler instructed as the last two remaining teams finished their final leg. As the wrestlers surrounded him, he began his blunt closing remarks.

"I hope today's performance was a result of the shock of organized practice. I was led to believe that you were working out during the off-season. It doesn't show."

The comment stung especially for Nick as he noted the coach looking at him and Kevin.

"In my book, team leaders earn their way by their actions. Castle and Hermanns, you are both fine wrestlers and likely deserved the leadership titles your teammates bestowed on you last season. That having been said, I'll decide who leads this team onto the mat this year. It won't be the same individuals every dual unless I see rare individuals who their teammates seem consistently willing to follow."

Nick watched Hermanns' face as the older boy nodded sadly.

His heart sank. He had worked so hard this past summer and taken so much pride in the effort he put into trying to make this team stronger. It dashed his spirits to think about having to re-start from ground zero but he immediately began contemplating how to get his role back.

Chapter 9

"…and as a tutor for underclassmen Engineering students, I've helped over a dozen students raise their grades. One with a 2.0 moved all the way up to 3.7 the semester I tutored him."

Sean was definitely bringing his "A" game to this interview. Because it was the final company interviewing on campus during the fall semester, he had no choice but to shine. He had been diligent, taking a night off from drinking to ensure that he would be fresh for the recruiter; an awkward, gangly man in his mid-fifties wearing a really bad suit. Judging by the amount of time the man spent avoiding eye contact, Sean pegged him for a pretty solid introvert.

Sean studied his interviewer while the man chewed on his pen. In a better economy, the young man was pretty certain that he would have had several offers by now. Unfortunately, lean times meant that few offers were being extended and Sean was among the desperate majority, still looking for an opening and a way to pay back his mountain of hospital debt and student loans.

At least as important as the salary was the benefits package. His research had unearthed an experimental brain surgery which may reduce or eliminate his severe post-concussion-syndrome effects. The right healthcare coverage would allow him to move forward with the operation whereas his current situation of having no insurance or money put him in a "catch 22." He needed his mind fixed to get a steady job but needed the income and healthcare benefits of a steady job to get his mind fixed.

His thoughts drifted briefly as he thought about how much this man reminded him of a recruiter from a month earlier. Sean had gotten that rejection letter just over a week ago, after finding that two students he had tutored had been invited to the corporate headquarters for office interviews. It felt slightly unjust that students who knew less than he did were being considered while he was still unemployed.

"Interesting. Let's talk about your grades," the interviewer finally continued, looking through a stack of papers for Sean's transcript.

The young man tried not to fidget as he got ready for the pending onslaught. Every interview seemed to focus on his declining GPA and his lack of an internship the prior summer, both stemming from his concussion the prior spring.

"I see that you had a 4.0 GPA but then dropped to a 3.9 during last fall's semester, and fell all the way down to 2.9 last spring. Can you talk about this trend?"

The young man inhaled deeply, trying to look confident. "I had a concussion right before mid-terms. I missed a lot of classes and fell behind. I still held full-time student status, despite missing so much school. You'll see that the 'C' was in a non-Engineering class."

"Were you in a car accident?" the man asked, feverishly taking notes and avoiding looking directly at his candidate.

Sean always struggled when the interviewers pressed him for more information about his ordeal. One time he had flat-out lied about it but the interviewer busted him when the story didn't hold together. Since then, he had tried to be vague with the details.

"No, I was assaulted."

"Assaulted?" the man asked with a tone of surprise.

Sean was suddenly self-conscious about the scar spanning the length of his left cheek as the man now seemed intent on looking him in the face.

"On campus?" the man continued, refusing to let it go.

"No, I was picking up a friend from a club and some guy hit me."

"So, you were in a bar fight," the man paraphrased.

Sean winced. "I'm not sure it's a bar fight when one person just gets blindsided and knocked unconscious."

The interviewer looked at him for a moment longer, now clearly studying the scar.

It was clear that the meeting had just taken a very bad turn. Sean wouldn't even end up having to explain the absence of an internship the prior summer due to missing spring recruiting.

While not quite as bad as the interview during which Sean had been hit with one of his killer migraines, it would end with the same rejection. He suddenly longed for a drink.

Chapter 10

Nick shot at the boy's legs, catching him off guard. Getting deep penetration, he picked the boy off the ground and drove him hard to the mat, straight to his back. As the boy flailed, trying to get any kind of control over his situation and turn to face down, Nick continued his attack, climbing the boy's torso but keeping between his legs, cutting off any opportunity for his opponent to stabilize or roll to his belly.

In fewer than twenty seconds, Nick had pinned the larger, more muscular boy. Nick looked around to see if he could catch Coach Tyler's eye. Fortunately, the man was looking straight at him. "Let him up, Nick," he commanded.

Nobody was going to keep Nick from his state championship, particularly not this football player who had never wrestled a match in his life. The practice mat was crowded with new faces. Nick had no idea how the coach had gotten them here or why they would want to take up the sport at such a late age. What he did know was that none of them would get the upper hand on him.

In the back of the boy's mind was paranoia. His head coach had hinted about being unhappy with Nick's failures in preparing the team during the off-season. The wrestler was out to prove his worth to this team and avoid further doubts.

Nick held out his hand as a gesture of sportsmanship to help the boy to his feet. The hand was eagerly accepted.

Facing one another, they started again. This time, Nick used a duck-under, took the boy to the mat, and began working to turn him. The session would continue this way for the next ten minutes until the coaches re-paired the wrestlers. Nick was determined to remove any question as to who was going to be the varsity star.

Today, he would prove himself on the practice mat. Soon enough, he would do the same in real competition.

"Let him up, Nick," the boy heard yet again. Once more, he was happy to oblige. The more times he heard the request, the more likely he was to gain his head coach's confidence.

Chapter 11

Ron stepped off the scale, glad to be safe at two pounds under. Tonight's win hadn't been a pretty one but a win is a win, even if only by a one-point margin. He was now five and zero on the season and pondered just how long his undefeated streak might last.

Overall, Ron was unimpressed with the way he was wrestling and sensed that his coaches must be as well. He certainly wasn't as flexible as he had been prior to his injury and it affected his technique significantly. Yet, he was finding ways to win and figured that consistency would have to suffice until dominance returned and he hit his stride. The boy's main concern was that he was not on track to be wrestling like a state champion by the end of the year. If it was even an attainable goal, it certainly did not show at this point.

"Are you on?" Nick asked, passing his brother and stepping on the scale himself.

"Of course," Ron replied, as if he would ever be over. "You?"

"143," Nick nodded.

The boy's skin fit so tight that Ron pondered for a moment what his body composition might be.

Ron's brother scared him a bit. The kid had gotten good. Even with minimal summer camp activity due to his ankle injuries, he was proving to be a solid practice partner. In fact, the two of them and Hermanns routinely had to pair up amongst themselves, the coaches or much heavier wrestlers to ensure that they were challenged during live drills.

As predicted, the Riverside team was showing signs of being strong up the middle as the Castles and Hermanns were the three undefeated grapplers on the roster after the first three duals and an ill-fated dual tournament. At three and two, Oscar was showing some spark at 130 as well. Yet, whenever Ron tried to spar with him, the smaller boy failed to wrestle with any kind of heart.

In general, Ron felt that the team was a bit weary or perhaps it was just him. The season was still young but the team had wrestled five duals in just over two weeks and would be turning around to attend a very solid dual tournament in two days. After keeping up with Coach Tyler's pace for over three weeks, Ron had to admit that even he was concerned about coming out of the weekend feeling sluggish. Twice the coach had invited neighboring schools to practice, which in Ron's book was essentially the same as a live match. Live wrestling wears a person down more quickly than any other workout.

"Wrestling as many different opponents as possible will help you build your skills," Coach Tyler had asserted. "Everyone brings a bit different talent and style."

Ron couldn't argue with the logic. He only hoped that his body, still in recovery mode according to his doctor, could hold up as well as he knew his mind would.

Chapter 12

May I join you?"

Nick was ecstatic as he looked up from his lunch to see Sandi's pretty face.

"Of course," he replied, hoping that he didn't appear over-eager.

The girl daintily sat her petite frame across from him, blonde hair bouncing softly as she organized some items on her lunch tray.

"MAN, SHE'S CUTE!" the boy thought, unable to take his eyes off of her face. He would stare at that face for hours if not for his inability to maintain eye contact.

"Say something, Nick," he coached himself but his spinning thoughts were moving too fast to come up with anything. Fortunately for the conversation, the girl didn't have the same issue.

"Are you going to the dance on Saturday?"

The boy's mind raced. He hated school dances, particularly given some embarrassing incidents his sophomore year. Yet, Sandi was asking if he was going. Did she want him to go?

"We've got a tournament on Saturday but maybe we'll catch the end of the dance if we get back in time."

He was elated when she smiled. It seemed to mean that she was glad that he may be there. Then, she quickly surprised him by changing the subject.

"Do you know of a wrestler from West Clay named Travis Spegidos?" she asked.

Nick's nose wrinkled, wondering if Sandi had any idea how silly the question sounded to him. Any wrestler in this state, or many other states for that matter, who didn't know of the Spegidos legend was clearly unfit for his sport.

"Of course," he replied.

"What do you think of him?"

Nick's skin suddenly crawled. He remembered the prior season's VC tournament and a brief conversation with Spegidos in the locker room. The boy was shifty and devious.

"Dangerous on the mat, that's for sure. He's only lost one match since half-way through his freshman year. He's on track to set the state record for most wins in a career."

While he didn't care for Spegidos, Nick was overjoyed at engaging Sandi in a conversation about wrestling, the one subject the boy could talk about for hours.

"What about off the mat?"

Nick's mind began to race wondering why she would possibly be asking so many questions about Spegidos. If she had somehow met him and was interested in the two-time state champion, it would be the end of Nick's dwindling faith that anything fair and decent still existed in the world. He answered the only way he could.

"He and Ron really don't get along so well so I can't say that he's ever been anything more than cordial to either of us."

The girl nodded slowly as the butterflies began to mix with Nick's partially-digested lunch. Trying not to be too obvious, he followed with a question of his own.

"Why do you ask?"

Sandi's look turned to frustration. "He beat up my cousin's best friend last week."

The story wasn't a big surprise. Fights happen.

"Al is a skinny, bookish kid and apparently this Spegidos thought it would be fun to beat him up. He told him he looked ugly and then punched him in the face and pushed him into some lockers before somebody broke it up."

Nick was at once relieved that Sandi didn't have interest in the champion and sickened by his choice of victim. Having been on the receiving end of some bullying, his natural tendency was to get angry with the antagonist.

"He could get suspended from the team for that," Nick commented.

"That's what's worse," Sandi added. "The wrestling coach got involved claiming that Al had started the whole thing. Al got two weeks of detention and a warning. Spegidos didn't even get a slap on the wrist."

The situation didn't sit well with Nick. Given the cast of characters and punishment of the victim, he suddenly felt a bit warm.

"It's just not right," he commented.

Sandi nodded in agreement and uncharacteristically reached across the table and gave his hand a pat.

The wrestler tried to avoid blushing as his usual self-consciousness swept over him. As he was pondering whether or not he looked goofy in any way, to his horror, he felt hands in his hair messing it to the left and right simultaneously.

"Hey, hot stuff," Oscar said to Sandi, emerging from behind Nick.

All Nick could do was quickly try to straighten his hair with his fingers. He glared at the boy, making himself a promise that he'd work the kid over during the afternoon's practice.

"Nice hairdo, Castle. What's up?"

"Do you remember Al, the boy who came up to see the university with my cousins a few weeks ago?" Sandi piped in.

Nick's ears perked up. Had Oscar been hanging out with Sandi and her cousins? There was a twinge of fear as Nick didn't like the thought of anyone spending time with Sandi when he was finally about to summon the nerve to ask her out.

"Yeah," Oscar reminisced, "what a nerd."

"He's not a nerd," Sandi shot back. "He's a very nice boy."

"Spegidos beat him up," Nick added, hoping to get Oscar to give some sympathy.

"Ha," Oscar laughed, "that kid deserves to get beat up, just for being a geek. Did Spegidos punch him in the face and fix his nose? The kid has a schnoz the size of a banana."

Nick was about to step in when he noticed Sandi visibly shut down.

"He's a very nice boy," she muttered again.

Nick gazed sternly at Oscar in a silent indication that he should shut up.

"Somebody will get Spegidos," Nick finally commented. He hoped the words would comfort Sandi even if he had a hard time believing they were actually true.

Chapter 13

Sean staggered up the stairs, completely inebriated. The sorority formal had been a blast for everyone until he had gotten completely out of hand. The young man snickered to himself as he thought about some of the harmless antics that drove his date, Susan, to call him an imbecile and leave the dance on a separate bus.

He had started the night a bit concerned, having accepted the date over the phone and, honestly, not remembering who the woman was. As such, he treated himself to a couple of tall "comfort" beers as he ironed his shirt. By the time Susan had shown up, he was already well into his first six-pack and his face was getting numb. He had been happy that her face was familiar and vaguely remembered dancing with her at one of the recent Beta Beta Beta parties. Unfortunately, they struggled to find a solid conversation from the start.

She had brought him to a pre-party at another fraternity where he quickly bonded with two of the fraternity's members, dates of Susan's sorority sisters, over a beer bong. As the night had progressed, the trio lost track of their dates and continued to find mischief. The final straw had been when the band went on break and Sean, with his two companions in tow, decided to raid the stage and serenade the party with a few choice songs of their own, earning them a prompt dismissal from the event.

As he reached the top of the stairs, Sean ran headlong into Otis who was kind enough to grab the drunk young man and prevent him from tumbling back down the flight he had just ascended.

"You all right, Sean?" the Southern sophomore had asked.

Sean closed one eye, trying to focus on his friend. He suddenly broke into a big smile and slurred out the phrase, "I'm naked."

"No you're not," the younger man assured him as he helped Sean down the hall.

"Well, I should be," MacCallister mumbled.

A similar strain of nonsensical dialogue continued as Otis half-assisted, half-dragged Sean into his room. As the underclassman tried to steer Sean to lie down, the senior resisted.

"I can't go to bed yet."

"Why?"

"I've got to set my alarm clock. I work tomorrow morning."

"Are you sure?"

"Yep … road trip … small but intense tournament."

Otis handed him the alarm clock which read slightly after eleven o'clock. As Sean set the alarm for 6:00, he was very glad that he would get nearly seven hours of sleep.

As he crawled into bed, still wearing his suit, he kicked off his shoes as Otis walked toward the door.

"Otis," Sean said, stopping the young man in his tracks.

"Yeah, Sean."

Sean pointed toward the little garbage can near the entry way.

"Will you please hand me that?"

Otis shook his head. "Sure. Are you feeling sick?"

"No. Not yet, but it's always best to be safe."

Otis handed the trash can to his friend, turned out the light, and left the room.

"Thank you," Sean mumbled, a few seconds too late.

His mind was numb as, on this night, the alcohol had disguised the inner darkness rather than multiplying it. Yet, the desperation soon returned as he lay there alone. The bottle had gotten him through another day.

"If I'm alive tomorrow morning," he thought, slowly filling with dread, "maybe I'll find a way to make it through that day too."

Hugging the garbage can, he attempted to say his prayers but passed out cold before the end of the first phrase.

Chapter 14

Sean lay on the cold hard floor of his childhood bedroom. His entire body ached from the night's run-in with his father but it was his face in particular that he feared had sustained some structural damage. He would have to go to the hospital to get it checked out.

"Another day, another beating," the boy thought as he tried to pull himself into a sitting position before realizing how sore his back was and just laid back down for another minute. He couldn't quite remember what the fight had even been about which was odd, given that it had just happened.

He felt numb, like he had been drinking and hadn't quite sobered up. How old was he? Surely he was in high school but why couldn't he come up with an exact age?

His cheek was broken. He would have to wear a mask the entire season to protect it.

Sean was very confused. How could he know that his cheek was broken and that he would have to wear a mask when he hadn't even been to the doctor yet?

"Junior year," he mumbled. It was his junior year when he had to wear the mask.

The loud clanging sound of metal on wood caused him to jump.

"Get up!" his father yelled.

He thought that the man had already gone downstairs. It just added to his confusion.

The second clanging sound abruptly resonated in his ears.

Sean opened his eyes to see a large man dressed in a cook's outfit towering over him.

"Get up!" the man repeated as he slammed his pancake turner on the table a third time. It was clear that he was irritated.

Sean looked around, trying to gain his bearings and figure out exactly where he was. His body ached, apparently from having slept in some kind of a restaurant booth. What confused him the most was that the restaurant didn't look the least bit familiar.

"Do you have a room here?" the man asked gruffly.

"Yes," Sean lied instinctively, still trying to figure out where the heck he was.

"Well, go find it. You can't sleep down here," the man growled before turning and heading back to his business.

Sean pushed himself forward, looking around. He was completely disoriented and noticed he was still wearing the suit he passed out in the prior night.

"Sorry," he called after the man but wasn't surprised to be completely ignored.

Finding his jacket in the booth's opposite seat, he donned it, located a door, and began heading in that direction.

"Jeez," he abruptly yelled, noting that the restaurant's clock read 6:20. He had ten minutes to get from wherever he was to Riverside High School before the bus would leave for the day's dual tournament. He only hoped that one of the other coaches had arrived on time to get the team weighed and organized.

"Keys? Keys?" he thought as he searched his pockets. Where were his keys?

Getting outside, he recognized the hotel. It was near the Interstate which would allow him to get to Riverside only slightly late if he could figure out where his keys and car were.

Hearing the growl of a familiar engine, he turned to see his Galaxie 500, parked in visitor parking, still running.

"Thank you, God," he remarked, for once grateful that his vehicle was such a monstrosity that nobody would want to steal it. Who knew what had driven him to come to this place or how long the car had sat there.

Upon entry, everything seemed okay. Sean was more unnerved that he couldn't recall the prior evening's events than he was that he had woken up in such an awkward position. He put the car in gear and raced out of the parking lot, toward Riverside.

Chapter 15

Ron stood quietly at the edge of the mat, watching Oscar get pummeled. It wasn't the first outcome of its sort during this dual. West Clay High School had been a power in the state in recent years and so far was doing a number on the lighter members of the Riverside team, leading by a score of eighteen to three.

He looked across the mat and found Travis Spegidos glaring at him. The chill that shot down his spine reminded him how thankful he should be that he was only wrestling Brent Decker, the state's number two 140-pounder rather than Ron's former nemesis from two years earlier.

Ron had caught Spegidos' first match of the tournament earlier that day. Referring to the event as a "match" was a misnomer as the returning state champion had thrown his hapless opponent to his back and finished him off within the first minute. Nothing was out of bounds for the West Clay wrestler; he was uncommonly strong, his technique was impeccable, and his angry intensity made him downright dangerous. Riverside's Travis Skinner, boasting a record of two wins and four losses, wouldn't likely provide much of a challenge.

The referee called for three points and a technical fall as Oscar rolled to the safety of his belly.

As Skinner prepared to walk out to center mat, Ron pulled off his warm-up pants in anticipation of the boy returning quickly. How quickly was even something that Ron underestimated as he saw the ref signal a forfeit for West Clay and raise his Riverside teammate's arm in victory.

Ron's heart froze as the realization overtook him and the crowd at the same time. Spegidos was moving up to 140; the rematch of the Castle-Spegidos state semifinal from two years ago was on. Ron felt desperately under-prepared and, for the first time, felt fear creep into his soul as he walked onto the mat.

* * *

Spegidos' eyes were cold and intense. He had only lost one match in the past two and a half seasons and appeared resolute on proving that said loss was a fluke.

Ron felt his opponent was something less than human as the whistle blew and the two wrestlers began to move in and circle. Whether Spegidos' aura was more that of a cold machine or some kind of jungle animal, Ron really couldn't tell; what he did know for sure was that he was being stalked by a very dangerous individual.

In an impressive show of strength, the champion drove Ron backward, popped the boy's arms up and lifted him for a moment before driving the older Castle to the mat. Ron's focus quickly changed from hoping to win the match to desperately trying to avoid being completely humiliated.

Lying on his belly, Ron took a forearm to the left side of his face and immediately got his arms up for protection. A moment later, a hand came across, nailing him in his right cheek. The onslaught was relentless, seemingly coming from every direction.

"Give me some kind of opening," the weakened wrestler thought as it took everything he had to avoid rolling up like a hedgehog and drawing a stalling call. As he attempted to rise to his base, he felt a heavy blow to his left side combined with his right arm being pulled all the way across his body underneath him. Suddenly, he was on his back.

* * *

Nick watched from mat-side. He had never seen his brother take a beating like this and the pummeling only got worse as the second period began.

Spegidos looked completely insane as he finally locked up Ron's arms. Nick cringed as the champion succeeded in pressing Ron's shoulders to the mat and the West Clay team went wild.

Just noting the way the boy left the mat made Nick angry.

"Somebody's got to beat that guy," he thought as he headed out for his own match, patting a very discouraged Ron on the back on the way.

Nick closed his eyes for a moment and took a deep breath. He was revved up to meet a highly ranked wrestler for his own match and relieved that Ron and Spegidos' differing weight classes would ensure that everyone had just witnessed the final chapter in the Castle versus Spegidos feud … or so he thought.

Chapter 16

Nick felt like a million bucks. Everything had gone right for him in this weekend's dual tournament. He had again gone undefeated and, absent an unlikely loss at this upcoming week's dual, was about to take a 10 and 0 record into the pre-Christmas tournament. He wondered if it was good enough to earn him the top seed at 145. In the end, it didn't matter. Regardless of where he was seeded, he was wrestling in an unbeatable way right now. The big pre-Christmas tournament would surely see him bring home his first high school championship.

Even better, he was about to take the momentum he had gained on the mat and parlay it into his love life. The team had gotten back to town in time for the final fifteen minutes of the school's winter dance. Sandi was there. Nick and Oscar had stopped to talk to her on their way into the school and, as soon as Nick dropped his gear in his wrestling locker, he was going to find her for the final dance, his first big step toward seeing if she might be interested in him. Of course, who wouldn't be interested in the undefeated wrestler on this day?

The boy smiled at the thought as his confidence overflowed. At this point, the only thing that kept him from feeling total elation was his brother's run-in with Spegidos and subsequent loss in the final dual of the day. It had been a major slap in the face for his brother to have to face such a dominant opponent so quickly after his return to the mat. Even completely healthy, Ron would not be likely to beat Spegidos. The senior had only lost one match since the middle of his freshman year. Yes, that loss had been to Ron but Nick's brother wasn't the same wrestler now … and Spegidos had only gotten better.

Nick punched his locker. The adrenaline flowing through his veins was making him feel aggressive. He didn't want to wait another week for the big tournament. He wanted a new opponent now. Who could beat him? Spegidos? The thought sent a brief shiver down his spine. The middle weight classes were always filled with solid competitors. However, nobody at 140 or 145 was the caliber of Spegidos. The boy was on track to win a third state championship and secure the record for the most wins by a wrestler in the history of the state. There was nobody else quite like him anywhere … and Nick was relieved.

The locker room door opened and Nick looked over to see Kevin Hermanns enter. Nick knew that he was blessed to have this senior on his team and so near his weight. Between Kevin and Ron, Nick always could count on having a solid practice partner, one who would push him and make him better.

"You don't get better by practicing with people that you dominate every time," Coach Tyler had said.

Nick agreed. Having the two-time state placer a weight class above him was a key component in Nick's development, not to mention a boon for the team.

"Is anyone else here?" Kevin asked.

"Nope," Nick replied, rattling off another quick flurry of punches into the steel of the locker door. Ron had taught him long ago how to hit the door so as not to injure his hands and, at the same time, create the maximum amount of noise.

"Good," came the response. There was a look of concern on Kevin's face that was uncommon for the undefeated 152 pounder. It suddenly shot into Nick, disrupting his good mood.

"Nick," the boy started, approaching his younger teammate. "I've been doing a lot of thinking …"

There was something about his tone that made Nick feel like he should be on guard.

"… I don't know that I can win the state title at 152."

Nick started to raise an argument but Kevin firmly continued his monologue.

"Willis and Troftgruben are both going 152 this year. Both of them are hungry to repeat as state champions. One of them likely will. On the right day, I match up well against either of them … but I'm not going to count on the state tournament being 'the right day' for me. Especially not twice."

A shiver ran down Nick's spine.

"145 is where I need to be," the Senior continued. "I can make the weight … but it means that you will have to move down to 140."

"140 is Ron's weight class," Nick countered.

"Maybe he can go 135?" Kevin argued.

"Spegidos is at 135. I'm not going to push my brother down there."

Any team camaraderie Nick had felt with his summer co-captain was quickly disappearing.

"Well, you're too light to compete at 152," Kevin pushed back.

"But you aren't."

"I just told you that I'm going to cut down," Kevin's voice showed more than a hint of frustration. "I'll wrestle you off and take your 145 spot by that route if I have to."

Nick was angry as he looked his teammate in the eye. "Apparently you'll try," he stated and walked toward the door, punching one more locker on his way out of the room.

Chapter 17

Nick was sick to his stomach as he wandered down the hall back toward the gym. His run-in with Hermanns had distracted him and shaken his confidence. Still, it would not stop him. He was going to find Sandi and ask her to dance if it killed him.

"One step at a time," he coached himself. "If she says 'yes' to dancing, it is a good sign. Asking her on a date is the next logical move."

He pondered whether or not it would have been a good idea to tell Oscar his plan. The smaller wrestler could be a bit of a pain but Nick's experience told him that, when he told Oscar he was going to do something, he would never live it down if he didn't follow through.

The DJ's voice in the distance echoed down the hall, "One more dance. If there's someone you've been meaning to ask, this is your final opportunity."

Nick broke into a sprint. How could he have misjudged the timing so much? He took consolation in the fact that he knew exactly where Sandi would be, sitting at the second table from the end of the gym with her obnoxious friend Kendra and Oscar. Beyond that, he was pretty sure that Oscar would ward off anyone who might be moving in on Sandi. It was only natural to keep others away from a buddy's would-be-girlfriend, right?

Fighting the crowd and racing into the gym, he pushed his way through the mass of bodies to find Kendra sitting at the table, alone.

Nick's adrenaline spiked.

"Where is Sandi?" he asked Kendra nervously, fearing that one of the guys from the theater crowd had swooped in and beaten him to the punch.

"Oscar asked her to dance," she replied. "They'll be back in a few minutes."

The boy's head began to spin and he felt a wave of bitter cold cover him. He looked out on the dance floor and saw Oscar holding the girl of his dreams. The only person in the world who knew that Nick liked her had just stolen her, preventing Nick from making his move.

Blood dripped from multiple proverbial knife wounds in his back as he stood gawking, his face covered with a look of disbelief, betrayal and pain.

Chapter 18

Sean entered his home feeling utterly exhausted after a day of emotional peaks and valleys. He had gotten severe tongue lashings from both Coach Tyler and Assistant Coach Kreitzer for being late. He knew he deserved the reprimands but the thought of the latter coach holding anything over his head made him feel a bit ill, especially given the man's on-time attendance record. Kreitzer had even given him grief about his suit, commenting that it looked as if he had slept in it. If he only knew the truth …

The young man still had no idea how he had ended up in a hotel restaurant that morning and it had bothered him the entire day. He thought of it less during the first few duals when Riverside wrestled well. But his hopes for the team came crashing down during a dual against West Clay that was a complete debacle, one in which his team only won four matches, one by forfeit.

Certain individuals, Nick and Kevin in particular, looked strong throughout the tournament but he knew there would soon be tension there. Kevin had formalized his request to wrestle-off for Nick's weight class to Coach Tyler and Sean after all of the other wrestlers had left the bus. Knowing the way his head coach worked, Sean suspected that this would be used as a tool to stir the pot and keep the team's intensity high.

He was glad to finally be home and slipped up the back stairs to avoid the partiers who were blasting music in the basement. He was optimistic that he could lock himself in his room, perhaps do a few shots and pass out unnoticed … but, unlocking his door, he soon found this assumption to be dead wrong.

"WHERE HAVE YOU BEEN!!!!????" Kelly started in on him before he could even take off his coat. His big friend's tirade continued for nearly a minute as he cussed-out Sean, informing him of how irresponsible he was and that people had been looking for him and worried about him for nearly twenty-four hours.

The imminent tension Sean felt between Nick and Kevin was nothing compared to what Kelly was dishing out. While Sean was disturbed to have no recollection of the prior evening's events, he was at least satisfied that Kelly could piece things together for him.

Around midnight on Friday, Randy Hordelman, back in town for the weekend, and his date had shown up at Beta Beta Beta needing a ride back to their hotel. Apparently they had rousted Sean out of bed and convinced him to let them drive his car to the hotel under the condition that he would be able to drive it on the return trip to make it to work Saturday morning.

Slowly noticing how inebriated Sean was, Randy had invited him to pass out on their hotel room floor. Unfortunately, that only lasted until Randy needed to use the restroom and Randy's date told Sean that he had two minutes to sober up and get out. He had staggered out and not been seen since.

"We've all been worried sick about you since the middle of last night," Kelly stated, turning back to his TV. Sean was too tired to argue with the man. Could he help it if he had tried to be a Good Samaritan the night before without even knowing it?

He paused for a moment to watch his roommate stare, mesmerized by some late night trash show. Sometimes, it seemed like the only thing in the world that Kelly needed was that blasted TV.

Sean's head hurt and he had no energy to continue the discussion. His life was out of control with insurmountable debt, nonexistent career prospects, bad grades, alcohol, lack of love life, and the recent strains on his and Kelly's friendship. He had to turn a corner sometime soon.

Amazed that he could feel worse this evening than he had with a major hangover when he woke up, he made a mental note to figure out how to mend fences with Kelly the following day … sleep was the priority of the moment.

Chapter 19

Nick sat at the kitchen table with the Monday morning newspaper. The boy's fists were clenched tightly on the outer borders of the broadsheet as the tension in his face pursed his mouth and wrinkled his nose. He didn't even look up as his brother entered.

"Riverside Wrestlers Battle for Position," read the column header. It was less the article's existence than Nick's perception of the backstabbing behind it that infuriated the boy. Still, the column pushed the conflict beyond the wrestling room for the entire community to see and judge.

"What are you reading?" Ron asked.

Nick sat silently, glaring at the paper for several more seconds before replying, "Garbage."

The battle to dominate the state's 145-pound weight class begins as an internal struggle for two Riverside wrestlers," the article began. *"Kevin Hermanns, who placed third at 145 at last season's state tournament, and Nick Castle, who came on strong late last season at 135 before being injured in the conference tournament, need to look no further than their own wrestling room for solid competition. Both grapplers sport perfect 9 – 0 records coming out of this weekend's dual tournament and both have their eyes set on the state's 145-pound crown.*

Hermanns has been wrestling at 152 pounds thus-far this season but indicated this weekend that he feels he is a bit light for that weight class and intends to move down. This will put pressure on Castle who will either need to successfully defend his current varsity spot, move to 152, or challenge his older brother Ron (7-2), the team's current 140-pounder.

A wrestle-off is expected to take place this week with the victor representing Riverside in the 145-pound slot at the big pre-Christmas tournament next weekend. The entire state awaits the results.

"I don't want to deliver this," Nick snarled as he put the paper down, giving Ron the opportunity to snatch it up and quickly peruse the column. "This is between Kevin and me. The whole city doesn't need to know about it."

In the back of the younger boy's mind, questions were being asked about who would read the article, who would bring it up in the halls, which teachers would ask him about it in class ... He didn't want to be put on the spot with everyone staring at him but now felt it was inevitable.

"It could be worse," his brother countered. "I don't know why they had to put my record in here. Do we have to trumpet to the world that I lost? It was already in yesterday's box scores."

Silence filled the room. It had been a stressful weekend for both boys. Yet, the weekend was now officially over. Practice would start soon, enabling them to focus on the future.

Chapter 20

Sean was beyond frustrated but tried to keep his composure. Trying to study the technique of two dozen wrestlers while at the same time keeping an eye on his stopwatch and keeping the boys from falling on each other was more work than he could expect to keep up with on a normal day, much less at 6:30 in the morning while he was mildly hung over.

He tried to focus on the fact that the situation was his fault. He certainly could have chosen to stay in the previous night but he had gone out and had a few anyway. It was the kind of morning in which he avoided live wrestling for himself to eliminate any potential bad influence on the students.

His animosity was not with the wrestlers but rather with Coach Kreitzer. The man had shown up late once again and had promised twenty minutes earlier that he would be right up to the wrestling room. Yet, here Sean was, still waiting and shouldering the load, flying solo.

"Don't reach backward!" he shouted toward a newcomer a moment too late as the boy's more experienced partner, from the top position, grabbed the boy's arm and used it as leverage to turn him to his back.

Sean stopped the contest briefly, giving the less experienced wrestler a few quick pointers before sending the two back into action.

He looked across the mat to see the Castle brothers battling for position. Ron had gotten reasonable penetration on a shot but Nick had gotten under his brother's arm with a whizzer and was valiantly holding him off. It was an interesting battle of wills and the assistant coach let the boys go for nearly another minute to see if one could prevail before whistling for a break.

Needing hydration as badly as anyone else in the room, Sean joined them in line at the drinking fountain.

"Nice moves against a very strong opponent," he commented to Hermanns. He had paired the highly touted wrestler against 215-pound Clifford Vassec which turned out to be a good test for both as talent challenged mass.

Kreitzer was supposed to lead half of the drills but the boys were now well over half-way done with practice, with still no sign of the assistant principal. Sean opted to improvise.

"Get your running shoes and then line up, smallest to largest," he instructed. "You're going to pair up with the wrestler next to you, close to your weight, and run with him on your back. When you reach the far end of the wrestling room, switch so that your partner carries you. We'll start with five circuits."

It was 7:20, nearly time to wrap things up by the time Kreitzer graced the team with his presence. Sean had just instructed Oscar to lead post-practice stretching when the man confronted him with a quick reprimand instead of an apology or note of gratitude for running the entire practice on his own.

"How dare you show up for practice sweating booze," the man growled.

Sean was caught a bit off guard. He had always taken extra measures to avoid any signs of alcohol when he was around the team.

"At least I show up," he responded.

"You have no idea how much work is involved with being an assistant principal," Kreitzer fired back.

"That's true," Sean again countered stepping closer to avoid arguing openly in front of the wrestlers, "but YOU have no idea how much work it is being a wrestling coach."

The relationship was continuing to move in the wrong direction. Their eyes locked for a moment of tension before Sean turned his attention back to the team and the final wrap-up.

Chapter 21

Nick walked into the commons with his salad, the smell of burgers and fries still lingering in his nose. It was Monday lunch and the boy knew that both he and Hermanns would be weighing in at 145 for the evening's dual. He just had no idea which weight class Coach Tyler would put him at. In any case, he had packed his salad with vegetables, fruits, meats and cheeses, ensuring that he was giving his body the proper nutrients to stay strong and lean. These characteristics would be important at any weight.

Spying Oscar at their usual table at the far end of the commons, Nick made his way across the room. The two boys had not spoken since the dance. He was bitter about losing his lead-in with Sandi and, at the very least, he wanted to know Oscar's intentions. Did he have designs on taking her out despite knowing Nick's interest? The memory of the dance made Nick want to punch the smaller wrestler in the head.

Oscar was as obnoxious as ever when Nick arrived. "You're lucky we have a dual instead of practice today," the 130-pounder stated. "I'd probably have to give you a smack, smack."

The smaller boy accentuated the "smack, smack" by giving a quick motion with his hand, as if slapping an imaginary opponent and then immediately following up with a backhand.

Nick let the words roll off of him even though they fueled the boy's craving to pop Oscar in the melon. He looked around to see whether or not Sandi was in the area.

"Is it just us today?" Nick inquired, trying to sound nonchalant.

Oscar shoveled another heaping forkful of food into his mouth instead of responding. Nick took it as a sign that they would be lunching alone and opted to not push the subject and cause an unnecessary public display. When the right time would be to discuss this, Nick didn't know. What he knew for sure was that it would be in a setting where he wouldn't risk Oscar causing a scene.

The two sat in near-silence throughout the meal. It was awkward enough that Nick's mind even started wandering to his post-lunch Physics class. The concepts they had been discussing made absolutely no sense and Nick found himself falling further and further behind. Having his grades at risk was a major concern to him, intermingled with all of his other off-the-mat headaches.

"Hi."

Nick's adrenaline hit the ceiling as he looked up to see Sandi's sweet face. Just being around her made the stoic youth antsy and borderline giddy.

Unfortunately, her visit was short lived. She just stopped by to mention that she needed to eat in the choir room to get some things done. The boy took consolation in the fact that she had felt compelled to come over at all and give a reason for not joining them … until he pondered that the message might be pointed more toward Oscar. How could he get a good read?

He tried to be discrete as he stared after her until she disappeared down the hall.

Oscar didn't say a word until Sandi was out of earshot.

"If you want, I can see if the janitors will lend you their mop," the smaller grappler finally commented, standing up to leave.

Confused, Nick could only wrinkle his nose and ask, "What?"

"You're going to need it to clean up all of your drool," he continued.

"Don't start with me," Nick snapped.

"Quit being a dork," Oscar responded. "You know you want to grab that little butt of hers, but you'll never have the chance."

Nick felt himself turning red.

"You knew I liked her and had one chance to dance with her and you still asked her to dance," he stated intensely yet quietly.

"… because you're so lame that I knew you'd never ask her," Oscar replied in a similar tone. "Then she would have been dancing with one of her geek friends, and I would have had to stand there staring at your ugly face."

As the boy started walking away, Nick wanted to tackle him and pound him for screwing things up at the dance. Maybe she'd be Nick's girlfriend now if not for Oscar's stunt. Yet, the last thing Nick needed was a highly viewed fight in the Riverside commons.

He finished his salad and moved on to Physics class, hoping that the coaches would allow him to give Oscar some payback during the following afternoon's practice.

Chapter 22

Nick glanced over his shoulder. How much time was left?

As if knowing the wrestler's question, Coach Tyler glanced at his stopwatch and barked out, "Twenty seconds."

Nick was getting desperate. He was down four to five and hadn't gotten a decent shot on Hermanns since the first period.

His opponent was clearly content with riding out the remaining time, locking up and trying to keep Nick at bay. It was borderline stalling to be sure, but Nick knew that his coaches would never call it.

Nick pushed Kevin's arms away, working to create a decent opening but none appeared.

"Ten seconds!"

Coach Tyler's update caused Nick to react with haste, taking a shot from way too far away. Hermanns easily sprawled, using his superior strength to ward off Nick's attack and drive the boy's head into the mat. With no hope of pulling his opponent's leg in, Nick was forced to let go, pushing Kevin away as time ran out.

"Time!" Tyler called out. "Hermanns five, Castle four. Kevin will be 145 at the pre-Christmas tournament, Castle 152."

Nick shook Kevin's hand. It was certainly no disgrace to lose to a wrestler of Hermanns' caliber but the whole situation still irked the boy. As a light 145-pounder, Nick felt that he could compete at 152 but did not have any confidence that he could bring home a championship while giving up nearly ten pounds.

"Staller," Nick's mind raced to the negative and he tried to shake it off. He wanted to be a team player but his mind kept going back to blaming Kevin for not doing what was best for the team in Nick's mind. Surely the team was stronger with Nick at 145 and the more powerful Hermanns at 152 than vice versa.

He felt a hand pat him on the back and looked to see Coach MacCallister's calming face.

"It looks like you've got an excuse for eating double lunches the next few days," the young man commented. "These guys might be bigger than you, but I'm still willing to bet that you can give the top guys a run for their money and more."

Nick's mood lightened slightly.   Leave it to Coach MacCallister to find some kind of a bright side and be Nick's advocate yet again.   While extra food was nice, Nick's main concern was how he would handle being the small guy in a weight class with two returning state champions.

He'd have a few days to think about that one. He crossed the mat to don his running shoes for the day's conditioning.

Chapter 23

Sean looked up and watched the clock closely. He felt ill and dehydrated. This was one of those days when 5:45 could not come quickly enough. He had to smile when he heard Coach Tyler bark, "Bring it in, gentlemen," at a mere 5:40.

Sean lumbered to the center of the mat. It would have been embarrassing to throw up in front of the team, certainly not something he would live-down quickly. He only needed to make it through the pep talk and then he would let the wrestlers roll the mats without his help tonight. He just didn't have it in him.

"If you think you're done, most of you are almost right," started Coach Tyler. "One more drill and then you get to shower up."

Sean didn't like the sound of this. He knew Tyler well enough to suspect that whatever he had planned, it wouldn't be easy.

Within moments, those suspicions were verified as the coach described the final drill. He would pair up wrestlers and they would wrestle until one led by three points. The winner would then leave for the locker room and the loser would have to wrestle another loser from within their bracket.

"I call it, 'Losers Advance'," commented the coach. "The final four losers run ten wind-sprints and roll-up the mats. Come see your pairings. MacCallister, you are not exempt as I need you to round out the pairings. However, I may need to re-consider your employment if you end up in the final four," he commented as he held up the bracket. Sean could not quite tell whether or not the man was jesting.

"Please Lord, give me someone easy," Sean prayed under his breath. His body was already beginning to shake. It needed rest.

"I've got you, Coach." Nick's voice was far too friendly as he tapped his mentor on the back. Sean cringed. This was not what he needed.

As he faced the boy, he tried to look well. However, he had a feeling that he was beginning to turn gray. The whistle blew.

"You're all mine, old guy," Nick teased. He had no idea how old Sean felt right now. "You're going to get stuck with the loser between my brother and Hermanns."

"Why today?" Sean thought. "I've got two finals tomorrow, I feel like death, and I've got an emergency meeting of the fraternity executive committee tonight." This was truly not the way for him to end practice.

Sean hoped that Nick would not see his body trembling. He tried to pass it off as extra movement. Nick took the first shot. As Sean sprawled, he could feel the nausea setting in his stomach. He felt weak.

"No!" he thought. "Not now."

Nick was climbing, relentlessly trying to pull Sean's leg forward and topple the man to get his two points. That would mean Sean would need five points in order to come back and win.

Sean looked for some way, any way, to keep his balance. He hooked Nick's arm, and drove the boy's head into the mat. It was much harder than he would usually push one of his wrestlers but Sean was getting desperate. He knew that the nausea was a precursor to the migraine. It would blast through his skull like a pile driver, but he doubted that Coach Tyler would let him use it as an excuse to end his participation in the drill.

Sean spun around behind Nick and got his two points.

Not surprisingly, Nick didn't let up. The boy was already pushing forward, trying to break free.

The dull ache started in Sean's head. "Not now, God, please, not now," Sean pleaded. He felt a small bit of vomit rise in his throat but quickly swallowed it before it left his mouth.

He had to turn Nick. It was the only way. He would get his two points and shuffle down to the locker room where he could cover his head and ride this thing out.

Nick was bucking. It was like trying to ride a freaking bronco. Sean tried to grab the boy's arm but his hand slipped right off from the sweat. Nick used Sean's loss of balance to come within an instant of turning the tables but the assistant coach was able to right himself and hold his position.

Sean's whole body was trembling with minor convulsions. When would the lightning strike? Would it be in two seconds? Four? If he turned the boy to his back, would he be able to hold him long enough to get his points before crumpling in pain?

These thoughts pounded through Sean's head as Nick continued to squirm. Would he still have a job tomorrow? How was he going to pay his bills? He flattened Nick out and quickly wiped a small bit of barf from his lips on his shirtsleeve.

The thudding in his head intensified. "Here it comes," he thought. "I need to put him on his back NOW." In a burst of strength, Sean threw in a half nelson. "Please turn," he thought. "Please turn now."

It didn't work. "Why?" he thought. Tears were coming to his eyes. He had to get Nick to his back. It had to work this time. With all of the power he had left, he inserted a clumsy chicken wing and moved toward Nick's head.

"Ow, coach!"

The boy's voice brought Sean back to reality as he felt something strain in Nick's shoulder. In the background he heard a whistle blow. Everything was a fog.

Coach Tyler stepped in. "Are you okay, Nick?"

"Ow, my shoulder."

Sean was horrified. "I'm sorry, Nick."

The boy lay there, face down, holding his upper arm.

"Go put some ice on it," came Tyler's voice. "Who was winning?"

"He was," Nick replied.

"Go shower, Sean."

Immediately, the feared migraine hit Sean.

Later, he barely remembered limping down to the locker room, leaning on the wall the entire way, lying down on the coaches' couch, and covering his head, in pain and shame.

Chapter 24

Nick trudged quietly along his paper route, pondering the upcoming weekend. He was only a day away from boarding a bus to the big pre-Christmas tournament, the third largest event of the year. Nick was eager to impress in his first showing as a competitor.

His shoulder was a bit tender but he refused to use it as an excuse. After the previous evening's mishap with Coach MacCallister, Nick's dad had taken him to a doctor as a precaution to get the joint looked at. Fortunately for the wrestler and his coach, all that was noted was some inflammation and possibly a minor strain, certainly nothing that should keep him from competing over the weekend. Ice and ibuprofen would do the trick.

Unfortunately, there was still no spring in the boy's step this morning. So much of his current mood reminded him of a year earlier when he missed the pre-Christmas tournament completely after having lost his varsity spot. He walked on, mulling over why an undefeated varsity star would be harboring the exact same feelings as someone sitting on the bench.

Granted, the boy's prospects for the upcoming tournament, not to mention the remainder of the season, looked daunting. His build was slight, not stocky and muscle-bound. At 145, it was his technique and leverage which made up for his average physical power. Against competition ten pounds heavier, he was bound to move to "far below average" in the strength category.

The biggest issue weighing on his mind was disbelief over how everything had changed so quickly. Just four days earlier he had been walking on air, feeling indestructible after maintaining his undefeated record coming out of a tough dual tournament. Today, he was looking for a way to regain any kind of momentum. It was a toss-up as to whether his recent issues with Hermanns or Oscar were more to blame.

"Pull yourself up," he reminded himself. "Nobody is going to get you back in focus but you."

While the words themselves seemed right, they didn't provide him with a map for getting back on track.

Chapter 25

Sean could only find two things to be the least-bit happy about as he staggered up the stairs; he still had a full bottle of rum in his room and the blood on his torn shirt wasn't his own.

It had been a rotten day that had turned even worse as it passed into the evening hours. He had gotten an assignment back and had been awarded a "D" for his efforts. A "D"? Sean MacCallister didn't get "D's," especially after the amount of sleep he had lost working on that project. The material just didn't click for him. Why didn't anything seem to click for him anymore?

His diminishing mental abilities both angered and scared him. With no money or insurance, he vacillated between pondering how he would deal with the situation for the long term and simply giving up, telling himself he didn't even deserve to be fixed. It all tormented him on good days and drove him to drink on most days, making the situation even worse.

He had still been fuming about the "D" as he arrived at wrestling practice and Kreitzer had ensured that Sean's late afternoon hours didn't improve his temperament. The man had shown up on time for a change and started needling Sean as the two got dressed in the coaches' office. Once they moved into the wrestling room, the man continued by consistently second-guessing and trying to change the drills Sean had spent a good hour developing. For a man who knew next-to-nothing about wrestling, he sure proved himself successful at finding fault.

The two assistant coaches had mixed words again in the office as they had gotten ready to leave, ensuring that Sean left Riverside in an even worse mood than when he arrived.

Unfortunately, Sean's next stop had been a new country bar for Thursday night drink specials; three-for-one bar pours were exactly what Sean didn't need in his current state-of-mind. He started the night with the cheapest tequila on the list and had downed it like water. He quickly lost track of whether he had gone through two rounds or three, certainly it couldn't have been four ... could it have?

The big man who had slammed into him and spilled his last remaining shot glass feigned innocence, but Sean knew better. He was a brute, just looking for someone small to beat on. Tonight, he had picked the wrong victim as the situation brought back a slew of memories of growing up in the MacCallister household.

By the time the bouncer tore Sean off of the man, MacCallister had a few minor scratches and abrasions, but his opponent's face was quickly turning into mush. The bouncers had thrown Sean outside where he had been fortunate enough to catch a ride home with some women from a neighboring sorority.

The whole way home, he believed that he couldn't fall into a worse mood than he was already in … he was about to find out otherwise.

* * *

Sean opened the door to his room. As usual, Kelly was sitting inside, eyes glued to the TV with a mound of empty beer cans by his side.

"You have a message from your sister," the big man noted, rising from the couch.

Sean smiled, a wry drunken smile as he sauntered to the answering machine. He and Kelly were the two poorest people he knew. Even sharing a phone line to save expense, they were still in grave danger of having their service cut off at any time.

"Let's see what my leetle seester has to say," the young man slurred as he pressed the button. The somber look on Kelly's face led him to believe that his roommate already knew the message's contents.

Sean was a bit surprised that the big man hadn't answered the call outright. Due to recruiting season, Sean had turned the phone's ringer up all the way so the two young men would never miss a call. It should have been loud enough to be heard down the hall or possibly even on other floors.

"Sean, it's Amy," his sister's voice had a tinny quality to it, as if she had been crying. Sean's anger turned to concern for a moment.

"Dad is in the hospital. He's real sick. Call me when you get this message. He wants … I want you to come home."

Instantly, he turned back to anger at the voicing of the request.

"Well, maybe I don't care what he wants … I want," he growled, picking up the phone. Kelly immediately stepped in to stop him.

"Sean, don't call her back right now."

"Why not?"

"Because it's almost midnight and you're loaded."

"Yes I am, and I'm going to tell her that I am already at my home and I won't be leaving here anytime soon."

Kelly grabbed the phone before Sean could dial.

"Sean, don't!"

His roommate's intrusion and insistence irritated Sean. Yet, with all of their recent run-ins, the smaller man thought better of forcing the issue at this time, backing down with only a stern look and a tone of resentment in his voice.

"Maybe you're right, where is my rum?"

To Sean's further annoyance, his roommate took the hard line with him on this subject as well.

"You've had enough for one night, just sleep it off, you'll feel better tomorrow."

Sean looked around and noted five empty beer cans on the end table near Kelly's couch.

"You should talk," he responded. "Now where is that rum?"

He tried to push Kelly out of his way but the big man wouldn't budge.

"I'm cutting you off, Sean," Kelly declared. "We need to talk about your drinking. Maybe, we need to talk about both of our drinking. But we need to do it when we're sober."

Sean's anger had almost reached its tipping point. Everywhere he turned, somebody was beating him down about something. Maybe he couldn't control his lack of career options or his broken mind or the people that were getting down on him about grades and everything else, but he could at least soften them by passing out and escaping. He spotted the bottle on the other side of the room, beyond Kelly, and tried to make a break for it, only to be restrained by his friend.

"Don't start with me, man. I just need one more drink."

"No more tonight."

Things suddenly moved in slow motion as Sean did the one thing he would consider unfathomable when he was sober; he took a swing at Kelly, catching his best friend squarely in the cheek.

The equally unexpected retaliation followed immediately as Kelly stepped up and pounded Sean with both hands, open palms catching him in the chest and launching him through their open door into the hall.

The physical part of the fight ended there as numerous fraternity brothers, hearing the commotion, grabbed the two men to keep them separated, saving them from themselves and each other. The swearing and threats continued as four brothers pulled Sean down the hall and down the stairs.

It was the last thing Sean remembered about the night.

Chapter 26

The blackness slowly began to dissipate and Sean found himself in a pre-waking fog. He pulled the covers closer to keep the cold out.

In this half-awake state, he slowly became aware of his body. His stomach hurt with the all-too-familiar, "hangover post-vomit" feel. Last night must have been a bad one as it hurt all the way through his chest.

He rolled over to pull the covers even closer to him and felt the pain in his chest worsen. This wasn't his usual post-vomit chest pain. It actually felt like something may be broken. Had he gotten into an accident?

Refusing to open his eyes, he pushed his face into the pillow, enabling himself to more effectively avoid the light which was too much for his condition. The fog would lift shortly, he knew, he just needed a bit more time to remember the events of the prior night.

"Concentrate," he thought, "where did I go after practice?"

The floodgates suddenly opened as he remembered the altercation at the bar, the message from Amy, and the run-in with Kelly.

"No," he thought as his mind raced through the scene. His blood ran cold as he remembered hitting the big man, his best friend, the only person on Earth that Sean truly loved and trusted … his brother.

And Kelly had hit him back but it was no regular hit. In all of the run-ins with Sean's father and fights throughout his adolescent and young-adult years, he never remembered having been hit that hard. He remembered the impact to his chest, flailing to keep his balance as his body was launched backward through the door, and vaguely recalled cutting his arm on the doorframe as he unexpectedly exited.

It all flooded back to him as he remembered both of them yelling, "I'll kill you!"

Now, in his calmer state, he was relieved that neither of them had gone for the revolver in the bottom drawer of their desk, leading to something not only regrettable but also irreversible.

Had Kelly broken Sean's ribs? It hurt to breathe. That certainly wasn't a good sign. Sean reached over and felt his left arm with his right hand. The cut on it had scabbed over and was sure to look unpleasant. He hoped he hadn't bled all over the sheets.

It wasn't until that moment that Sean was jolted by the realization that he had no idea where he was. He felt like he was living in a Gear Daddies' song as he slowly removed the pillow from his face to see off-white residence hall walls and a very tidy room. The substantial amount of pink in the décor filled him with an immediate dread of who might have brought him here and what they may have done during the wee hours of the night.

He could feel that he was wearing his boxers but the rest of his clothes were suspiciously absent as he scanned the floor and furniture. He wasn't sure whether to be relieved or scared that his hostess was also missing.

"What have you gotten yourself into this time, MacCallister?" he pondered. "A broken body, no clothes and nobody to call to pick your sorry butt up."

He momentarily contemplated whether or not he had finally hit bottom but pulled his mind away, concerned that he could possibly jinx himself and find an even lower level. He shivered at the thought of what a lower level could possibly be.

The sound of a door opening behind him made him jump, taking the breath out of him as the pain in his chest surged.

"You're alive." Even her welcome voice was hard on his pounding head.

"I wish I wasn't," he admitted, craning his neck backward to take a look at her.

She was tall and blonde although he couldn't make any kind of judgment about her face or her build due to the lighting, her enormous bathrobe and the apparent layers she was wearing under it.

"That could be because of the hangover," she responded, handing him some aspirin and holding out a glass of water for when he was ready. While her voice housed a hint of irritation, her actions were those of an angel.

"Thanks," he said, downing the pills and praying that his stomach wouldn't reject the accompanying water.

He tried to figure out a sly way to ask about the prior night's events. This woman did not look the least bit familiar which scared him considerably. Unable to be creative in his weakened state, he finally just blurted out.

"I really don't remember anything about last night. May I have my clothes back?"

The woman looked annoyed. From the pale glow of the hall light, he could make out some attractive facial features, despite the aggravated frown.

"Well, if you're thinking that you being in your underwear means anything happened between us last night, you're sadly mistaken," she started, shaking her head and looking sternly at him.

"You were inebriated and, lucky for you, my friend Sara knew you because she lives in the sorority next door to your house. You told me that you would be killed if you went home, and since I didn't want to deal with the guilt of reading a story about you being found frozen to death in some parking lot, I brought you back here. You rewarded me by puking all over yourself and my rug. You'll have to excuse me if I'm not especially pleasant to be around right now, but I spent most of the night in the laundry room, cleaning up your mess."

Her halo was getting shinier and shinier all the time.

"Thank you for putting up with me. Would you be offended if I admitted something else?"

"Let me guess, you don't remember my name."

He nodded sheepishly.

"I'm Julee Novak," she said.

As he reached out to shake her hand, he noted, "I'm Sean MacCallister."

"I know," she responded. "I was sober last night."

Chapter 27

Ron glared intently at the face in the mirror as he brushed his teeth, glad that he and Hermanns had finished their argument before Nick returned to their hotel room. They would weigh in for the pre-Christmas tournament in nine hours and the last thing he needed was Hermanns telling him what to do.

The boy didn't mind the argument itself; he liked confrontation and getting his adrenaline up. What he resented was that Hermanns, or anyone else, would imply that Nick was a better wrestler than he was.

Perhaps part of it was the history. Ron had always outshined Nick. The older Castle brother was always, "The Legend" while the younger was "The Follower." Their records this year implied otherwise.

What cut Ron to the core was Kevin's assertion that having Nick at 140 would be of greatest benefit to the team. 135 was supposedly the slot for Ron as, in Hermanns' words, "it would give Riverside two legitimate contenders for state titles," implying that it was time for Ron to give up his dreams and let the other two boys assume the spotlight.

Hermanns, along with everyone else in the state, had written Ron off. It made Ron so angry that he wanted to break something, preferably something human.

The boy finished brushing his teeth and spit. He only hoped that he had this exact same feeling while on the mat the next two days. Ron refused to be forgotten or a has-been. With the right mix of focus, anger and adrenaline, he believed that he could still be unstoppable. It just felt like he was the only one to still have any faith that his goal was reachable.

Chapter 28

Coach Tyler had stressed to Nick how important it would be to over-prepare for this tournament. Nick had prepared both physically and mentally by taking his already-intense workouts to a new level. As the seconds ticked down to end his 152-pound semifinal match, one thing was abundantly clear; Nick had not prepared himself to wrestle Chester Troftgruben.

"What else could I have done?" Nick wondered as he peered up at the match score. It was Nick's first loss of the season; he didn't expect it to be a 14 to 3 routing.

Nick had seen Hermanns wrestle Troftgruben twice last year with Hermanns coming up on the short end during both contests. He was aware that Troftgruben was the golden boy, the Cinderella story who had gone on to surprise everyone his sophomore year by winning the state championship at 145 pounds. However, it was not until tonight's match started that he realized just how solid of a competitor this boy was. Nick shot in on his opponent's legs and experienced the feeling of trying to uproot a tree. Troftgruben's strength and experience had put Nick on the defensive for the remainder of the match, an unusual place for him.

As the final three seconds ticked away, Nick continued to fight being turned. He did not want to end the match on his back and add being pinned to the night's woes. As he pushed all of his muscles to their limit, he realized that the extra ten pounds that Troftgruben carried above Nick's own weight was a solid ten pounds of muscle. The only person he could remember being this much stronger than his opponents was Dino Benz.

The buzzer sounded, creating a combination of glee and heartbreak. As happy as Nick was to finally end the hopeless debacle, he was equally distraught that his winning streak had come to an end.

Walking to the center of the mat to shake hands and watch the referee raise Troftgruben's hand in victory, Nick's thoughts flowed back to Dino. When Dino had beaten Bota in the prior year's heavyweight conference championship, Bota had outweighed him by 70 pounds. What had Dino done to counteract that weight and strength differential? Nick wished that he had seen that match as it was potentially Dino's greatest accomplishment and his last great success before his untimely death.

Thoughts of his friend suddenly spiked the sorrow that Nick felt. Why was it that he felt Dino would have the perfect bit of advice at this point? It would probably have been in the form of a solid punch in the shoulder followed by an invitation to either work out or watch match video. Regardless, Nick felt that the big man would have had the right answer after this thrashing.

As he reached his corner, he was greeted by the next-best thing as Coach MacCallister clapped and patted him on the back, serving in his ever-supportive role.

"That was a good effort against a tough kid. I'll spend some time with that match video as I think I saw some of his gaps," the young man offered before being interrupted by the head coach.

"You're going to have to beat him if you are going to be a state champion," Coach Tyler said bluntly. "Do you have any idea how you are going to do that?"

Nick was tired, sore and more than a bit angry about his performance. He didn't want to be wrestling at 152 and wanted even less to work up some impossible plan with his coach. He could think about that tomorrow. Right now, he just wanted to be left alone.

"No," the boy replied.

"I suggest that you spend some time watching the video of that match this next week," the coach continued. "That kid has his weaknesses but you're going to have to watch very closely to find them. You'll need to watch his championship match as well. You will learn something."

Why was it that if Dino had been there to offer the same advice Nick would have readily accepted it, but when Coach Tyler commanded it, the boy's first instinct was to resist? Something about his coaches, with the exception of Coach MacCallister, made him feel like he was fighting each battle alone.

Nick nodded as he put his warm-up tee shirt on and walked away. His head hurt, not only from the physical beating it had taken but also from this new expectation that he would find weaknesses in this opponent who had just beaten him so soundly. It seemed like it would be easier to just figure out how to beat Hermanns and regain his varsity spot at 145. Hermanns was headed for the championship, a place Nick knew that he would have ended up had he been in the lighter weight class.

Hermanns was still on his mind as he entered the locker room. He really wanted his teammate to win the championship. The boy was his friend and each title won would reflect well on the Riverside team. Yet, if Hermanns did win, would the coaches reject Nick's request for a wrestle-off to get the 145-pound spot back? The thought of it made him a bit angry. Why did the only people on the team that could possibly beat him have to be competing with him for the same varsity positions?

He rubbed his eyebrows as he thought the situation through. His headache was not helped by some loudmouth jabbering across the aisle.

At first, Nick was so deep in thought that the exact words that were being babbled didn't register. It was not until he heard his own name enter the mix of comments that he even realized that the boy was talking both to and about Nick.

The weary wrestler looked up to see Paul Bezdok, rambling on.

Nick didn't know Bezdok well. They had been at wrestling camp together the previous summer but Nick's only real recollections about the heavyweight wrestler were that he wrestled for a school on the far western edge of the state and that he didn't wash his hands after using the bathroom, the latter of which seemed like an odd point to recall. Perhaps it only stuck in Nick's mind as he remembered the boy coming out of a bathroom stall just before practice and he pondered what might be on the boy's hands that would soon be wiped on some unsuspecting practice partner.

"Yeah, I'm talking to you, Castle," the boy continued, making Nick half wish that he had paid attention to the first portion of the chunky boy's ranting while wishing even more that he had chosen an area where he could change clothes in peace. Unfortunately, it was too late as Nick had already ditched his warm-up top and tee shirt and was starting to unlace his shoes.

"What?" he replied, hoping that acknowledgement and entry into the conversation would change its apparent negative tone.

"You heard me," the boy continued. "How did you like having your butt handed to you by Chester tonight? You probably felt pretty tough facing those geeky eastern wrestlers but you come out here and take on the western guys and you crumple like a cheap suit."

Nick was glad that his face was still red from his match as it would help disguise the similar shade from frustration and embarrassment that were beginning to flow over him. He had passed a good half-dozen wrestlers in the locker room when he entered and was certain that several more were in the showers or other areas within earshot. It was a painful spot for one who shunned the spotlight.

"Of course, you can take consolation that you did better than your loser brother … so much for the celebrity of Ron Castle, given his fish impression during the quarter finals. He'll be lucky to place."

Nick was splitting his concentration between trying to find a motive for Bezdok's tirade and looking for an opening to blast the boy with a snappy comeback. Picking on his brother's performance dug into Nick even deeper. And, to make matters worse, a crowd was beginning to form.

"Yeah, Spegidos beat the crap out of your brother last week. He told me that the only thing Ron Castle is good for is adding to his streak of first-period pins. By the end of the year, I bet he'll own the quickest pin record for every tournament. He would have pinned old Ronnie in the first minute if the freak hadn't been doing his best Dino Benz impression and stalling like a rented mule."

At the sound of Dino's name, Nick sat straight up, eyes open wide, and crossed the line to become officially irate as Bezdok continued, "Old Thunder Thighs Benz had stalling down to an art, it apparently rubbed off on …"

"What?!!!" Nick interrupted the boy's raving and crossed the aisle in two swift steps to get in the boy's face.

Whether it was a build-up from events with Oscar and Hermanns from the past week or just sheer rage at the disrespect being shown to Nick's fallen idol, the boy had taken enough and was determined to take action. Driven by faithfulness to his friend, he was completely oblivious to the notion that his night and his season's plight were about to get worse.

* * *

Sean walked toward the locker room as briskly as the pain in his chest would allow, kicking himself for not doing a better job of encouraging Nick after the boy's loss. Troftgruben was clearly in a league of his own but it certainly didn't mean that the returning state champion was altogether unbeatable. He wished he had passed on that kind of sentiment before racing off to huddle with the other coaches.

Nick needed someone to remind him that an occasional loss, especially to a wrestler of Troftgruben's caliber, was to be expected. More than that, he needed to know that Sean was in his corner and committed to doing whatever was necessary to help the boy achieve his dream.

He opened the locker room door and held it a moment for a grouchy-looking tournament official who was headed the same way. Neither of them was expecting what this trip was about to deliver.

* * *

Entering the locker room, Sean was annoyed at the sound of voices shouting. However, that annoyance turned to alarm as he realized that one of the loud voices belonged to Nick Castle.

The young man picked up his pace, rounding the corner just in time to see a fat kid shove Nick. As Nick caught his balance and took a step forward, Sean called out to him to intervene.

"Nick!" he yelled.

As the boy turned to acknowledge his coach's call, the fat kid took advantage of the distraction and caught Nick in the face with a fist to the nose. Nick crumbled as suddenly everyone in the locker room seemed to get involved.

Sean was to Nick in a moment as another coach grabbed Bezdok, who seemed to be elated over catching the smaller wrestler off guard.

"How did that one feel, Castle? A cheap shot is worth a thousand words, huh?"

Nick held his face with both hands as blood poured out from under them. Sean quickly pulled his wrestler into a reclined position.

"You'd better teach your boy to not mess with the big dogs," the adrenaline-filled heavyweight yelled to Sean.

His concern for Nick was the only thing keeping Sean from instinctually pummeling the kid for picking on someone a hundred pounds lighter than himself. He was soon covered in blood as he looked for ways to stop the continual flow of crimson coming from Nick's face.

The tournament official who Sean had held the door for was quickly taking charge.

"Get him out of here," the official yelled at the coach who had grabbed Bezdok. "He's out of the tournament."

A wrestler stepped over to Sean and handed him a towel to use as a mop as he cradled his 152-pounder's head in his arms.

"What about him?" a coach asked the official, pointing to Nick.

"He's out too," the man responded, causing Sean's rage to suddenly change direction.

"What?!!!!" Sean argued. "He gets a cheap shot to the face and you're going to eject him?"

"It takes two to tango!" the man responded in a manner which made Sean want to pound him on the spot, bruised ribs or not.

"Take care of your kid," the official continued. "He participated in a fight and he's not wrestling any more this weekend."

Sean knelt by Nick, still trying to control the red river oozing from the boy's nose. He suddenly felt queasy.

"Nick, can you apply some pressure?"

The boy only shook his head; it was clear that the pain was excruciating.

"It's broken," a trainer commented who had entered the room in the meantime. "You had best stabilize that bleeding and get him to a hospital.

Sean suddenly felt like he may be in for a very long night.

Chapter 29

Nick sat in his parents' hotel room, reading *The Outcasts of Poker Flat*. The story was the single bright spot of the day. For a required reading for English class, he was enjoying the tale of the gambler, Mr. Oakhurst, holding a rag-tag group of survivors together after the whole group had been run out of town. In the back of his mind the main character reminded him of Coach MacCallister, always calmly in control. Certainly the group would pull through and the story would have a happy ending. A happy ending was what Nick really needed on this particular day.

Mr. Castle and Ron walked in but Nick kept focused on his reading. He knew how angry his dad was about Nick being involved in what the man called a "senseless Neanderthal moment." His father had even commented that he hoped the boy learned something from his ejection from the tournament. Nick wondered what his dad would say if he had heard what Bezdok had shouted about Ron. He guessed that his dad's reaction would have closely mirrored Nick's own.

It had been a long time since he had seen his dad that angry. Combined with his mom's paranoia about either of her sons getting hurt, Nick knew he would be walking on thin ice if he did anything other than focus on his studies. The last thing he needed was to be benched by his own parents.

The whole ejection situation made him angry. Bezdok's coach had made Nick out to be a hot head but, under the circumstances, Nick wondered how long an average person would have listened to a fat kid's trash talk before snapping. Nick momentarily pondered his faithfulness to his friend and how nobody alive was quite as close to him as Dino had been. It all seemed a bit sad that none of his living friends were worth getting kicked out of a tournament due to a zero-tolerance policy.

"You've become quite a celebrity," Ron commented.

Nick furrowed his brow and peered over the book at his brother.

"In some versions of the story, you were giving Bezdok a beating until some other kid jumped you from behind. There is a rumor that the two of you are going to duke it out after the finals tonight."

"There will be no fight and there will be no finals for either of you," their dad interrupted. "We're getting on the road as soon as you're done wrestling, Ronnie, so we can get ahead of this weather."

"Even though he's a celebrity?" Ron pried.

"One more word about this and you're going to be as far on your mom's and my bad side as he is," their father countered, causing the boy to zip his lips.

"Ugh," Nick thought. If it wasn't bad enough that he wanted to hide his mangled face due to the disfigurement, he now had a deep-down need to hide it to avoid publicity.

Chapter 30

Ron grimaced as he lay in the back of the Castle family van. How long had it been since he had placed fifth in a tournament? It stung the boy's pride to be that low on the platform, even at such a sizable event.

He was secretly glad that his parents had been paranoid about the oncoming weather and wanted to get on the road during daylight before the storm hit in full force. The weather, coupled with Nick's broken nose and ejection from the tournament, justified a unanimous family decision to get out of town quickly.

It wasn't just that Ron didn't want to admit to himself how poorly he had wrestled; there was one thing that hurt more than Ron's pride and, unfortunately, it was his back.

He felt something give when he shot a double-leg in the third period of his final match. He should have known that he was not quite in position. Yet, to finish the move, he had lifted with his back while trying to get his legs under him. It was a bad combination as Ron felt the tearing immediately.

Fortunately, he had held on through the remainder of the period, showered quickly, and gotten to the family van, only walking slightly stiff. Now, the muscles continued to tighten as the journey wore on. From time to time, he bit his lip as he felt the sharp jolt of a spasm. As he lay on the floor in back, Ron contemplated how he would possibly explain his injury without causing his parents concern. His worst fear was that they would get scared and reconsider their choice to let him wrestle.

"Listen to your body," the voice inside his head demanded. It was the same voice that had guided him through his rehabilitation. Yet, he didn't know what to make of it tonight. Back then, there had been no consequences to disobeying. Nobody was going to stop him from pursuing his goal of walking again. Now, it was different. He knew that anything resembling a re-injury to his back would send his mom in particular over the edge and make her withdraw her always-hesitant support of his return to the mat.

The van hit a bump and another spasm rocked Ron's world. He wanted to scream. He wanted the entire world to hear his pain but just couldn't deal with the consequences.

Quietly, he removed the top from his McDonald's cup and, careful to not make any noise, poured the ice into the plastic bag which had come with his salad. He folded the makeshift ice pack and stuffed it into the back of his pants so that it fit firmly against his lower back.

He was a bright kid. Surely he could come up with a "best of both worlds" compromise for this predicament. Alternating between looking for the solution and getting some much-needed rest, Ron braved the cross-state trip in painful solitude.

Chapter 31

Sean took another drink and felt a cold sensation sweep over him. It was well past four a.m. and he sat on the couch; depressed, drunk and alone. He pondered turning on Kelly's TV but really didn't want the distraction. He had gone back inside himself, deep into the Sean MacCallister that nobody else knew, the one he would never show.

He stared out the window a long while into trees and blackness. It was how he felt: sheer blackness interrupted by small intermittent fingers of gray.

One more swig and he burped up a taste that warned him he was overdoing it yet again. He stared blankly at Kelly's note. The big guy had used every curse word known to man in the document, clearly relaying the story that Sean was worthless, and when Kelly returned, he would be living somewhere else. The shiver that raced up the young man's throat seemed to indicate that every word was true as he read the note for the twentieth time. The two had not seen each other or spoken since their fight.

"Why do people live?" he pondered. "What about this existence is worth the pain?"

He had always forced himself to get by with a promise to himself that things were eventually going to get better. Tonight, the doubt was far too deep. Could this possibly be the way that life was supposed to be? Did people truly drown in debt and loneliness and live endless lives of hopelessness?

Where was the sign? Shouldn't there be some kind of indication that things would eventually improve?

He took another tug, this one smaller than the last, more for taste than effect, hoping that it wouldn't push his stomach past the expulsion point. Then, he put his head back and listened to the silence. Anyone who found silence calming was clearly cracked. The eeriness in the stillness was completely unsettling.

Sean closed his eyes and put his fingers to his forehead, wishing that Kelly's note had been the only message waiting for him. Amy's tear-ridden voice filled his ears again, pleading with him to come home and giving him an earful for not returning her prior call.

How ironic that he had pushed the only two people who had ever mildly understood him past the point of resentment. Did they truly despise him as much as he despised himself and this miserable existence?

His neck started swaying as he half-fought to stay awake. If he cowed to Amy's wishes and drove back to Wisconsin, he would most likely miss the VC tournament the day after Christmas. As worthless as Kreitzer was, it would essentially leave Coach Tyler coaching the entire team by himself. Would that cost Sean his job?

One more sip and he laid his head on the backrest of the couch. It didn't matter. His job, his friends, his family, his life ... they could all just go away. He didn't care. The gray fingers vanished as the blackness completely engulfed him and he drifted from consciousness.

Chapter 32

Ron smelled the chicken, mashed potatoes and gravy and knew that his plan was coming together ... for now.

He had not moved from his bed since his father had carried him in from the van in the middle of the night. Ron had faked sleep the entire way, fighting back the urge to scream from the spears radiating from his lower latissimus dorsi. For once he was happy with his loving dad's occasional episode of child-like treatment as he had no other viable plan for getting from the vehicle to his bed in his current pain-ridden state.

He let his eyelids drop to keep up the charade as he watched his dad entering the room.

"Feeling any better, champ?" his dad questioned.

"No," came the boy's quiet response.

He wasn't lying to his father. Not this time. It was earlier when he had claimed to be nauseated and feverish that he had cashed in on the untruths. The fake illness had provided the perfect excuse to stay in bed all day as he dealt with his latest back problems.

Holding his hand briefly to Ron's forehead, William countered, "You don't feel feverish."

"The fever broke a little while ago," Ron lied again, keeping up the farce. "I guess I'm lucky that I have my check-up tomorrow."

He had the feeling that his dad knew more than he was letting on. Yet, if he wasn't willing to call Ron's bluff, the boy was dedicated to continuing to play.

"Doc will fix me up if I'm not feeling better by then," he continued.

"Of course he will," William added, kissing his son on the forehead before leaving the room.

It pained Ron to look at the meal his father had just left. Sadly, this was the decoy meal. Ron had devoured his real lunch, brought in earlier by Nick, almost as soon as the younger boy had left the room. The plate was tucked away behind Ron's bed. Picking at the feast his father had brought in would provide further proof to both of his parents that Ron was far too sick to get out of bed and, if his back didn't improve substantially by the following morning, far too sick to go to school.

"Listen to your body," the voice echoed in Ron's head again. He felt a faint twinge of guilt about listening to the voice while at the same time completely ignoring his parents' would-be wishes for this situation. Yet, the pain hadn't radiated down his legs so he didn't feel that the injury was as serious as it might be.

"You're going to get better," he told himself, "and you're not going to get caught."

As long as his dad and brother didn't compare notes when Nick got home, Ron was pretty sure that both thoughts were true.

Chapter 33

Ron walked stiffly toward the coaches' office. His stomach was feeling queasy from all of his medications and he was fairly certain that his complexion bore a tint of green. Perhaps it wasn't only the medication medley that was upsetting his stomach. In his hand, he held a doctor's slip which he would use for the inevitable conversation he wanted to avoid.

Without the pain killers, he could hardly move. His back was tight and he was getting hit with spasm after spasm. Even for Ron, who had lived through a far worse spinal injury, the pain was completely debilitating. There was no choice for him to do anything but sit out the practices leading up to Christmas and the following VC tournament. A wrestler who can't move can't compete.

"Listen to your body," echoed again in his mind.

The sole bright spot he could find was that his doctor's appointment had gotten him out of a few afternoon classes and, more importantly, would give him an opportunity to talk with the coaches with nobody else around. The last thing he needed was for his teammates to hear him groveling and using a doctor's excuse to spend time on the bench.

The slip from Doctor Whalis was vague. "Ron Castle should not participate in practice for a minimum of one week." As with his parents, he would try to insinuate that he had a bad case of the flu which could be contagious. Would they suspect that he was injured? Was there any chance that they would make him sit longer?

These questions were still going through Ron's brain as he came within earshot of the coaches' office and heard voices. He paused for a moment, feeling a split second of shame about his weakness. Would a stronger wrestler tough it out? Could anyone perform at all with the kind of sharp pain he was feeling?

"NO!" Coach Tyler's voice echoed loud and clear from the room, apparently in a heated debate with someone.

"Ron Castle is NOT a leader on this team!" the man continued. "His role is to push his brother so that his brother can lead this team. When he stepped off the mat at state two years ago, yes, he had a ton of potential. But all of that has changed. He has a new 'support' role and we need him to stick to that responsibility."

The boy stopped in his tracks, suddenly feeling as though he should not be here. What he had just heard would make his request to miss practice less of a challenge. However, it would certainly be tough to look his coaches in the eye feeling that they had lost faith in him. He turned around, opting to take another five minutes before approaching them.

Chapter 34

Nick sat on the steps in the garage, holding Chewie on his lap. The dog leaned into his chest, a single warm spot on a very cold morning.

"At least somebody loves me," the boy thought as he gave the animal a hug, taking in the musty odor of the golden retriever's fur.

Someday, he would like to get his arms around Sandi and hold her close like this. The two hadn't spoken for more than a few seconds since the dance, not that there had been many opportunities to converse. In addition, his discussions with Oscar had been brief at best.

Had Oscar asked her to dance simply to make Nick angry? Did he have a crush on Sandi as well? Was he possibly oblivious to Nick's intention of asking her to dance and asking her out?

To a large extent, none of the questions mattered at this point. None would change the fact that Nick was still alone and, at minimum, two steps away from asking the girl out.

Why couldn't he be someone who would just take the risk and inquire about a date? Why did he have to be so paralyzed with fear at the possibility that "no" could be her answer?

"You'll always be here for me, won't you, fur face?" he asked the dog.

The face full of bad breath and wet tongue that immediately crossed his cheek gave him the feeling that the dog's answer was "yes." The boy gave the dog a kiss on the muzzle to show that the feeling was mutual.

Chapter 35

Sean felt completely ill as the Galaxie 500 rolled slowly into town. The previous night's over-indulgence may have been partially to blame and the ten-hour drive and accompanying gas station cuisine were likely contributors. Yet, his indigestion did not peak until he entered the streets of his hometown. The sight of the main street's buildings alone made him nauseous.

The young man could feel completely at ease pretty much anywhere in the world with the exception of this particular location. It was only a drawn-out phone conversation with Amy two days earlier that had forced him to make the trip.

"Why can't you do this one simple thing for me? You're so selfish!" she had shouted, adding to his lingering guilt from his run-in with Kelly.

With Coach Tyler exercising a rare move by making practice optional on both Christmas Eve and Christmas Day, Sean's excuses had worn thin for not making the trip. He worked the boys hard the morning of the twenty-third and reluctantly got on the road.

He pushed his focus back to the morning's workout, wanting desperately to think of anything other than his present location. Poor Nick had looked as lousy as Sean had felt, wrestling in an outdated mask which he complained restricted his vision and rubbed on his nose, ironically the very appendage it was meant to protect.

Turning off main street, Sean's heart began to race. He was getting close now … too close. He slowly crept along for two more blocks before he stopped at the intersection, refusing to go any further.

One right turn and he'd be able to see it, camouflaged by the trees and likely looking as rustic and sickly as ever, the worn-down shack he had been brought up in. Headlights in his rearview mirror forced him to move the car from its perch and face the unthinkable.

He was pretty sure that he was going to hurl as he pulled into the driveway. His hands were shaking so bad that he could barely hold the wheel. With goose bumps the size of pebbles, he sat and stared at it – facing down a structure holding memories and stories that would make the most freakishly intense haunted houses seem lackluster to him.

Opening the car door and his mouth simultaneously, he filled the gravel with the contents of his stomach, convulsion after convulsion until there was no more. Then, letting the vehicle roll forward a few more feet to pass the mess, he closed his eyes and waited for the shakes to subside.

* * *

He watched his sister move around the room and tidy some papers that had been sitting on the end table. She had offered him something to eat but the very smell of the house had killed his appetite. Instead, he settled for a traveler of rum.

"Are you feeling all right?" she asked.

Sean hadn't felt all right in ten months. He had moved straight from his concussion to a surreal period in which he couldn't remember a single moment of feeling better than slightly below-average … not counting the occasional "up" he got from drowning his inhibitions with liquor.

"No," he finally answered. "I feel like crap. Tonight is worse than most but it's generally pretty consistent. I just feel like crap all of the time."

Listening to his own voice, there was a nervousness in the tone, like he may crack under the pressure at any moment.

"Is it because of your drinking?"

His blood boiled for a moment and he fought to maintain his composure.

"The only time I feel somewhat normal is when I'm drinking," he countered. "This darkness is even worse than in high school. It's been there since I got my skull cracked. I didn't start drinking again until two months later."

"But you don't think of suicide, do you?"

"All the time," he thought but refrained from answering out loud. He had made the mistake of mentioning these tendencies to his sister once while he was in high school and suddenly found himself in therapy and spending his lunch hours with the school counselor. He didn't have the means or the patience for repeating that period of his life.

"Of course not," he lied, putting the bottle to his lips.

The upward motion of the swig caused him to change his gaze and catch a glimpse of himself in the mirror. He resembled something out of a classic horror movie with sunken eyes underscored by large black bags. His face was pale other than the stubble from two days of not shaving. On top of it was the general unkemptness and, of course, the scar.

"Horrifying," he thought and looked away. Any child approaching this rundown shack and seeing someone who looked like him lurking inside would surely be terrified out of his or her skin.

Sean rested his head on the back of the sofa and closed his eyes. He heard his sister approach and could smell her light perfume as she leaned over and gave him a light kiss on the forehead. It was nice to have someone thinking about him, caring about him, if only for a moment.

She moved away and as the perfume scent in the air dissipated into the stench of this dwelling, so did any remote feeling of being loved. His mind returned to where he tended to dwell, lost in the darkness that seemed to constantly consume him. He wanted to be anywhere but here. He would certainly prefer to be back at Beta Beta Beta. But most of all, he wanted to just disappear.

With his broken mind, financial ruin and loss of friends, he wondered what the final straw would be to drive him past his breaking point.

Chapter 36

Nick took a minimal dollop of mashed potatoes and passed the bowl on to his father. As hungry as he was for the Christmas feast, he could only let himself partake in a very small portion of it.

He looked across the table at his brother whose plate looked nearly the same as his own. In a show of constant support, his dad's plate also held only a sparse portion.

"Why do we wrestlers do this?" Nick wondered. He thought back to all of the Thanksgivings, Christmases, and other feasts at which he had picked at a morsel or two of food while everyone else at the table had gorged themselves.

"When the ref raises your arm at the end of the match, it makes it all worthwhile," Ron would say. Then again, that was the old Ron. This new brother of his was using a doctor's excuse to get out of practice for a week and miss the VC tournament. What had happened to the boy who knew no fear and never quit? This seemed an awful lot like quitting to Nick.

Nick took a moment to ponder the whole "quitting" concept. Even when the cards turned up against him, he had always held his own. He was always angry with Mr. Kreitzer and Coach Tyler scared the crap out of him, yet he would never let the two intimidate him into quitting. There was no honor in backing down from a bully.

Ron's hiatus left the team down one strong wrestler. The only silver lining Nick could find in the situation is that he got a temporary reprieve from the 152-pound weight class. He was cutting to 140 for the VC tournament in hopes of getting his legs under him and getting his season back on track. Why the tournament had been planned for the day after Christmas was beyond Nick; it almost seemed sacrilegious. Nevertheless, Nick would find a way to make the weight and he would wrestle.

"The VC tournament," Nick traveled down memory lane. "This is where it all started."

The boy had been having a miserable season his sophomore year until he moved up a weight class to 140 for the previous year's VC tournament. Thanks to some creative maneuvering by

Coach MacCallister, Nick had gone into his first match believing that he would come out on top. Although the match ended with Nick losing by a point, he gained a ton of confidence when he found out that his opponent had been one of the top 140-pounders in the state. From then on, his sophomore season had taken an upward turn with his success on the mat translating to confidence off the mat.

So what had changed this year? He pondered his current list of shortcomings. This year, he wanted to date a girl but there were complications involving Oscar. This year, he had been legitimately bested for the weight class at which he could surely take home the state title. This year, he had gotten expelled from a tournament after having his face smashed in for defending the honor of his deceased friend.

Late last season, he had been hungry and unstoppable. During every match last January and February, it had seemed like he was in the zone. But as he looked at life in general this year, everything seemed gray. It was like watching a black-and-white movie and feeling that there should be color which just didn't want to appear.

Where was the spark? What had given him that extra drive last year?

It wasn't like Nick wasn't motivated. All he thought about was winning a state title. This was why he arrived early and stayed late. Why did he feel so lethargic? It was like he was just going through the motions. Even while wrestling his better matches, he felt that he still had another gear but lacked the clutch for making the shift. He didn't have the answer and he didn't want anyone at this table to even know that he was asking the question. Who could help him? He would bet Dino could have.

This is what he pondered as he continued through the meal. He'd have plenty of time for reflection the next few days while his parents and Ron were at his grandparents' house … lots of lonely solitude during which he could search for answers.

He grabbed a second sliver of ham and avoided his brother's "should-you-be-eating-that?" glance. There was plenty of time this afternoon to work off this meal. The bigger question was whether or not, once he made weight, he would have the fortitude to get his arm raised in the championship match.

Chapter 37

Sean sat at the bar staring blankly into space and pondering how long Amy had been gone. Fifteen minutes? Half an hour? It didn't really matter. He could sit in silence alone just as well as he could sit in silence with her.

The two weren't talking … only drinking. He was angry about having made the trip to this godforsaken town while she was livid at his behavior during their short stay in their dad's hospital room.

The visit had started out well enough. Sean had been taken aback by the old man's appearance. At only 42 years of age, the man could have easily passed for 60, thanks to his years of hard living. Yet he somehow managed to keep a thick head-full of salt and pepper hair.

Twenty minutes of small talk had seemed to drag on for an hour. All the while, Sean shifted from foot to foot, regularly looking toward the door and thinking of the relief he would feel to finally leave.

When the subject changed abruptly to his father's revelation about being clinically depressed, Sean had gotten irritated.

"I just felt like hell, all the time…" the man had commented, "anxious … sweaty… nervous."

Not understanding the disease, Sean's thoughts had turned steadfast to his own point of view, "Whether the man was sad or not, there was no excuse for the way he had treated his kids. Everybody felt anxious and nervous, right?"

Sean was amazed when the old man launched into a lecture about how Sean should be checked for the disease as well and, at the very least, curb his drinking.

"I don't want you to hurt people you care about … to injure your kids. You're so much like me …"

At the last comment, Sean had reached his tipping point and exploded at his father, informing him that he did not have any disease and certainly, accentuated with about every curse word he could fit into a sentence, was nothing like his crusty, violent old man.

He had burst through the coveted door without a "goodbye" and with no intention of ever seeing the man again … alive or dead.

The fact that he threw that last comment at his father before leaving the room had been a major piece of contention between him and Amy.   It felt odd that he didn't regret having said it, even several drinks into the evening.

Where he would go from here, he really didn't know.   He dreaded having to spend even another moment in the shack but the storm forecast to come in from the West would certainly make a ten-hour drive difficult.

For as long as Amy had been gone from their table, he was pretty sure she had taken the Galaxie 500 and gone home.   He pondered the vehicle and how, for all of its aesthetic and functional shortcomings, it had never truly let him down.   He wished that humans were as dependable.

So he sat drinking, with no company, no plans and no options. It seemed to be his situation far too often these days.

Chapter 38

Nick stepped off the scale and scurried to don his workout gear.

"How much do you weigh?" Hermanns asked.

"140," the junior replied.

"Really?" Kevin asked, surprised.

"Plus tax," Nick continued.

Hermanns shook his head.

"I hope it's a low tax rate because we've got to board the bus in ten minutes. Besides, we need Dino's leadership from you, not his sense of humor."

"I'll make the weight," Nick replied.

The wrestler would hold to his word. Making weight was something he had figured out. Motivating the team was the area that still needed work.

Chapter 39

Sean's lips were pulled into a snarl as he stood in his childhood bedroom, hastily throwing his clothes into a duffel bag.

"How dare he ..." the young man raged.

For Don MacCallister to imply that his son was anything like him was an insult. Not only did it make Sean angry, it made him sick to his stomach. Moreover, the old man's stated assertion that Sean had some sickening mental disease like his old man had made Sean want to pummel anyone in sight. He needed to get out of this town and needed to do it now.

Sean approached his closet. This would be his last venture to this godforsaken house; he may as well snatch whichever remaining childhood belongings still carried favorable memories.

As he pulled on the closet door's knob, the warped door opened only inches before embedding its base in the room's thick shag carpet.

Sean lost it. He punched the closet door with his right fist creating a large opening in the flimsy wood. A follow-up blow with his left fist opened a second, matching hole. In his current state of mind, the destruction felt way too good. He hit the door again, continuing to shatter the door's face with his fourth blow breaking through the back of the door. A dozen more punches in rapid succession followed by an equal number of kicks left little more than splinters smattered with his blood. Reaching into the carnage, Sean grabbed the upper frame of the door and pulled it toward the ground. Applying pressure for a number of seconds, the weakened structure collapsed, enabling him to gain entry.

Sean trembled as he entered the opening. Was there anything inside that he really needed?

He instinctively put his right knuckles to his mouth, trying to soothe the pain as he searched in the dim light. His letterman's jacket could stay as could the toys and box of letters from friends long forgotten. He had hoped to find something of value, a lost box of football cards or anything else that might garner him a few dollars or at least a smile on a miserable day. Nothing of the sort stood out.

Sean shook his head. His hands were all cut and filled with wood splinters and all he found was a rack of outdated clothes and some garbage he'd rather forget. He grabbed one of his old favorite sweaters so that the venture wouldn't be a total loss and turned to go before a contrast of black and white caught his eye.

Hanging from a hook on what used to be the back of his closet door was the mask. Sean stopped short before slowly reaching for the object. He had done his best to disfigure the device, longing to make it as gruesome as the broken face it had once hidden and protected. Yet, there was only so much that the officials would tolerate. In the end, it just looked as weathered and downtrodden as Sean felt.

He turned the mask around, studying it from all angles and wondered if Nick may be able to use it. The device wasn't going to do any good in the local landfill and he could just as easily throw it in the Beta Beta Beta garbage if Nick rejected it.

The noise behind him broke his gaze but did not cause him to turn and look.

"You never did have much of a stealth mode," he commented over his shoulder.

In the doorway, Amy's tone reflected the sadness on her face.

"You're leaving?"

It was clear that their confrontation from the previous day was over.

"He broke my face," Sean commented, holding up the mask. "Over the course of half a dozen years, he hit me in pretty much every part of my body."

"We weren't the easiest kids to raise," she interjected. "Maybe things could have been different if we weren't so headstrong and spirited."

"He never broke my spirit," Sean replied, "only various physical parts."

The young man closed his eyes and squeezed the mask like it were Ted Graham's neck.

"I can't stay for him," he finally concluded.

Amy walked over to her brother, studying the cuts on his knuckles.

"Will you stay for me? The weatherman says a storm is coming."

"You're the only reason I came here in the first place but I just can't stay any longer," Sean retorted. "Besides, the only time I ever let the weather hold me back is when I don't want to reach my destination."

Careful not to get blood on her clothes, he gave Amy one last hug before loading his car and getting on the road.

He never looked back.

Chapter 40

Sean had turned north nearly 40 minutes earlier, starting the final 75-mile leg of his trek. The snowfall had been constant the entire way but was coming down much harder now. His speed had been kept well below the limit so far but the big flakes he was seeing were sure to push him down to 40 miles per hour or less.

He pondered what he would give for a nice soft bed. Stopping and sleeping-out the mounting storm would have been the prudent thing to do had his budget for getting a hotel room consisted of more than the two dollars and change that remained after filling up with gas.

The added money from working a few more days would be a nice benefit of arriving home sooner than planned, helping pay some bills for a while longer. He took his final swallow of coffee and a twinge of fear set in as darkness continued to fall and the road-weary traveler's visibility and speed decreased.

The radio had fizzled a couple of hours earlier, likely from a combination of sub-standard weather conditions and generally being a piece of crap. Sean's salvation was that the music he had brought was still engaged and helped to keep him somewhat alert.

"…who all did I offend last night? And I tell myself for the thousandth time, today I start to live right," Sean sang along with the Gear Daddies as he slowed down again. This time, he slowed to crawling at less than 35 miles per hour. The crunching of snow under his tires was a bit unnerving. It was getting deeper and he had not seen any signs of plowing, very odd given the amount of snow.

Perhaps he should stop in the next town he came to. Even without an option of staying in a hotel, he was bound to be able to find a gas station that would let him sit and wait-out this storm. He could sleep in a booth in a cafe. He groaned as he thought about his recent past experience in this area.

The minutes passed as he inched along. Gradually, his speed decreased to 30 miles per hour, then to 25, then to 20. His eyelids got heavy and his dashboard lights dimmed, certainly an indication that his eyes were playing tricks on him. All at once, the music stopped as his "Check Engine" light came on, the combination jarring him to reality and kicking in his adrenaline.

"No, not now, girl!" he pleaded with the vehicle. "We can't have far to go. Just a few more miles and we'll be home."

He noticed now, for the first time, that the air from the heater was a bit cooler. As the engine began to falter, Sean barely got the Galaxie 500 pulled off to the side of the Interstate before the car failed completely.

"Well, what do you do now, MacCallister?" Sean asked himself. He watched the snow swirl across his windshield, driven by the howling wind that gently rocked his Galaxie 500 and began to ponder all of the news reports he had seen over the years of motorists stranded in sub-zero temperatures.

He knew that he would need the coffee can filled with winter survival supplies from his trunk. He pulled on his jacket and ski cap as he remembered a story he had read on hypothermia and what a painful way it was to die. Dreading the pending cold and taking a deep breath, he pushed open the driver's side door.

The wind that bit him was even more painful than expected as he clamored out of his vehicle. It stung his face and neck the most but even his legs, covered with denim jeans, were not impervious to the icy nip. The minute it took Sean to grab his sleeping bag and wrest his can of supplies from the trunk seemed like an eternity as the wind and snow seemed intent on cutting his body. He knew the can's contents could mean the difference between life and death; candles and matches for warmth, several candy bars for energy, and flares for visibility.

Scrambling back into the driver's seat, he pulled the door shut behind him. It took Sean several minutes to stop his teeth from chattering. He knew now, beyond a shadow of a doubt, that walking anywhere was not an option. He would just need to sit there and keep warm until someone …

A miracle! Sean rejoiced. He hadn't even had the chance to finish his thought about waiting for someone to come along when he saw the dull glow behind him, slowly making its way through the snow. Again, he held his breath and pulled his hat tight. "Thank you, God," he quickly prayed. He would wait until the car was almost upon him before braving that wind.

Sean's heart was pounding both from the dread of facing the wind and excitement over his pending rescue, giving him an adrenaline rush. He counted to three and again pushed open the door as the car approached in the far lane. He walked out and waved, making himself as large as possible as the car passed him … and continued down the road.

Sean was dumbfounded.

"Hey!" he yelled, running a few yards and trying to hit the car on the trunk. "Aren't you going to stop?!! You're not going to stop?!!!"

He hurled every curse word he knew at the vehicle as the tail lights gradually disappeared into the stormy distance, wishing he had something to throw besides words.

All alone in sub-zero weather with frozen clothes and a dead car, he ran back to his only shelter, knowing he must quickly get the candles burning and have the flares ready. Another car would be by shortly. He only had to sit and wait.

* * *

Sean stared at the candle. He continued singing but the chorus of "Born in the USA" had diminished to a whisper. How long had he been sitting here? He wanted to look at his watch, but he was too cold, too tired to pull his arm out of the sleeping bag.

Drowsy … drowsy … Sean's head bobbed and his chin hit his chest.

"No!" Sean recoiled, quickly reviving himself. "Born in the USA, I was born in the USA," he shouted, hoping Springsteen's anthem would have some impact.

How much longer could he hold out? He had been tired, not to mention hung over when he started the drive more than 12 hours earlier. Now, after sitting in the freezing vehicle for well over an hour, he was completely exhausted.

Singing was his last resort. He had tried every technique he knew to stay awake. He had tried continually moving his arms and legs but had eventually grown weary. He followed that by trying anger, thinking of everything from his upbringing to Mandi and Ted Graham, to his father's fresh remarks, but eventually his adrenaline had waned and his spirits dampened. All his body wanted to do was sleep.

"No!" Sean thought again. He had read too many stories about people falling asleep in the cold. Once you lose consciousness, you're as good as dead.

Still, he reasoned. Wouldn't it be better to just succumb now? Only the one car had passed him since his own car had died. The weather had grown steadily worse. Was anyone else crazy enough to be out in this blizzard?

He stared down into the coffee can again. The lone remaining candle was keeping his thighs and hands warm. The other candle, which he had used on the floor to dry out his feet and lower legs had burned out within the past ten minutes. He made a mental note that, if he did make it through this situation, he would invest in better candles for next time.

"Better candles AND better candy," he thought. The Snickers bar had melted during the summer months and frozen sometime recently. It still hit the spot but Sean would be sure to renew his stash each fall once he had more money and more time.

Drowsy ... drowsy ... Sean's head bobbed again. He folded his hands to pray. "Thank you for this life, Lord. I'm sorry I didn't do more good things. Please forgive me for the bad ones, and look over Amy and Kelly and Nick and ..."

With those words, the candle in the coffee can on his lap flickered one last time and went out, plunging the car into darkness.

"... and ..." Sean's head bobbed a final time and he was asleep.

Chapter 41

Nick stared out the bus window, keeping his focus away from his teammates. It had been a long bus ride after an equally long day. He wasn't ready to face his coaches yet as he couldn't believe that he had just placed third at the VC tournament.

A year ago, he had placed fifth so, technically, placing third was an improvement. Yet, he was so far beyond disappointed in his performance that all he wanted to do was crawl into a hole somewhere and disappear for a while.

With two teams bowing out due to weather-related issues, Nick found himself seeded second in a seven-man bracket. After pinning his first opponent, he ran into a brick wall in the semifinals. Up by two points going into the third period, he simply could not explain what had gone wrong. He would like to have blamed it on coaching as Coach Tyler had left the match after the second period to coach Hermanns, the team's only champion, in his 145-pound semifinal.

For some reason, Nick had simply lost focus during that third period. He gave up an escape about half-way through it and then found himself wrestling defensively but getting taken down with 15 seconds left. Together the two mishaps gave his opponent exactly the three points he needed. Coach Kreitzer had been little more than a cheerleader, as usual. Again, Nick would have liked to blame the man for being more of a distraction than a guide but knew that the responsibility lay on his own lean shoulders.

He was glad that his family hadn't been there. Ron would have decimated that kid had he been wrestling, Nick was sure of it. His big brother would have taken home the 140-pound title, eating all opponents for lunch. Yet, it was Nick who had wrestled and Nick who had failed. He couldn't blame coaches, his family, or his mask, as uncomfortable and awkward as it was. This one fell solely on Nick who had rounded out the tournament with two lackluster wins.

With the weather continuing to loom large, the tournament officials had eliminated all breaks and wrestled every round, including the championship, on four mats. As soon as Hermanns stepped off of the awards stand, the team had loaded the bus and headed for home.

Nick had been glad when big Clifford Vassec had chosen to sit by him on the bus. The big boy had largely blocked Nick from sight and dozed for most of the three-and-a-half hour trip. In better weather, they would have made it in two hours but, at times, a person could see nothing but white while looking through the windshield. The department of transportation had closed the Interstate, forcing the team to snake its way via back roads for the final 75 miles of the journey.

There was a small cheer as the vehicle entered the city limits. Despite his bad mood, Nick couldn't blame his teammates for being upbeat. Surely none of them wanted to end up as a popsicle, which could very likely have happened had the bus ended up in a snow drift.

The radio had reported the storm continuing to get worse. As they pulled into the Riverside parking lot, all Nick could think about was that, even as the darkness began to fall, he still planned to run all the way home. Bounding through snow banks like a buck was sure to be good for toning his leg muscles. Then, in the solitude of his house, perhaps he could spend enough time watching his matches from the day to figure out why he still wasn't making the grade.

Chapter 42

Thud!

A loud noise echoed somewhere in Sean's subconscious.

Thud!

There it was again. Why did things have to be so noisy all of the time? And why did his feet and hands hurt?

Thud!

What was that noise?

A loud creaking noise came from Sean's left, accompanied by a dim light and a painful burst of cold.

"What is happening?" he asked himself as he tried to get his arms up to protect himself, wearily opening his eyes a crack.

"Are you okay?"

It was a man's voice. Of course Sean was okay. He felt very relaxed, despite the pain in his extremities. He was surprised that the best response he could muster was a quiet, "uh, huh."

"At least you're alive," the man agreed. Sean felt arms around him. He felt some pain as the figure pulled him from the car and out into the cold.

"Can you walk?" the man asked.

Sean didn't respond verbally and was only able to shuffle his stiff legs as the man half-carried, half-dragged him along the side of the road past a waiting set of tail lights, and finally into the warmth of the passenger seat of some type of sport utility vehicle.

The heat was so welcome to Sean. His body could barely contain his joy as the man propped him up and pushed the door shut behind him. If he had the strength to move, he would have danced a little jig. As it was, he just sat, with one eye open, focusing on the driver's seat.

Momentarily, the man re-appeared, entering the car from the driver's side with Sean's duffle bag. In the brief glow from the dome light, Sean was able to make out a man in a ski mask wearing several layers of clothing.

"You picked the wrong night to sleep on the highway," the man commented.

Sean could barely smile in response. He wanted to say, "thank you" but the words only came out as a mumble as Sean fell back to sleep, basking in his new-found warmth.

Chapter 43

Sean slowly started regaining consciousness.

"The music is good," he thought although he couldn't name the band. His extremities in particular felt painfully sore but he felt warm and, at this point, that was really what mattered to him.

He kept his eyes closed, not quite ready to fully wake up. There was a faint smell of grease and gasoline which reminded him of days spent working on his car. Yet, these smells were mixed with an unfamiliar high-end cologne. The combination seemed out-of-place, but somehow soothing at the same time. He heard a series of small clicks and the flow of warm air shifted from blowing on his face to thawing out his feet. There was no bad place for warm air at this point.

At long last, Sean came to his senses enough to ponder whether or not he was being rude. As nice as it felt to sit back and relax, the least he could do was acknowledge his savior and see if there was anything he could do to help. Sean opened his eyes to a squint.

Through his slits, Sean could see the dull light of the dashboard as the vehicle crawled along. He gradually turned his gaze to the driver. He was a young man, within a year or two of Sean's own age. His dark hair was a bit wavy and his beard and mustache were neatly trimmed. Having thrown off his jacket, Sean could see the man's flannel shirt which had the appearance of being neatly pressed.

The man looked vaguely familiar causing Sean to ponder whether the well-kempt young man was a model or a movie star or something.

He studied the man a bit more. There was a calm look on his face, despite the near white-out conditions outside.

"Are we making progress?" Sean finally asked.

Without taking his eyes off of the windshield, the man replied with a wry smile, "I'm glad you're awake. At five miles an hour, progress has been slow."

"I'm surprised they're keeping the roads open," Sean offered.

The man chuckled a bit as he commented, "They closed the Interstate over two hours ago. It's only those of us who are insane enough to do a little off-road action to get around the barriers who are driving at this point."

The man's composed demeanor despite the horrendous conditions was encouraging to Sean. He turned his attention to the outside and was suddenly amazed that they were still on the road. He couldn't see a thing other than white.

"How are you keeping us on the road?" Sean quickly asked.

"It's a bit of an art," the man replied. "Every tenth of a mile, I can see a glint from a reflector off to the right. They add a bit of confidence but I'm mainly relying on the rough warning bumps on the shoulders to keep me honest. Once I hit them, I know it is time to move back toward the middle."

"Resourceful," Sean thought as he stared out the window. Seven or eight seconds passed before he caught a pale glimpse of a reflector. It shocked him how bad the road conditions were and made him curious as to why anyone with an option of staying indoors would choose to drive in this weather.

"You must have a really hot date tonight to be braving this madness."

The young man smiled and held up his left hand to show his wedding ring.

"My baby girl is being born tonight," he responded. "I was in my dad's Quonset working on his snow blower when the call came that my wife's water broke. I told her that I'd be in the delivery room or dead on the Interstate when the baby was born. I let her down big time once and I swore that it would never happen again."

Sean grinned, wishing that he could be in such a devoted relationship. It wasn't often that you found a person willing to risk his existence to make someone else happy. It made Sean like the man even more.

"Do you go to the University?" Sean continued his questioning.

"I will start again in January," the man answered. "I took last spring semester off to get my life back in order and get married. We didn't plan to have a baby so quickly but, when I found out she was on her way, I took the fall semester off too in order to save up some cash. I've got three semesters left to finish my degree. It won't be easy while raising a child but I want to make sure that I can get a good job and raise her right."

Dedicated and hard working, the man was quickly becoming Sean's idol. He made a mental note to start hanging out with this man during spring semester. He was even pondering offering to help by contributing his babysitting services when it occurred to him that he didn't even know the man's name.

"I'm Sean," he stated, holding out his hand to shake.

The man grabbed it with a firm grip, once again without taking his eyes off of the road.

"I'm Ted, Ted Graham," the man replied.

Sean's stomach lurched upon hearing his sworn enemy's name as his countenance changed from admiration to disdain. He suddenly felt as if he were going to vomit.

Chapter 44

Nick filled a plate with Christmas leftovers, feeling like Pavlov's dog as he began to salivate at the very thought of the feast he had declined a day earlier. His mind wandered as he thought about being alone in his family's house. It was unusual for the boy and he wasn't sure whether he liked the feeling or not.

Ruling the roost was sure to have its advantages. The prior night, Nick had weighed himself each hour as his parents and Ron packed for their trip. He had filled his evening with low impact exercise, intent on working off the small dinner he had consumed, leaving him just shy of two pounds over weight. Unlike that evening, he now had complete control over what he could eat and how to spend his time. He only wished he had complete control over his thoughts.

His brain fixated on the conversation he had with Coach Tyler an hour earlier in the Riverside parking lot. He didn't know how to read the man and it drove him crazy. The coach had alluded to Nick's excuses for not winning; his ankle, his weight class, his nose and that ridiculously uncomfortable mask … all were valid handicaps, but the coach seemed to know, as Nick did, that something else was holding him back.

The youth's tendency to dwell on the negative was frustrating even to himself and it began to impact his appetite. He was most exasperated by his coach implying that the entire team lacked leadership from within, the very thing that Nick had spent eight months trying to instill. The assertion that it didn't exist was an agonizing slap in the face.

"What is it that keeps me off the top of the awards stand?" he pondered. "What is driving the two and a half periods of brilliance offset by a single minute of disaster?"

"Dino certainly would have known," he told himself as he walked to the couch with his feast. Ron probably knew as well, but Nick certainly couldn't count on his older brother to share.

He flipped on the TV and surfed through the channels to no avail. As a last resort, he dug through his own movie collection, intentionally ignoring the shelf filled with footage of his and Ron's wrestling matches.

Nick needed to escape, even if only for a few hours, from the thoughts that reared their heads during his times of solitude. He loaded the movie, pressed "play" and allowed himself to retreat and enjoy his dinner.

Chapter 45

Sean stared out the window into the white nothingness, waiting to catch a glimpse of the next reflector off to the side of the road. How long had the two young men sat in silence? It felt like at least an hour.

"I'm going to take Ted Graham out back and beat him within an inch of his life." The words were still fresh in Sean's mind. How many times had he uttered them over the past year? What were the chances that, when the paths of the two young men did cross, it would be under such fortuitous yet dire circumstances.

He looked over at the driver and quickly looked away. How could Sean have not recognized him from the beginning? True, Ted had grown a mustache and beard and the light from the dashboard wasn't providing the best illumination. But given Sean's fierce revulsion of this man, he thought he would have recognized him instantly.

Was Ted feeling as angry and uncomfortable as Sean was? Sean glanced again quickly out of the corner of his eye. Ted didn't seem to have noticed the change in mood. He just continued to watch the road with the same regal look in his eyes.

The tension was getting to Sean. He had thought when he had woken up this morning that he couldn't move any closer to the edge. Now he felt as if he could burst at any moment with no logical outlet for his rage.

"Do you live on campus?"

The question broke the silence, causing the irritable passenger to jump slightly.

"What?" Sean asked, buying time, and trying to read into Ted's query.

"If you live on campus, I can probably drop you off at home on our way into town. If not, I may have to ask that you hang around the hospital while I check on my wife's status. Would that be all right?"

How could Ted be so calm about all of this? Didn't he already know where Sean lived?

Sean thought back to the men's previous encounters. How many times had they actually met? Five? Maybe six? He thought harder. He vaguely remembered their initial introduction a year and a half earlier. Sean had been on his sober streak and Ted had been liquored, surrounded by women. Perhaps Sean hadn't been at the top of the young man's mind? His memory raced through a few more scenes. He had never really had a true conversation with this man, until now. Even the morning at Mandi's apartment, there had been no real dialogue between Sean and Ted. Sean had been far too focused on getting out of there.

"I live at Beta Beta Beta," Sean finally replied. He watched as Ted winced, trying to read the man's body language.

"Oh," the reply finally came. Ted seemed to struggle for words for another moment before continuing.

"Do you know a guy named Mac or Matt or something like that? He lived at Beta Beta Beta last year ... a really preppy-looking guy."

"You've got to be kidding me," Sean thought. With all of the hours of anger Sean had thrown Ted's way and the man didn't even know his name? And what was with the "preppy looking" comment?

"Yeah, I know him," MacCallister replied.

Ted was silent for a while longer, seeming to get a bit nervous.

"Do you think he's around?" Ted finally asked. "I heard that he wants to kill me and I really don't need any more trouble, especially tonight."

Sean noticed Ted's eyes getting a bit misty. "Kill him?" Sean didn't think he had ever stated anything that drastic.

"He went home for Christmas." It was as good a half-truth as any given the situation. Ted just nodded in reply.

Several more awkward seconds passed as Sean pondered who was spreading rumors that he was a murderer in waiting. It bothered him enough to eventually break the silence.

"I've never heard of Mac being homicidal. Why does he want to do you in?"

Ted sighed heavily as he pondered his reply for several seconds. His previous self-assuredness quickly dissipating.

"Do you ever get drunk and do things that are completely stupid?" Ted finally blurted out.

Wow, this man knew how to talk Sean's language.

"If I had a dollar for every time that has happened, I'd be able to retire," Sean replied.

"A little over a year ago, I went to a concert. In my infinite wisdom, I got completely loaded. There was this woman named Mandi that I had a few classes with. We had been flirting back and forth all semester. She gave me a ride home and we hooked up that night. Apparently, she was this Mac's girlfriend and now he wants to throttle me. I guess I can't blame him, but had I known she had a boyfriend, maybe I would have been smarter about things."

Sean suddenly felt like he was in the Twilight Zone. Mandi had told Ted that Sean was her boyfriend? It was suddenly like role-reversal from when he had accidentally ended up with Kevin Lakes' girlfriend nearly two years earlier. His head began to pound as he realized just how much he had in common with this man. He shook his head, feeling empathy for him before suddenly remembering the morning that he had seen Ted at Mandi's.

"So that's it? You didn't go back for seconds?"

"That is certainly not it," Ted continued. "Things only got worse from there."

Sean patiently waited for the remainder of the tale to unfold.

"My wife and I had just started dating at the time. I certainly didn't consider us to be 'exclusive' but I decided to be upfront with her about what had happened instead of trying to hide it. Of course, right in the middle of that conversation, Mandi came over. Fireworks ensued and I had to ask Mandi to leave. She went home and got all drunk and took a bunch of pills."

The young man, calm as a stone driving in white-out conditions, was starting to look a little shook up.

"Anyway, a few days later, I jogged over to her apartment to tell her that it was a mistake, accept responsibility, and let her know that we couldn't be together anymore."

Sean thought back to seeing Ted at Mandi's apartment in sweatpants and a sweatshirt with his hair completely messed up. Suddenly, it was logical that this could be the appearance of a man out for a jog on a frigid winter's day.

"Well ... as we were starting to talk, this Mac guy comes over. It was fairly early in the morning but he was dressed to the nine's looking like he had just stepped out of an *Esquire* photo shoot. He went berserk when he saw Mandi and me together and stormed out of there. Mandi told me that he was irate about us being together and that I was lucky he hadn't killed me right there but he would get me someday."

Sean's head hurt as he mulled over all of this information from a new angle. He moaned quietly, painfully confused. He wished that he had a bottle of liquor or, at the very least, a bottle of aspirin to help him escape from his throbbing headache brought on by this whole discussion.

Chapter 46

Sean couldn't remember having ever been quite so happy to see the city limits signs.

"Thank you for picking me up," he finally managed to eke out.

"Anyone would have stopped," was the driver's only reply.

"The person before you didn't," Sean thought but didn't pass this on, realizing the true gravity of his earlier predicament.

"You always hear about people freezing to death in the winter because they fall asleep. Why is that?" he asked.

Ted seemed to ponder the question.

"I've never really thought about it. I suppose their circulation slows while they're unconscious which speeds up the process. I'm not really sure. If you have to die in a tragic way, I suppose falling asleep in the cold is the least painful way to go. You just don't wake up."

"I suppose so," Sean echoed. "I suppose so."

As they pulled to a stop in front of the Beta Beta Beta house, Ted made a final request.

"When Mac comes back from Christmas break, could you tell him that I didn't know Mandi was seeing anyone? I'm trying to start fresh here and don't need any trouble."

Sean opened the door but looked back at Ted, noting the sincere, almost pitiful look on his face. He looked the man directly in the eye.

"Nobody from this house will ever touch you. I PROMISE you that."

He stepped out of the vehicle and extended his hand.

"Thanks," Ted said, gripping Sean's hand.

"Thank YOU," Sean replied. "I hope everything works out for you and your new family."

In a scenario which would have been impossible a day earlier, the two men shook hands before Ted made his way into the night to see his wife and meet his new baby girl.

Chapter 47

Sean calmly climbed the stairs slowly noticing the odd numbness overtaking him. The past few hours were like a dream, some surreal experience that certainly hadn't happened, but somehow still lingered in the back of his mind.

Reaching the third floor, the only things he truly noticed were the low buzzing of the hall light and the fact that not a single other sound came from within the house as the wind howled outside. He was completely alone.

Seven steps later, he was at the door to his and Kelly's room, inserting the key into the lock as he had done hundreds of times before. His head drooped lazily to the side, completely lost in a daze.

Pushing the door open, his eyes fell on a dark spot on the inside of the door casing. Trying to gain focus, he looked more closely at the rusty brownish hue of dried blood. While his eyes wandered instinctively to his left arm, he slowly put the factors together, realizing that he had left the stain the night of his and Kelly's run-in.

His body jolted like the recoil of a rattlesnake as it all came back to him, his arm catching the door casing as his body flailed helplessly backward … he saw the image of his roommate standing before him that night looking back at Sean after having been punched. There was a vacant look Sean had never before seen in the big man's eyes.

MacCallister's body shook violently as everything he had repressed the past two weeks suddenly hit him: the fight with Kelly, the "Losers Advance" match with Nick, the argument with his father, his near-death experience beside the highway, and being rescued by one of the two people he despised most while fleeing the other.

The jarring onrush of emotion momentarily crippled him as he was hit with the mother of all migraines. His body went limp and collapsed in a pile on the floor. The pain of the fall and collision with the solid surface did not register at all; Sean's world faded to black during his descent.

Chapter 48

Ron lay on the hardwood floor in his grandparents' living room, quietly stretching and exercising his back. Everyone else was in the kitchen playing cards so he didn't fear being discovered. Even if someone did walk in, it wasn't uncommon for Ron to be strengthening his back. He'd just have to make sure that nobody discovered the secret of his re-injury.

He hadn't had a spasm in two days. While not an absolute assurance that everything was fine, at least it was progress.

The boy briefly paused from his routine and wondered how his brother had done at the VC tournament. Had he taken the title? Was he truly on a trajectory to surpass Ron as the family's wrestling standout?

A twinge of guilt shot through him. He knew that he should be happy for the boy. His feelings of emptiness over imminently losing his legacy shouldn't sour his pride in his only sibling. Yet, the superstar who was once on his way to becoming a three-time state champion was now struggling to find a way to not have his name be completely forgotten.

"One thing at a time," he murmured. "Get your body back in line and worry about everything else later."

He pushed all of the jealous and remorseful thoughts from his mind and went back to his stretching.

Chapter 49

In the eerily dim light that seeped through the cracked blinds and splintered the darkness, the room appeared quiet, still … dead.

A body near the point of exhaustion lay half-buried under a jacket and a blanket emitting occasional moans echoing from the nightmare that engulfed his soul. In his unconscious mind, a battle raged – a search for truth and a fight over what the future would bring … if there was to be a future at all.

Thoughts and memories flowed through Sean's head, one blending into the next. *"I'm going to take Ted Graham out back and beat him within an inch of his life,"* Sean's voice told Kelly. As the scene then changed to the events of earlier this evening, he saw Ted's face, and looked into the young man's eyes. *"Nobody from this house will ever touch you. I PROMISE you that."*

The sharp contrast in the two statements brought a groan to Sean's lips as they played and re-played over and over again in his mind.

"I'm going to take Ted Graham out back and beat him within an inch of his life."

"Nobody from this house will ever touch you. I PROMISE you that."

"I'm going to take him out back and beat him within an inch of his life."

"Nobody from this house will ever touch you. I PROMISE you that …"

"I'm going to take you out back and beat you within an inch of your life."

Sean's body recoiled as he let out a yelp like a puppy that had just been struck. The voice in his mind had changed from his own to that of his father. Now, clustered in a fetal position, his breathing was rapid and inconsistent as he saw himself as a little boy, watching his father and listening to his words.

"I just felt like hell, all the time … anxious … sweaty … nervous." The words played against a backdrop of the MacCallister living room as Sean saw his mouth telling Amy, *"I just feel so crappy all the time."*

"I don't want you to hurt people you care about …" Sean's fist caught Kelly square in the cheek bone. It was a scene that had gone through his mind at least a hundred times in the past few weeks, but it was not until now that Sean had truly read the look in his best friend's eyes. It was not until now that he witnessed the stunned, hurt expression, like a small child experiencing pain for the first time. It wasn't the pain of a physical blow; it was the pain of betrayal.

"… to injure your kids." *"Ow, coach!"* Nick screamed as Sean pulled his shoulder too far.

"I'm nothing like you," Sean mumbled angrily as he began to cry, entering the foggy area between slumber and being awake.

"You're so much like me …"

"I'm just like him," Sean said as he pulled himself to consciousness. "I'm just like him."

Tears rolled down his face. He hid his face in the blanket and could not stop blubbering.

"I'm just like him," Sean thought again. How had he not seen this before? Who else had seen it? Clearly Kelly had. Kelly had seen Don MacCallister's image, refused to give him alcohol, and was rewarded in typical Don MacCallister style, with violence. Sean put both hands on the back of his head and buried his face into the mound of blanket.

Had others seen it? Had Coach Tyler? Was Sean going to lose his job? It was no wonder the young man was in debt and friendless. It was the MacCallister way.

What about the recruiters? Clearly they had seen it and didn't want him around. A person capable of this kind of evil would not be a good employee. An evil person like this should not even be allowed to live.

"You shouldn't be allowed to live." Sean spoke the words aloud. He clumsily stumbled to his feet. Steadying himself against the desk, he saw his ghastly reflection in the mirror.

He knelt quickly, fumbled to get the key into the lock and moments later pulled open the bottom drawer. He scrounged through the contents in the dark until he found the revolver. While not the cleanest way to end it all, this would certainly be the quickest and least painful. To minimize the mess, he laid down on the couch with his left cheek against the back cushion. He held the gun to his right temple.

Uncharacteristically, he chose not to say a final prayer for forgiveness. Who he had been and what he had done was as twisted and inexcusable as the crime he was about to commit.

Sean closed his eyes and took one last deep breath.

An ear-splitting burst rang out, illuminating the dark room with sound. Then, there was silence.

Chapter 50

I've lost R2."

Nick sat on his couch sulking. *Star Wars* was typically the best cure for his being down but tonight, this scene in the movie just exemplified his feelings. Like Luke, hurtling down the Death Star's trench having just lost his final trusted companion, Nick felt very alone.

As Vader closed in on Luke, Nick thought about his coaches. Coach Tyler and Coach Kreitzer just didn't seem to understand him. Their lack of faith coupled with animosity over Nick getting kicked out of the pre-Christmas tournament was causing some of his teammates to alienate him, particularly when the two coaches were around. Nobody wanted to be on these coaches' bad sides so Nick was finding plenty of solitude. It felt like early sophomore year all over again.

He pulled himself back to the movie, his eyes were glued to the screen, anticipating what was coming.

"I have you now!" Vader declared. All was certainly lost … or was it?

"What?" Vader was startled.

"Yahoo!" Han Solo exclaimed, coming out of nowhere.

Nick grasped a couch cushion as he waited for his favorite part from any *Star Wars* movie.

The *Millennium Falcon* burst forth. Nick was sure that the ship was coming right out of the sun, despite his brother's argument that coming out of the sun was impossible and that the bright light behind the *Falcon* was just the ship's engines. Coming out of the sun seemed much more glorious to Nick but, in the end, it didn't matter. Han Solo swooped in and cleared out Vader and his wingmen, saving Luke, his mission, and the galaxy.

Nick needed a Han Solo right now. He needed someone, anyone, to come in and be there for him. Someone who wouldn't let his coaches get him down and would help Nick do right by his team. But who?

It would be nice to talk to someone right now to break the monotony. He pondered who might be up at 11:30 at night whose parents wouldn't lecture him for calling. In the end, there was only one clear choice. Even if he could only leave a message, at least his voice would eventually be heard by someone he could count on.

He picked up the phone and began punching buttons.

Chapter 51

The silence lasted only a moment before the second burst shook the room. Sean lay motionless on the couch.

A third time, the sound rang out.

The desperate young man opened his eyes.

The ringing of the phone was downright painful in such an enclosed space. When he had maximized the ringer volume weeks earlier so that it could be heard down the hall, he had no idea what kind of lungs the device had. Now he found out in a very painful way.

Groggily, he wondered who might be calling at this hour on a night when he wasn't even supposed to be home. His curiosity outweighed his inglorious intentions for a moment.

The call was transferred to the answering machine. Sean lay patiently as he heard Kelly's familiar voice, "Sean and Kelly aren't here. You must not be here either or you wouldn't be calling. Leave us a message." After the beep, there was silence. Sean looked through the darkness in the direction of the phone.

"Coach?" Nick's voice sounded unsure but hearing it was enough to get Sean to set the revolver aside.

"I'm hoping you can help me," the boy continued. "I didn't do so well at today's tournament but I just can't see what I'm doing wrong. Can you help? I don't know …" the boy paused, fumbling over his words, "I don't know what's wrong, something just, isn't right … well, anyway … thanks, I'll see you this week … when you get back. Bye … thanks."

There was one more click and the silence returned.

Sean lay motionless for several more seconds before putting the revolver on the floor and holding his head in his trembling hands. He felt queasy.

"How can I help you?" he wondered in answer to Nick's question. "I can't even help myself."

He lay there for another minute, staring at the ceiling, more frightened than he had ever been … even as a child. What was he doing? Was his life truly that useless? Nick didn't seem to think so.

Tears flowed down his cheeks as he emptied the revolver and shoved it back into the drawer which he immediately locked. He felt terrified and wired. He needed to be around people.

Sean grabbed his jacket and raced out into the night.

Chapter 52

Nick, we can't coach you if you're not willing to be coached."

Cole Tyler paced the coaches' office, practicing his speech. Did that sound right? He needed the kid to turn the corner soon if he was going to lead the team through January and February. The coach was frustrated with himself for not being able to find the right lever to make the boy excel.

At this point, he didn't care how he was perceived. He could be the good guy, fighting for the good of the team, or the villain, someone for Nick to rise against. The key was to get the kid to show some emotion and rally the troops, making the team gel.

This morning presented the perfect opportunity for a "good cap, bad cop" routine. Nick should be expecting a stern talking-to after his performance the day before. The conversation could then morph into something with significant tension and finally into a mutual understanding which would spur Nick to align with the coaching staff and lead the team to the next level.

For once, the man wished that MacCallister were there. He was more than annoyed at the young man for missing the VC tournament and leaving Tyler with Kreitzer as his only assistant. The assistant principal was politically adept but had absolutely no clue about how to guide wrestlers. Cole had left Kreitzer alone to coach Nick for one minute and the boy had completely collapsed.

"Kreitzer," the man grumbled under his breath. The plan was for the two of them to meet at 6:45 and discuss how to best motivate Nick. The boy always arrived early for practice so they would have a good ten to fifteen minutes alone with him to push some buttons … if Kreitzer would ever arrive.

Cole's frustration turned to anger as the clock turned to 7:00. Why couldn't Kreitzer ever be on time? He tried to think through the anger management techniques he was forced to learn six months earlier after crushing that hockey player at the bar. Life was so much simpler when a person could just pound their problems away. He momentarily pondered whether slapping the crap out of Nick would help him respond but quickly pushed those thoughts from his mind. He wished he could get in a good workout this morning to burn off some of that rage. As it stood, that would have to wait until later.

"Nick, we want to be able to coach you and enable you to lead others." It sounded goofy but if Kreitzer could memorize it, they might pull off this "good cop, bad cop" routine yet.

"Get with Kreitzer, get to Nick, get the team moving," he thought again. He heard the click of the locker room door and knew that it must be the younger Castle brother arriving. Tyler's blood pressure rose.

Twenty seconds later, Kreitzer meandered in.

This was it. Cole would teach the man his lines and they would make a break for it, bracing himself for possibly having to knock some skulls together if his carefully laid plan were to go awry.

Chapter 53

Nick sat in the locker room, methodically re-taping his ankle. He was as frustrated with himself for doing a poor job of taping it before his paper route that morning as he was with his coaches for their negative tone.

The pre-wrap was securely in place and he started rhythmically applying the tape; down, around, up … down, around, up … He would be sure to lace his brace tight enough as well. On his paper route, he had slipped on a spot of ice and suddenly saw his whole season flash before his eyes as he felt the ankle give. Fortunately, it was only his imagination getting the best of him. The damage, if not completely in his mind, appeared to be largely superficial.

Through the wall, he could hear voices in the coaches' locker room.

"Ugh," he thought as he was reminded of his frustration with the two men, separated from him by seven inches of cement and all the difference of opinion in the world. It made him tired just thinking about how impossible it was to please Kreitzer and Tyler. No matter what he did and how hard he tried, they always found issues. For Kreitzer, it seemed like more of a social thing. Nick would never measure up to the popular kids in his assistant principal's eyes. With Coach Tyler, Nick just wasn't sure. Each time he felt like he had done something deserving of reaching the top of the ladder, the man added another rung.

Though muffled, Coach Tyler's tone was unmistakable. He wondered what the head coach was saying. "No matter," Nick thought. If he was lucky, maybe he could get his brace on and get upstairs to start his run before the coach saw him and decided he needed an ultimately de-motivating one-on-one pep talk.

Nick grabbed his wrestling shoes and mask from inside his locker. Shutting the door quietly, his heart sank as, out of the corner of his eye, he saw the door to the coaches' locker room open.

Coach Tyler walked in with his usual "I'm here to shape you up" look on his face. Coach Kreitzer followed a few steps behind, his face locked in a cold glare.

Instinct told Nick to be on the defensive. As he braced for the onslaught, he thought, "I don't need a lecture right now."

Why did these men make Nick so uneasy? Every time they were around, it was like Nick felt he had to watch his every move. What should he do? He couldn't avoid the men completely. Maybe he could just acknowledge their presence and get out?

"Hi, Coach. Hi, Mr. Kreitzer."

Nick's pleasant greeting did nothing to change the expression on his coaches' faces.

"Nick, we need to talk to you about yesterday," the head coach started in before Nick had any kind of chance to get away.

"We went into a weak tournament and ended up placing fifth out of seven teams. The guys are looking to you as a leader, but if you continually underperform and show them that you can't make it to the top of the podium, how can you expect others to get there?"

Nick's hair raised on end as he heard his coach's words.

"I've got thirteen other wrestlers on this team, Castle ... and over a dozen more on JV that are hungry for a varsity spot. You claim to lead these guys, but you're not acting like a leader. Why would I continue to put you on the mat when every time I do, I know that you're going to drop in the semifinals? Why should I waste my breath coaching you when you're not willing to listen and react?

"I really can't coach you if you're not going to give me your best. I know there is more in there but you don't let it out and I apparently don't know how to make you give it."

What would the next line be? Nick hoped that his sweatshirt covered his arms well enough so that the men could not see him trembling.

"Well, do you have anything to say?"

Yes, Nick had plenty to say. He just didn't know if he could say it and remain on the team. He wished there was some way to disappear. He wished that he hadn't arrived early. He wished that he hadn't taped his ankle. He wished there was some way, any way, to get to the locker room door without having to look the two men in the eye and acknowledge their existence. What was the coach saying? Was he going to completely replace Nick as a team leader? Was he really thinking about taking away his varsity spot? How could he not see Nick's desire? Why couldn't he just let up and trust Nick to pull through? Where was the man's faith?

"I can't keep on this way. We're not moving forward, it feels like we're moving backward. It's an impossible challenge for me. I can't coach you if you won't be coachable."

Kreitzer broke in as Nick's heart sank deeper. "Why would he want to coach you if you're not going to listen, Castle?" Nick was so frustrated. He didn't know whether he should start swinging at the men or just break down and cry. "The way you're wrestling, you might as well not even be here. Nobody wants to coach you."

Kreitzer's final words cut especially deep, causing Nick to involuntarily clench his teeth and his hands simultaneously. Was this how they operated? Two on one? Nick wasn't sure if the explosion rising within him would come out as words alone or if it would get physical and he would go down swinging. He only knew that he was about to end this mess. He took a deep breath and braced for the imminent detonation.

Chapter 54

The cold electricity zapped Ron's spine as he winced and looked away. He was used to seeing Nick's face with scrapes and bruises gained in live matches and practice but the sight before him was too much. He held back a whimper as he looked at his little brother, appearing more like a lump of hamburger than a human being.

For some reason, he knew the words before they even left his brother's mouth. There was something about the angry glare in those pitiful eyes. Ron had to bite his tongue to keep from preempting the words before they flowed from his brother's bloody lips.

When they finally emerged, they were more of a bark or a growl than a sentence, yet the meaning of them was fully evident, making Ron feel guilt-ridden and helpless.

"Why weren't you there for me?! Why weren't you EVER there for me?!"

Ron sat straight up in bed, looking around blindly as he tried to get his bearings.

Something was wrong. Something was happening to Nick, and Ron wasn't there to do anything about it. He quickly got to his feet and crossed the room to look at the clock.

7:10 a.m.

Was it truly just a dream? Why did it seem so real?

Ron didn't believe in the supernatural but this encounter made him pause. Had he noticed something that could be putting Nick in danger? What could possibly be causing him harm at this early hour? Practice wouldn't even be starting for twenty minutes.

A bead of sweat slid down his right temple as Ron pondered what to do. It was a three-hour drive home in good weather. The past day's storm would surely add another hour to that … if the roads were even open.

The stiffness in his back reminded him of the possibility that his season, not to mention his wrestling career, was over. Yet, Nick's was not. What could an older brother possibly contribute at this point? How was he supposed to help his brother? And why was he scared to death, fearing that he may be too late?

Chapter 55

I'll coach him!"

The words rang out from somewhere near the coaches' office entrance. Nick swung his head and both Coach Tyler and Kreitzer spun around with a look of shock.

Coach MacCallister entered the room looking tousled and unkempt but was the most welcome sight Nick had seen in days.

"I don't know what happened at the VC that made you not want to coach him," the young man commented, looking straight at Kreitzer, "but I'll be happy to put extra time in with him as needed to work on any rough spots."

The boy looked back and forth between his favorite coach and the other two who seemed more than a bit uncomfortable and agitated by MacCallister's presence. There was no apparent grand plan at stake here for Nick to save the world but in the back of his mind, the *Millennium Falcon* had just appeared out of the sun.

Chapter 56

Cole Tyler could only cringe as he thought about what had just happened. He had one inept assistant coach who had turned a "good cop, bad cop" routine into two bad cops bordering on police brutality and, worse yet, didn't seem to realize or care that anything had gone wrong.

Beyond that, the second assistant had worse timing than a mongoose at a cobra convention.

How he would right this ship was unknown. What he did know was that he now faced a greater uphill battle to pull his team and staff back in line.

Chapter 57

At practice that day, Nick wrestled with a renewed sense of determination. Coach MacCallister had given him a new mask and, as battered and disfigured as the contraption was, it served the purpose of protecting the boy's nose while only minimally restricting his vision.

He actually began liking the concept of wearing a mask. Behind it, he could be anybody. He didn't have to be the shy kid who longed for respect. He could be Dan Gable for all the rest of the world knew. The boy would just have to wrestle in a way that showed it.

After practice, Nick and Sean spent the rest of the morning watching and dissecting matches and discussing mat strategy. For some reason, watching his matches with Coach MacCallister wasn't like watching with Coach Tyler or Ron. Nick didn't feel belittled by this coach's comments.

The early part of the afternoon found them hanging out and talking, more like friends rather than as a coach and a wrestler. Nick was elated to not have to spend all day in his depressing house and was engrossed by the story of his coach's near-death experience on the frozen Interstate just the day before.

"I knew I wasn't going to die," the assistant coach asserted. "It would be a complete miscarriage of justice for me to kick off without seeing you win the state championship."

Nick looked at the young man. There was something different about him today, a vibrancy that hadn't been present over the first several weeks of the season.

For the first time since the locker room run-in with Hermanns, Nick felt the pendulum shift. He wanted to win the state title to make this coach proud. Even if he had to move back to 152, he suddenly had the confidence that, if Coach MacCallister believed he could do something, there was no doubt in his mind that he could achieve it.

The boy even felt comfortable enough to ask his coach about leadership traits, confiding in the man that he was completely at a loss on how to motivate his teammates. This was something he never could have admitted to his other coaches. In general, he felt he needed some glimpse of what was most important.

While he was anxious for a moment as the man sat speechless, he was more concerned when he heard the answer.

"Integrity is the key," Coach MacCallister finally replied. "People look for leaders who live up to the standard they are setting. No excuses, no compromises; set the goal and accept nothing less."

The boy sat in awe, wondering how the single phrase could be so enlightening and terrifying at the same time.

It remained on his mind, well after the two parted ways mid-afternoon.

Chapter 58

Sean's mind was consumed with questions stemming from a single inquiry posed by Nick.

As the two left the school, the boy had actually asked him, "How do you always stay in such a good mood and not let anything bother you?"

Given recent events, Sean could only answer with an "I don't know" shrug. Yet, the question had him pondering "perception versus reality" the entire way home. How could anyone believe that Sean was perpetually upbeat? It was such a misrepresentation of the truth that it had captivated the young man's thoughts the entire frigid two-mile walk to his home.

If this was truly how Sean came across to at least one member of the outside world, was there a chance that he could change things in his own life to make it the truth for himself as well?

The boy seemed so wrong, but the question was something Sean wanted to contemplate further.

Chapter 59

Sean looked at his watch.

11:54.

The library would close soon, forcing him to go back home and face his demons.

Since returning to campus late afternoon, he had done his best to stay away from anything and anyone that would lead him to drink. There was a spark of pride as he realized he was about to earn a number on the calendar he kept to show consecutive sober days. While only a number "2," it would be far better than the X's he marked on the days when he had succumbed to the bottle's call.

Making him especially proud was his ability to get past two disappointments of the late afternoon.

The first had come at the career services office, seemingly his location of endless suffering. He had checked the recruiting schedule for the spring semester only to find it devoid of any Engineering postings. A single company was scheduled, looking for graduate students to be project managers. Unqualified, Sean could only shake his head and walk away.

The second disappointment completely broke his heart.

His Galaxie 500, the vehicle which was both an extension of Sean himself and also the bane of his existence, was gone.

The woman who had left the message had been kind enough, simply calling to inform him that his car had been found along the side of the Interstate by a snowplow driver who, due to limited visibility, had collided with the vehicle causing minor damage to the plow but making the Galaxie 500, in all likelihood, irreparable.

The sense of loss was similar to that of losing a friend. The car had developed its own persona; it had been battered, on the edge of death since it had come into Sean's life. Yet, there had always been a comfort each time Sean turned the key and heard the engine roar to life. Despite its tarnished appearance, the car seemed to feel a sense of responsibility, which provided the peace of mind that Sean could always get where he needed to go.

At the core of its tangible value, the car had been made in an era when computers did not rule every facet of a vehicle's being.

Sean could make nearly any repair himself; a bent frame was one of the few exceptions that lay outside of his abilities.

Ironically, the car must have met its final fate somewhere near the time that Sean thought he was meeting his.

In all, it seemed like a good evening to do some research on clinical depression. While he still refused to consider that he may have the disease, he certainly took to heart some of the symptoms and tendencies he and his father both displayed. In particular, he zeroed in on some of his father's traits such as a sedentary lifestyle, which fed the disease and in turn caused disinterest in physical activity … a vicious circle.

Alcohol was an especially dangerous vice of the depressed due to the impact it had on the brain's chemical make-up. He took this information and several other tips, trying to gauge his own likelihood of having the disease and staving off further degeneration because of it.

12:01.

Sean was packed and headed for the door before the security guard could find him and ask him to leave. He would enter the "2" on his calendar as soon as he arrived home and would add a "3" as well on the day that was just starting.

He had reached the point where his drinking days just had to be over. There was no way he was going to give in and drink within the next 24 hours. The "3" was an extra step to ensure that.

Chapter 60

Ron didn't know whether to be proud of himself or completely disgraced as he walked from the wrestling room with Hermanns. It was his first practice since his injury a week and a half earlier and while simply returning to the mat was a victory, his stiffness put him on par wrestling with the likes of Oscar, far below the bar he set for himself.

The boy had been cautious to avoid risk of re-injury, refusing to even take a shot. He cringed, reminding himself that defensive wrestlers often won matches … but rarely state titles.

The cold stare Coach Tyler gave the power duo as they passed made him uneasy until they started down the stairs and Hermanns interrupted Ron's thoughts at a low whisper.

"You might do well to stay away from me for a couple of days," the 145-pounder commented. "My dad had a run-in with the coach yesterday."

The situation intrigued Ron enough to ask why.

"My dad tried to step in and coach me at the VC tournament. It angered Coach something fierce and he made Dad go sit in the bleachers. Dad has been coaching me since I was five so he stopped in to talk to Coach about it yesterday. There was steam coming off of both of them by the end."

Mr. Hermanns had coached at Roosevelt Junior High for years and Ron had wrestled against many of his wrestlers. He knew how high strung Mr. Hermanns could get and hated to think what could happen if the man pushed the wrong buttons on Coach Tyler.

"What was the result?" he finally asked.

"Coach finally told him that any wrestler on the team who makes it to the state championship will have Coach Tyler in his corner. If that wrestler thinks that having an additional coach in his corner will help him win a state title, he's welcome to invite that person to fill the second chair. Then he told him that, if he heard one more word about this before the state tournament, the entire deal was off."

As gritty as the coach tended to be, Ron hoped that Mr. Hermanns wouldn't do any more to ruffle his feathers.

Chapter 61

Sean stared through the window of the diner. It was nearly 2:00 a.m., snow continued to fall, and he was more than 250 miles from home. His head was spinning at the evening's events which had the possibility of leaving him in a bloody mess on the diner's floor.

The adventure had started around 7:30 as Sean sat at Beta Beta Beta, studying an Engineering textbook and sipping a water. He had been sober for nine days and counting, thanks to the support of newfound friends in the local Alcoholics Anonymous chapter who had gotten him through the New Year's holiday without a single drink.

The same could not be said for Darrel Zok. The young man had broken Sean's solitude at the house, showing up with whiskey breath on New Year's Eve and remaining largely inebriated for the following few days. Zok annoyed Sean whenever possible by insisting that the two get liquored together. It had been Darrel's drunken ramblings that had tipped off Sean to the pending disaster in which MacCallister quickly inserted himself.

"I'm going to pick up your buddy tomorrow," Darrel had slurred. "We should drink to his freedom."

With those words, Darrel poked a bottle of rum in Sean's face, which elicited the immediate response of the wrestling coach tackling the drunk, wrapping him up, and pulling his forehead across the carpet, ensuring that Zok would have a very visible rug burn just above his eyebrows for days to come.

After the altercation, the two went to their separate sofas as Darrel continued babbling.

"Kelly's got a meeting with the Dean Monday morning at 8:00 so that he can explain why he should still be a student here with the grades he's been pulling."

"You mean he's got a meeting on Tuesday morning," Sean had corrected. "Today is Sunday and you're not picking him up until tomorrow."

"It's Saturday," Darrel insisted, his eyes glazing over. "The message is on my machine."

The machine had confirmed Sean's fears to be true that Kelly's parents had dropped him off at a diner half-way across the state, waiting for Darrel to pick him up today.

With Darrel passed out and his car nowhere to be found, Sean had ventured out, praying that he could rent a vehicle with the few dollars that remained from his most recent paycheck. It was at this point that his angel had re-appeared.

Julee Novak pulled up as Sean trudged through the snow and asked him if he needed a ride. Sean was still a bit sheepish given their previous encounter but was happy to get a chance to make up for a poor first impression, not to mention the chance to jump into her car to warm up.

"Let me get this straight," she replied after hearing his story. "You want to rent a car with money you don't have to drive 250 miles in a snow storm to pick up a person who, the last time you saw him, slammed you in the chest and bruised your ribs as the two of you threatened to kill each other?"

"That about sums it up," Sean responded, realizing from the woman's look of disbelief just how ludicrous the situation sounded.

She stared at him for several more seconds before turning and putting the vehicle in gear.

"Thank you. I appreciate the ride," Sean acknowledged. "If you could take me to the airport, I'm sure I can find someone who will rent me a car."

"I'm not taking you to rent a car," she said. "I'm taking you to get your roommate."

Then, shaking her head, she added, "This will be a story I'm pretty sure I'll leave out when I have children someday and am trying to teach them about acting responsibly."

* * *

Five hours later, Kelly seemed irate as he watched Sean saunter into the diner. Before he could speak, Sean cut him off.

"I'm sorry about everything," the young man started. "We've got just enough time to get in the car, get home, and for you to take a quick shower before your meeting with the Dean. You don't have to talk to me, you just need to let me help you get back into school."

Lacking other options, the big man simply nodded and walked past Sean toward the door.

Chapter 62

I don't want to talk about it," was Ron's only response to Nick's obvious question of "why?" The words left the younger boy very confused.

In the time since Ron had returned from his sick leave, the team had wrestled two conference duals and four more duals in a tournament. In each instance, Nick and Hermanns had both weighed in at 145, giving the team flexibility at the 145 and 152 pound weight classes. The boys combined record was 12 – 0 in those matches. Ron, on the other hand had not seemed to completely find his footing, going four and two at 140 through the same events.

As the Capital Tournament drew near, Nick's mind had begun to fill with anxiety. As well as he was wrestling, he knew that nobody he or Kevin had faced at 152 was anywhere near the caliber of Troftgruben, the returning champion both Riverside wrestlers feared with good reason.

Perhaps even more frightening was that Troftgruben would only walk into the tournament as the second seed. Willis had beaten him in the pre-Christmas tournament championship, earning the top ranking among the state's 152-pounders.

The thought of facing either boy made Nick cringe. The possible match-ups were making him lose sleep until he was unexpectedly called into Coach Tyler's office the Wednesday before the big event.

"Can you make it down to 142 in two days?" the coach had asked. As if reading the obvious question in Nick's mind, the man continued, "Your brother has asked to cut to 135."

It was a move that made absolutely no sense. Ron would be going into the year's most difficult tournament, moving to a no-win weight class, and having to certify at scratch weight all while not wrestling like his old self. Was his brother nuts?

Ron's refusal to give a reason for his choice bothered Nick but the younger boy knew that getting his stubborn older sibling to change his mind, either about his decision to drop a weight class or his refusal to discuss the subject, would not be a battle worth fighting.

Making the weight wouldn't be difficult given Nick's recent history. The bigger challenge would be in forcing himself to express his gratitude to his brother, the boy with whom he could be a poster child for sibling rivalry.

Chapter 63

Sean was ecstatic as he raced up the stairs with the large envelope addressed to Kelly. It had been a week and a half since the big man had met with the Dean. Surely this package from the university was good news that his re-admittance request had been approved.

Mending the friendship was taking time but there were several factors playing in their favor. Five hours cooped up in a car could lead to tension or camaraderie. Fortunately for Sean, their driver ensured the latter.

Julee was very charming and won Kelly over right away. She was well versed in subjects that the two men rarely pondered and it led to several friendly debates. She seemed to know a lot about nutrition, and Sean locked some of her trivia in the back of his mind related to the connection between excess carbohydrates, the kind found in alcohol, and diseases such as depression.

Sean briefly pondered why she had gone well out of her way for him and Kelly, given that she repeatedly professed to hate men. Ironically, despite the two men's history of run-ins and fights, she claimed that she found the two of them harmless.

By the time they arrived at Beta Beta Beta, the two men found themselves lightly joking with one another. Sean was able to put in a good word with the few people he knew at the Dean's office, and everything seemed to be moving back to normal with one significant exception.

Kelly insisted that neither of them would drink the entire semester as both seemed incapable of doing so in moderation. The big man needed to focus on his studies and Sean needed to get his life together in general, thus Kelly declared their room a "No Drinking Zone."

While most of their fraternity brothers doubted the duo's ability to keep their commitment, most were supportive of the general concept.

When Kelly peeled open the envelope and it contained documents that aligned with Sean's expectations, the two celebrated with a pizza and glasses of ice water.

Chapter 64

That's it. I just lost my last chance to wrestle under the big lights."

All Nick could do was absorb the comment as his brother walked away. It wasn't as much the words that caused the chill to reverberate down Nick's back as it was the way in which they were said. Ron's eyes were vacant, and if Nick was not mistaken, it almost looked like the older boy had begun to tear up before he quickly turned away and headed toward the locker room.

Nick watched him go and thought about the words: "... last chance to wrestle under the big lights." The reference was clear. The Capital Tournament was one of the few events left that held its championship round as a single string of matches, starting at 103 and continuing through heavyweight with no other distractions. Two wrestlers were the sole focus of the audience's attention at any one time, unlike so many other tournaments that ran concurrent championship matches in order to move more quickly through the event and get spectators on the road.

Completing the majestic environment of the Capital Tournament's championships was the enormous light display which adorned the underside of the middle scoreboard at the capital city's civic center. Illuminated only during the championship round, these lights poured down on the epicenter of attention, a single wrestling mat and its two grapplers. All other lights in the facility were faded or doused completely. It was an awesome spectacle and experience for high school athletes.

It hadn't occurred to Nick until now that this was Ron's last chance for so many things the older boy considered "unfinished" after his sophomore year and "missed" during his junior year. For all of Ron's individual titles as a sophomore, the Capital Tournament championship was a big one that had eluded him. In fact, losing to Spegidos in the semifinal round two years ago and losing one more match in the wrestlebacks had caused Ron to place fifth. This was the single largest factor in dropping Ron's ranking to fourth in the state that year, the seeding he held going into the state tournament which set up his historic semifinal match with Spegidos.

Having just been pinned by Spegidos in the first period of the quarterfinals, Ron's ranking was sure to suffer again this year.

Nick thought about the way he himself had been wrestling during this tournament. He had barely scraped by some unranked opponents on his way to the quarterfinals and clearly was not wrestling with the intensity he needed to bring home the gold.

He looked in the direction his brother had just walked, but his older sibling had disappeared from sight. What if Nick lost in the semifinals this year? What if he lost in the quarterfinal match he was about to wrestle? Would he be dejected a year from now after a repeat performance? Would he miss all of his chances to wrestle under the big lights?

That was not going to happen.

"Next up on mat number two, Nick Castle from Riverside versus ..." the rest of the words did not register for Nick. He had already gone into his own little world as he mechanically snapped on his head gear and mask, ditched his warm-up shirt, pulled up his singlet straps, and marched into battle.

Chapter 65

Nick's stride was vigorous as he headed for the locker room. The boy was completely pumped having just pulled off an overtime win against a previously undefeated wrestler in the semifinals.

His mask was proving itself to be more of a help than a hindrance. The self-conscious wrestler was looking forward to his upcoming championship match aided in part by the anonymity the mask provided.

In the match's aftermath, he was overflowing with confidence and had enough adrenaline flowing through his system to make him an even match for your average lion. It was in this state of mind, preoccupied with reaching his destination that he nearly collided with Travis Spegidos and Brent Decker as they entered from an adjacent hallway.

"Watch it!" Spegidos thundered, pushing Nick's shoulder and knocking him off balance. Instinctively, Nick countered by shoving the two-time state champion in the chest, knocking him back a step. He was suddenly aware of how sick he was of the soon-to-be legend's treatment of wrestlers and others and was instantly prepared to do something about it.

"I've already slapped your ugly brother around. Are you stupid enough to want in on that action?"

Nick didn't break the older boy's stare. Spegidos could intimidate a lot of people but not Nick. Not tonight.

"I'd love to teach you some manners," Nick replied after a moment, not noticing the small crowd starting to form.

"The only thing I could learn from you is how to bleed all over a locker room. Meanwhile, I'd be finding interesting ways to re-break your nose. Heck, we've always called your brother 'the ugly one' and you 'the scrawny one' but now I'd be hard pressed to say who's uglier."

If the boy was trying to goad Nick into something, he'd have to do better than picking on the boy's looks.

"You may think you're hot stuff, but you aren't showing me anything."

"I showed your brother how to count the civic center lights this afternoon. If you guys didn't work so much on stalling at practice, I would have gotten to set a new tournament record for the fastest pin."

"You'll be setting the WORLD record for having the deepest mat burns on your shoulder blades by the time I'm done with you," Nick shot back.

Nick had never been much of a trash talker but felt like he was holding his own in this particular exchange. He felt his blood pressure peak as Spegidos cocked his fist and he immediately donned a defensive stance.

Before the scene could move any further, Nick was stopped by a familiar voice in his ear.

"Nick, stand down!"

The boy only tensed further until he felt Coach MacCallister's arm coming around his chest and pulling him backward.

"Stand down!" Sean repeated a second time, a bit louder, pulling Nick away from his tormentor.

Nick kept his eyes firmly fixed on Spegidos' glare. This may not result in him besting the boy in a hallway fight but he would make sure he got his point across.

"You're lucky you've got your guardian angel to pull you out," Spegidos commented snidely.

"You're lucky you've got the 135-pound weight class to hide in," Nick retorted as Sean got more aggressive about pulling him away. "Come to 140 and I'll beat you like a circus monkey!"

He didn't break eye contact with the boy until Sean lifted him off the ground and turned him to march away.

The gauntlet had been thrown down.

Chapter 66

Nick couldn't sleep. He wanted to roll over again but intentionally stayed still to avoid waking Ron. One of them needed to get some rest.

Why did everything have to happen at once? As if Nick didn't have enough anxiety with his pending championship match and run-in with Spegidos, Oscar had to choose this night to pull a stunt which nearly drove Nick over the edge.

The boys had returned to the hotel after the semifinals and Oscar had immediately gone out on the prowl, surprisingly returning half an hour later with two girls. One was borderline cute. Of course, Oscar had his eye on her. The other could best be described as having a good personality.

After several minutes of cajoling, Nick had reluctantly agreed to accompany the three back to the girls' hotel room. He tried to be polite and talkative but there was a constant conversation going through the back of his mind.

"I really don't want to kiss her."

"How much time is left until the coaches come by for room check?"

"What if Sandi finds out? Would she ever date me if she knew?"

It was one of the most uncomfortable evenings of the boy's life. Forty-five minutes seemed like a month before Oscar's girl popped open the refrigerator and started handing out wine coolers. Nick completely panicked.

"I'm going to get kicked out of the tournament … off the team for six weeks … out for the season," his mind raced, pondering if there were further things Tyler or Kreitzer would do to make an example out of him.

"I've got to go," the flustered boy eked out.

"Miss Personality" tried to dissuade him and Oscar had a short tirade, chiding Nick for being lame, but all Nick could see was the door … and freedom.

Two hours later, Oscar still hadn't returned. Nick would fake sleeping when the boy did to avoid confrontation for one more night.

He wanted to explode, and reflexively jerked his leg away as his brother brushed against it.

"Why does he have to be so hairy?" the agitated youth asked himself. "It's like sleeping with a dog."

His adrenaline wouldn't allow him to drift off for quite a while, giving him plenty of time to ponder comebacks for when Oscar and others inevitably started heckling him about missing a prime make-out opportunity. Ideally, he would be thinking through possibilities for his pending match, but those would have to wait until he had a clearer mind.

Chapter 67

Sean was very concerned as the seconds ticked down on Ron's match. The boy was continuing to slide and was about to place sixth in the Capital Tournament.

When he had coached Ron a day earlier in the quarterfinals against Travis Spegidos, he had noticed a significant turning point. Ron had fallen in a worse showing than even their December confrontation as Spegidos pinned him in the first period. But to put things in perspective, Spegidos was Spegidos, an incredibly strong wrestler who did not show any intention of having his year-and-a-half undefeated streak broken any time soon.

Now, in his final match of the weekend, Ron just looked like he didn't care. There was no more spark in his eyes, no intensity, no desire. He just looked defeated, and the scoreboard showed that he soon would be, again.

Sean looked to his left and caught Kreitzer's gaze for a moment. The man just rolled his eyes before getting up and walking away. The breach of coaching etiquette astounded MacCallister. With Nick and Hermanns both in the finals, there couldn't be another Riverside match on deck. He couldn't imagine where the man would be going in such a hurry. Leaving your wrestler, unless you are leaving to coach another, was inappropriate regardless of the match's outcome.

The match complete, Ron walked slowly away from center mat toward his waiting coach. He didn't look Sean in the eye as the young man patted him on the back.

Sean hated these situations and didn't say a word. What could he say? "Good job," certainly was not appropriate. "He's a tough kid, you'll get him next time," wasn't true either. Ron had just lost to some guy he had never even heard of from the southwest corner of the state. Apparently his name was Goetz. Who the heck was this kid?

He looked across the mat to where the other boy was glowing, using a lot of body movements as he discussed portions of the match with his coaches. It was a victory that was sure to get some press in the boy's hometown, "Local Sophomore Defeats Former State Runner-Up."

As Ron walked to the showers, Sean considered how he might be able to help the boy turn the corner again. This boy was more mature than and not nearly as impressionable as Nick had been when Sean had helped him to ascend a year earlier. His greatest concern was that Ron had peaked too early and that he would spend the rest of his life dealing with ghosts from his sophomore year, ghosts that caused him to undervalue his own current capabilities and fail to respect the abilities of others.

Chapter 68

Ron sat in the stands with his parents, silently watching the 140-pound championship. After entering the tournament seeded fifth, Nick had won 11 – 3 in the quarterfinals over the fourth seed, a boy that had beaten him three weeks earlier. In the prior night's semifinals, he continued his march by upsetting an undefeated wrestler.

Upon first glance, a bystander would clearly favor Nick's opponent in this match. This boy was a good three inches shorter than Nick and made up for it with a solid muscular frame that made Nick's slight build look frail. His team hailed from Oklahoma where he was ranked first in the state. Despite these facts, the boy had spent the entire match on the defensive, never quite finding the answer to Nick's methodical attack.

The score of 12 – 4 made the match seem less lopsided than it had actually been. Nick had been unstoppable, only giving up escapes in pursuit of subsequent takedowns.

From the bottom, Nick sat out, stretched his arm back and his hand found the perfect spot, just inside his opponent's thigh. From there, it was artwork. He found his leverage point, driving his opponent's body to the mat as he pivoted behind, completing the switch and ending in the dominant position.

"That one could end up in a 'How To' video for switches," Ron thought.

"Two points green," bellowed the ref.

Ron thought he could detect a twinkle in the eye of the younger Castle brother behind Nick's mask, possibly letting out a gleeful smile. He controlled his opponent and his destiny as he broke the boy down to his stomach again.

The match had seemed all too easy. Sitting on his lead in the third period, it looked like Nick was backing off a bit, opting to not go for the pin. He had already broken the boy's spirit, there was no need to try to push things to embarrass this competitor. He worked for hand control and was careful not to get too high, checking his hip position as the remaining seconds ticked away.

The foghorn blared and Ron and William sprang to their feet as they roared with a majority of the crowd. Nick burst to his feet as well, racing back to the center of the mat with a level of elation he had never shown before.   His first high school tournament championship had come at the largest tournament the state hosted each year, under the big lights for everyone to see.

Nick just clenched his fists and made gestures with his arms as he walked to the center of the mat. His mask completely hid any facial emotion as the crowd looked on.

The champion shook his opponent's hand, popped across the mat to shake the hands of the Oklahoma team's coaches, and then did something that seemed completely out of character for the stoic younger Castle.   Nick sprinted back to his own corner, dropping his headgear and mask along the way, and jumped directly into the waiting arms of Coach MacCallister. The cameras flashed as the chapter of "Nick the underachiever" officially ended.

Ron watched his brother's victory celebration in silence. He had never felt close enough to a coach to revel together in a success like his brother just had. Today was Nick's day, the baton had been passed, and Ron watched in awe as his brother made the most of it.

Chapter 69

Sean felt the best he had in a long time as he accompanied Nick from the mat. His sobriety stint was 22 days and counting, Nick had just won his first title, and the team, in general, felt like it was beginning to gel. Despite the number of teams and quality of their wrestlers in the Capital Tournament, Riverside had performed well. Six of its fourteen wrestlers had placed in the top six with two making it all the way to the championship.

"Thank you, Coach!" Nick's words broke into Sean's thoughts.

"Thank yourself, Nick, you're the one who did all of the work."

Sean was very proud of the way Nick had progressed both on and off the mat. He just hoped that the boy didn't have a MacCallister-like temper that would get him into trouble.

Nick's parents interrupted the conversation, racing down from the stands.

"Coach MacCallister?" Mrs. Castle asked. "Can I get a picture of you with the champion?"

Sean knelt by his wrestler and Nick put his arm around his coach as his mother snapped the picture.

"Are you glad you came, Mom?" Nick asked, knowing his mother's aversion to seeing her boys on the mat.

The woman did not reply. Sean moved out of the way to allow room for Nick's mother to give the boy a kiss. Mr. Castle then moved into position and hugged his boy as well. Sean stood in silence as he watched the fourth member of the family, Ron, move in and pat his brother on the back.

"You did well, little brother. You did well."

Immediately Mr. Castle gave his older son a supportive hug as well.

"Ron needed that tonight," the coach thought.

There was a brief lonely feeling in Sean's gut as the family walked Nick toward the staging area for the awards ceremony. Sean had won his share of matches and even several championships during his wrestling career. However, he couldn't imagine how the boy must feel as, surrounded by a family who loved him, he went to wait to receive his award.

"Someday …" Sean thought.

"Coach!" Sean looked up to see Nick motioning for Sean to join them. He happily, albeit sheepishly, followed the champion and his family.

Chapter 70

Nick was beaming with a gritty look of feistiness on his face. He sat on the warm-up mat with Coach MacCallister, waiting for the 140-pounders to be called. While he was proud of his accomplishment and the way he had dominated his most recent opponents, he was hungry for more. He didn't want another title quite as much as he wanted Spegidos.

The undefeated senior had been too cocky for too long and was the primary reason that Sean would be by Nick's side constantly until they left the building and headed home. Nobody wanted an altercation between the two boys with the possible exception of Nick and Spegidos themselves.

Nick only had the doctor's permission to cut to 140. In some ways he was glad as scratch weight had been a challenge for him. Yet, he wanted to chase the boy. What harm could losing seven more pounds cause? He knew that he wouldn't be allowed to find out and that he must pull his adversary up to 140 if there was to be a match.

"It seems like a long wait, doesn't it?" Sean commented, interrupting Nick's thoughts.

The Capital Tournament's awards ceremony followed the final championship match. All weight classes waited to receive their plaques until all wrestling was finished. This helped keep additional spectators in the stands through the heavyweight match.

"Yeah," Nick responded, semi-oblivious. He was watching his mom and dad make their way across the floor, back to their seats.

"You keep this guy out of trouble," Nick's dad had instructed Sean as he left.

Nick hoped that it was just a general jest and that his parents didn't know about the hallway clash from a day earlier. If there were two people in the world who weren't afraid to pull him out of wrestling for bad behavior, they were the ones.

* * *

Nick felt Ron pat him on the back as the 135-pound placers left the podium and the 140-pounders took their places. From his perch on top of the platform, Nick had one wrestler on his mind and in his sights. Spegidos returned the boy's glare while he watched his teammate, Brent Decker, receive the plaque for fourth place.

Nick broke eye contact briefly as he smiled, shook the athletic director's hand, and accepted the champion's plaque. He then looked to the cameras as they flashed and flashed.

As the boys stood for another moment, waiting for a signal to leave, Nick returned his gaze to Spegidos. Slowly and silently, he raised the plaque above his head for the older boy to see and hoped that the unspoken challenge was clear, "You know where I am. COME AND GET ME."

Chapter 71

Nick was certain that he saw a shadow move in the wrestling room as he walked by. He paused, briefly wondering who would be in there at 3 a.m. on a Sunday. The team rarely arrived back at the school this late but it had been a long drive from the capital city.

A week ago, the boy would have been unnerved by the prospect of some prowler or social deviant lurking in his territory and just moved on. Not tonight. The Capital Tournament champion wasn't about to let anyone, real or imaginary, interfere in his domain.

Edging to the door for a closer look, his eyes adjusting to the pale lighting, he was surprised to note that there was indeed someone lurking within. Rather than a thief or a fiend, however, the boy quickly recognized the form of his own brother, standing silently in the middle of the room, staring intently, seemingly into space.

"Ron?" he asked, opening the door.

The older boy didn't respond, continuing to just stand there, as rigid as a sculpture.

Nick followed his older sibling's eyes, focusing in on the Ring of Honor, names of Riverside state champions carved into the upper walls of the wrestling room, just above the padded mats. The mats were there to protect the wrestlers, the ring was there to pay tribute to the great ones.

They stood a few moments longer in silence before Ron finally chose to speak.

"Six years," he said.

He didn't need to say anymore. Nick knew exactly what he was thinking. Six years earlier, Riverside had won its most recent state team title, completely routing the competition by putting five individual champions on top of the podium with seven additional grapplers placing in the top six. Sheer dominance.

"Welsh and Beshey," Nick followed the names as his brother read, "Palmer, Grunseth, Fuller and the Eischens brothers … did those guys ever lose a match?"

Nick couldn't remember anyone on that team ever faltering. He had been in fifth grade and Ron in sixth. They had begged their dad to bring them to every dual and every tournament. The elder Castle was always quick to comply, within a reasonable driving distance, and sometimes beyond. It was the team that had made Ron and Nick want to be wrestlers.

"… and we were going to overshadow them."

The last comment caught Nick a bit off guard, in part due to remembering that they had both believed it to be true, but also because of the hint of sarcasm that entered Ron's voice as he said it.

Another moment of silence passed as Ron turned to walk away. Nick noticed an awkward stiffness in the boy, almost a limp, and soon realized the origin of the trip down memory lane. Ron had yet to win a tournament this year and seemed to be regressing as the season progressed. Nick at least had one gold medal. He struggled for some reply.

"We will," was the only thing Nick could come up with.

He thought he heard Ron mutter something as he felt the boy pat him on the shoulders and move away.

* * *

"One of us will," Ron said under his breath and walked toward the door looking completely disheartened.

Chapter 72

Are you serious about taking on Spegidos?"

Nick looked up from the newspaper. Seeing the western boy's championship pin in one minute fourteen seconds in black-and-white solidified his resolve even more.

"Of course," he finally replied.

"Good," Ron continued, turning on the TV. "We're going to start training today. The state tournament is only a month and a half away, which isn't nearly enough time, but we'll make use of the time we've got."

Nick smiled. The day after the Capital Tournament was designed to be a day of rest for the Riverside team. Being Sunday, the school was locked and Coach Tyler had vowed that it would stay that way. "Most of you should be proud of this weekend's performance," the coach had stated. "All of you should let your bodies recover for one day before we hit it hard again on Monday."

Ron hit the play button and, to Nick's surprise, the image that began to play was Spegidos' championship match. "We'll honor the coach's request for a physical reprieve," Ron stated, "but we're not taking a day off from preparing."

It wasn't much of a match to watch. Spegidos was relentless, ravenous-looking as he took it to his opponent. There was no need for defense, he attacked from the first whistle, going after Don Holter's upper body and forcing the boy to avoid locking up. Holter was a fine wrestler in his own right but there was a look of pure fear on his face as Spegidos locked and launched him.

It was clear that Spegidos was having fun. Even though Holter found a way to scramble to his belly, his prevailing opponent had a big grin on his face as he put in a double chicken wing and applied pressure, walking toward Holter's head and turning the boy's entire body.

Nick had a quick twinge of fear. Was he really signing up for this? He had wrestled Don Holter at wrestling camp the prior summer. He knew that the boy was no slouch. Still, Spegidos made beating him look like child's play.

Holter turned red as he struggled, using every ounce of strength he had to adjust his body and stay off of his shoulder blades. All gestures turned out to be futile. He was just no match for the superior strength and leverage of his opponent. The referee counted for near fall but Spegidos was out for more than three points. He squeezed harder and all Holter could do was hold on for a few more seconds, not nearly a minute as needed. Finally, Spegidos got the right angle and forced Holter's shoulder blades to the mat.

"Slap ... whistle ... over," Ron commented as his brother looked on. "We've got our work cut out for us."

It seemed odd to Nick to be partnering with his brother, the boy that had always been his tormentor as well as his idol (although he would never admit to the latter). The two had never truly bonded; Nick had always been the tagalong and Ron the leader. Yet, for once, it seemed like they were taking on a worthwhile project together. If the two of them working collectively couldn't find a way to beat the returning champion, nobody could. Although, to add to their chances, Nick made a mental note to include Coach MacCallister in their preparation.

The two spent the rest of the afternoon watching every Spegidos match they could round up – Ron's two losses this current season, the prior year's state championship match, and Ron's state semifinal match his sophomore year, which was the only match that found Spegidos on the losing end. Yet, he had progressed so far since then. As the brothers dissected a variety of angles of the boy, a daunting question remained locked in both of their minds.

"Was it possible for anyone to beat Spegidos this year?"

Chapter 73

Don't lock up with him, Nick. Focus low."

Ron's logic seemed sound although it seemed to Sean that the boy should focus on wrestling and leave the coaching to others.

For two weeks, Sean had stayed after practice with the Castle brothers, focusing on live wrestling and preparing Nick for a potential bout with Travis Spegidos, one that the assistant coach cautiously doubted would ever happen. When, after the first few days it became clear to Sean that Ron had neither the strength nor the agility to be a solid surrogate-Spegidos, the young man had recruited Kevin Hermanns to make it a foursome.

The boys all seemed to enjoy the extra competition but the coach was becoming more and more concerned that the older Castle brother was resigned to taking a back seat role. Even in live competition, the boy still wrestled with heart but stayed on the defense, waiting for his opponent to shoot so that he could sprawl. The coach was particularly worried that it was costing the boy a good twenty-five percent of his matches.

With the state tournament only a month away, something would need to change soon if Ron hoped to place or even qualify. Sean hoped that all three wrestlers were gaining something of value from their added efforts.

Chapter 74

Nick stared at the actors. He really hadn't expected to enjoy this musical but was finding himself getting caught up in the plight of several of the characters.

The show's name was *Les Miserables*, which his limited French language skills led him to believe was a story about being miserable. The school's French teacher had arranged the outing at a local theatre and Nick jumped at the chance to attend, less for the extra credit being offered than for the chance to inconspicuously spend some time with Sandi.

Initially elated that the show had been translated to English he was finding that the plot was really pulling him in.

"If I speak, I am condemned. If I stay silent, I am damned." The lead character was agonizing, trying to decide between two really bad choices. He could either admit to the law that he was a parole violator or quietly let a man who looked like him take the fall.

The ethical choice seemed to be to admit to the crime and go back to jail. However, a wrinkle was thrown in that this main character had hundreds of people working for him who may not survive in poverty-stricken France if he were to return to prison.

Nick thought about Coach MacCallister's comments on integrity and leadership and was relieved that painful choices like the ones in this show didn't exist in his life … at least not on such a grand scale. Sure, he was tormented about wanting to date Sandi, but it certainly wasn't something that would affect hundreds of lives or cost Nick his integrity.

Could she ever be interested in him?

He peeked over at the pretty girl beside him. His heart beat a bit faster as he watched her gazing wide-eyed at the stage. She was mesmerized, which enabled him to steal some extra glances at her.

How could she be so nice to him and so clever, fun and beautiful all at the same time? She was everything Nick had ever wanted in a girlfriend … but was he even in her league? He wished that she would give him some kind of a sign that he could understand. His ability to interpret her hints, if she was even truly giving hints, was sorely lacking.

Chapter 75

Ron was all smiles as he walked up the championship podium. He took the long way, patting the guys who took sixth, fourth, and second place on the back as he rose to the champion's platform. These were all solid wrestlers; he recognized their faces, even if their names did not come to him immediately. He was proud to be among them and even more proud to have won the gold in their bracket.

The gentle breeze caught Ron slightly off guard as he passed behind the runner-up, patting the boy on the shoulders. It seemed a bit odd that a tournament of this importance would let him advance to the top of the platform without putting his warm-ups back on or, for that matter, even pulling up his straps. Yet, he had earned the title of "champion," and apparently that entitled him to do pretty much whatever he wished.

The boy's mouth was locked in a silly grin. He was far too giddy to relinquish it as the tournament official asked each of the placers their names, shook their hands, and handed them their respective plaques. Ron was absolutely elated by the time the official got to him.

"Your name, son?" the official asked.

Ron could see the golden "champion" plaque glistening in the man's hand as the crowd noise dwindled to a low whisper in the background.

"Ron Castle," the boy proudly announced, reaching forward to shake the man's hand.

Ron's heart lurched into his throat as the man suddenly withdrew his hand.

"Excuse me, your name please?" the man repeated as he studied the bracket sheet in his hand.

"Ron Castle," Ron repeated, suddenly confused, his body unexpectedly feeling cold and bare.

A look of confusion crossed the man's face as he continued to study the bracket sheet.

"I'm sorry, son," the man remarked. "We don't have anyone of that name listed."

Ron's adrenaline kicked in and he was downright jumpy as he saw a figure begin to ascend the platform the way Ron had just come.

"Do you guys know of a Ron Castle in this tournament?" the official inquired of his team, all standing nearby. "Does anyone know a Ron Castle?"

His question was only met with the shaking of heads as Ron saw the dark figure continue to ascend, now within an arms-length of Ron's perch. Back and forth, back and forth, the heads of every one of the officials shook. The shaking soon became a pattern, spreading into the first rows of the crowd and continuing upward.

"I'm Ron Castle; I just won the tournament," the boy continued as the crowd suddenly began to murmur, a sound that grew into boisterous laughter as Ron continued to plead his case to no avail.

The dark figure reached the top step and jolted Ron awake.

In the solitude of Ron's bedroom there was no official, no figure, no crowd, just a cold student, lying coverless in his underwear.

"They don't even know me. I've been completely forgotten," he whispered to the shadows in his semi-conscious state.

Alone and ashamed, he hid his head under his pillow and drifted off again, praying for more peaceful dreams.

Chapter 76

WHAT DID YOU DO TO YOUR BACK?!!!"

Ron wasn't quick enough to dodge the verbal shrapnel or the irate woman marching toward him the moment he entered his house. Seeing his equally angry father standing behind her made him wish that he had stayed at school to study with Nick and Coach MacCallister.

"How did she know?" he wondered for a split second. No matter. Past experience had taught him that playing innocent would be a losing battle, thus he immediately went on the offensive.

"There is nothing wrong with my back," he stated, knitting his eyebrows and bracing for the retort, which as he suspected, came before his words even landed.

"I've got a bill from Doctor Whalis that tells a completely different story!" his mother argued. "There are five different tests listed, x-rays, the whole gamut, DO NOT LIE TO ME, RON!"

"There's nothing wrong!" he repeated with a bit more bite. "I pulled a muscle at the pre-Christmas tournament."

"Do you want to spend the rest of your life in a wheelchair?!" his angry mom continued.

"I KNOW MY BODY!" Ron now felt himself getting hot. "It wasn't anything like my accident! I let it rest for a few days when we went to Grandma and Grandpa's, and it's been getting better every day since."

"And you didn't think it would be good to let your parents know about this little issue?" his dad piped in with a shade of frustrated sarcasm.

"Given the way you two are blowing this all out of proportion, I'd say I made the right choice."

"DON'T you talk back, young man!" Ron had rarely seen his father get this aggressive. "Even if you don't care about your future, WE DO! You're going back to see Doctor Whalis tomorrow at 3:00."

Ron froze.

"Not tomorrow, Dad, team pictures are tomorrow before practice."

"You're not stepping foot on the mat again until we get this resolved," the elder Castle asserted. "Your mom had a choice between 3:00 tomorrow due to a cancellation or 3:25 on Wednesday, two weeks from now."

Ron knew that there was no way for him to win this round. He was on the wrong side of a two-on-one with minimal weaponry. All it would take was one word from his parents to his coaches and his season was over.

"I'll go tomorrow," the boy responded after a long pause. "But you're going to feel awfully silly when the tests come back saying that I'm fine."

"They had better," his parents responded in unison.

Chapter 77

It clicked.

Nick stared at the paper. He looked over at Coach MacCallister, and then looked back at the paper. It made sense. He had completed the Physics problem and it actually made sense. Not only did it make sense, it made sense in a way that made other problems make sense as well.

Nick's eyes moved to the next problem on the page. Yes, this was doable too. He punched a few numbers into his calculator, drew a couple of diagrams on his grid paper and showed Sean the answer.

"Is it right?" Nick asked.

Sean smirked.

"Of course," he answered.

Nick's mind was a blur. He raced through some of the other problems on the page. They weren't hard. In fact, they bordered on being easy. How could this be? In less than an hour, Coach MacCallister had shown him how to master a subject that had been his albatross after months of lectures and countless hours of study.

Once again, his coach was "the man." The boy marveled at how Sean could not only bring out his best on the wrestling mat but could also expand his mind, allowing him to master this class-work. Every time there was a problem, the solution seemed to stem from Coach MacCallister.

The youth watched his coach as the young man's roommate entered the Riverside commons area. Sean slapped his hands down on the table and pushed his chair back. "It's time for me to get to my own studies," he exclaimed as he began loading his materials into his backpack.

"Ready?" Kelly asked. "I've got Otis's car."

Sean looked around.

"Give me two minutes," he responded. "I need to grab my jacket from the coaches' office."

With that, he hustled down the hallway, leaving Nick and Kelly alone.

Nick was amazed at Sean and how he could just get up and go as if this had been all in a day's work, an unpaid day's work at that. Suddenly, a new question of "why?" filled his mind.

Nick looked to the behemoth standing close to the door. The man was intimidating but Nick's curiosity was roused. Was this a weird question?

"Does he take care of everyone at home, too?"

The man looked a bit confused. "What do you mean?"

"It's just that …" he started. "It's just that he took the time this evening to explain half a year's worth of Physics to me. He found me a reasonable mask when the school didn't supply one. He believed in me when other coaches didn't. Why is he like that?"

The question seemed to catch the big man off guard. He straightened his stocking cap while he thought through Nick's words, looking at the ceiling, then down at Nick again.

"When he was growing up, nobody was ever there to stand up for him. I think he just tries to make sure that nobody else he knows has to feel like that."

Nick nodded, contemplating the words as the two stood in silence until Sean appeared down the hall.

"Make him proud," Kelly said, before Sean got within earshot.

Nick only nodded again.

"Do you need a ride, Nick?" Sean asked moments later, approaching the two.

"No thank you, I always run home," the boy replied.

"All right, that figures," Sean answered. "I'll see you tomorrow."

The three walked together toward the door that would lead them into the frigid February night.

Chapter 78

Ron's face was expressionless as he rode into the Riverside parking lot with his dad. The man was oblivious to the pain in his son's eyes as the boy's heart sank. Those eyes stared straight forward, watching the Anderson Photo truck pass on its way out of the parking lot.

If his dad noticed the truck, he didn't say anything. As such, Ron surmised that the man clearly did not know what the departing truck meant. On the surface, it appeared only that Ron had missed the team pictures. However, at this point in Ron's season, the void left by the vehicle encompassed much more than that.

Ron was already resigned to his role as a bit player on this team. Missing the photo meant that he had reached the bottom of his downward slope. He had gone from being a star two years ago, to a cripple last year, to a comeback story, a let-down, and was now about to complete the 180-degree turn as he ended up a complete nobody.

Ron thought of his brother and the season the boy was having. Nick would be the Castle brother featured in the yearbook. He was well on his way to winning the state title that had eluded both boys their sophomore years. Even more important, Nick would have the opportunity to repeat as a senior the following year.

Where did all of this leave Ron? The boy who had blazed such a bright path as an underclassman was now about to be forgotten with all traces of him completely erased. At best, he would qualify for state and at worst, spend the last weekend in February dressed in street clothes, watching his brother from the stands.

Ron closed his eyes.

"It doesn't matter," he told himself. He would go to the locker room and dress for practice as if it were any other day. His mark would rest on something, someday. He accepted that the state wrestling title he had dreamed of since his youth would simply not be it.

"Here you go, Champ." His dad's words were distant as the car rolled to a halt.

Ron tapped his fist on the dashboard, said a brief, "Thanks, Dad," and stepped out of the car. He would practice today as the doctor had not found any reason to hold him out for now. As an added precaution, the doctor had ordered an extra review of the results of Ron's most recent MRI.

Ron's destiny would start with today's workout. He just wished he had some more clarity as to what that destiny held.

Chapter 79

Nick felt an internal jolt of electricity as he stared at the Sunday newspaper. A new rush of adrenaline wiped away any hint of drowsiness in the pre-dawn hours.

Oddly enough, the boy's moment of combined excitement and fear had nothing to do with the small article covering Nick's championship performance at the previous day's tournament. He was focused on what most people would consider minutia in the box scores of a tournament on the other side of the state.

The 140-pound weight class championship match box score showed Spegidos pinning his opponent in the second period.

"What does it mean?" the boy wondered as the quick adrenaline hit pushed him out of his chair. He paced the kitchen with fists clenched. "Is he really taking the bait? Is the stage truly being set for a Spegidos versus Castle showdown at the state tournament?"

There was no way for him to know for sure. Still, in any case, he would need to be prepared. For starters, he would run extra hard on his paper route this morning. Afterward, he would roust Ron out of bed for help in dissecting the dozen additional videos of Spegidos matches they had been able to collect.

If he had in fact lured the state's most formidable grappler into his weight class, the one thing he knew for sure was that he would need to redouble his efforts if he hoped to have any chance to come out on top.

He cringed, thinking about what it would feel like to lose in what would undoubtedly be a highly touted state championship match. For an adolescent who shunned the spotlight, there surely could be no worse fate. No mask could hide that kind of embarrassment.

He shook his head, flinging the distasteful thought from his mind like a dog shaking off water.

"That's not going to happen," he told himself as he motored toward the door to deliver his papers.

Chapter 80

Sean lay on the floor, no longer able to move. His chest was sore and his throat hurt as he reached a weary arm to his face to wipe the tears from his eyes ... and it was all his father's doing.

Sean hadn't laughed that hard in years, nor had he ever before had a phone conversation last longer than five hours. The physical and emotional demands of the call had left him feeling utterly depleted as he lay on the floor with a small grin plastered on his lips.

Conversation can sometimes be the best medicine and this long talk had been just the dosage the two men had needed. After the first half an hour, there had been no anger or blaming, just two reasonable adults talking about their lives and doing their best to understand each other's perspectives which, surprisingly, had been fairly easy as they discovered more and more ways in which they were truly alike.

For the first time Sean could remember, he had listened to his father. He listened to the crazy stories about college road trips before the older man's first stint at college had been cut short by having to raise a family. His ears piqued as they were filled with accounts of making hard money choices over the years in order to make ends meet and holding off groups of creditors long enough to ensure that the monthly mortgage payment was made.

The two discussed bar fights, bar maids, and being barred from several establishments due to their involvement with the first two. There had been no animosity, just two men who bled the same blood coming to grips with how painfully alike they were despite having seen each other as polar opposites for Sean's entire lifetime. It was all point of view.

Sean squinted as he looked toward the clock.

"Ugh," he thought, realizing that he was going to have to pay for a phone call that had been nearly the length of two football games. The phone company would turn off his phone for sure this time. Yet, Sean had seen enough situations like this one that he knew he'd eventually find a way to pay the bill.

He wished that he could be home with his dad and promised himself that he would find a way to make the trip as soon as wrestling season was over.   Spring break would be a great opportunity to get back home for some one-on-one time.

The afternoon of forgiveness and rebirth had taken everything that Sean had. Still, he wished the call would not have ended.

Chapter 81

Don MacCallister lay in his hospital bed with tears in his eyes. As exhausted as he was from the conversation, he also felt 50 pounds lighter. When had been the last time that he and his son had ended a discussion without yelling? Had they ever?

For the first time, he realized that he did truly love the young man. Sean was his son, regardless of what had or hadn't happened between Don's wife and other men. Sean was the one who would carry the MacCallister name long after Don was gone and, if Don were lucky, would restore some dignity to the name's standing in society.

He wheezed a little bit. The pneumonia certainly wouldn't subside if he kept up this schedule. He shook his head, suddenly aware of the fact that he hadn't told his boy that he loved him today. Then again, had he ever? How would Sean respond if he had?

Don shivered a little bit and pulled his blanket more snugly around him. What if he said it and all he heard was silence on the other end of the line? Would that be the end of him? Would he just write it off as a character flaw in the boy and send the two back to their prior animosity?

He shook his head. It didn't matter what the response would be. Don had to say it for himself and his son to hear. He would do it when he woke up in the morning. His eyelids fluttered as he fought off sleep for another moment. He would do it tomorrow. He would call his son and tell him he loved him tomorrow.

For the first time in a long time, he said a quick prayer and felt himself relax. He closed his eyes and went to sleep.

Chapter 82

For possibly the first time, Nick was glad when Sandi left the lunch table.

The boy had enough on his mind with the conference tournament quickly approaching. He was confident that he would fly through it and make it to the final step. However, he was less confident that, should Spegidos choose to move to 140, he could stop the juggernaut from steamrolling him at State. He and Ron had watched match after match of the returning champion, looking for a vulnerability to exploit but finding none.

The brothers continued after-practice training with Coach MacCallister and Kevin Hermanns to ensure that, if nothing else, they would all be prepared for the state's other contenders. They had been surprised that, recently, the foursome was not alone. Coach Tyler was staying nearly every day to work with them in addition to several other wrestlers who seemed to view the extra sessions as an opportunity to rise in the standings.

Pulling himself back to the present situation, Nick could only shake his head at how rude Oscar had been to Sandi. Kendra had also joined them for lunch, and when she and Nick took Sandi's side, Oscar unloaded with both barrels, accusing Sandi of turning everyone against him.

The whole situation was so incredibly uncomfortable. Caught between his interest in Sandi and a loyalty to a friend that, quite honestly, he didn't even like most of the time, Nick was elated when the two had chosen to angrily march off in separate directions.

Everything in his life was moving so fast. The last thing he needed was to catch shrapnel in this crossfire. He exchanged glances with Kendra, hoping for some kind of stress reprieve sometime soon.

Chapter 83

Nick was frustrated with himself. Given the way he had wrestled his brother tonight, there was absolutely no way that he would be prepared to face Spegidos. Ron had cut the boy off at every turn, allowing only a single takedown as Nick focused on being aggressive during their post-practice match.

"Focus," Nick thought as he and Hermanns circled. The two boys would go full steam in this six-minute post-practice match. Nick certainly needed something to go right in this bout after the debacle with Ron.

Kevin shot and Nick sprawled which was exactly what Nick felt this contest didn't need. Spegidos loved to throw these days and go for the quick pin. Nick didn't need a practice partner who was going to go "lower body" on him. His frustration mounted as he got hip position and broke Kevin's grip, temporarily avoiding danger.

Hermanns finally relinquished his waning grip on Nick's leg and fled backward to prevent Nick from getting behind him for an easy defensive takedown. How could Nick have missed that opportunity?

"Focus," he told himself again.

Back in neutral position, Nick's frustration was beginning to turn to a hint of anger. He pushed Hermanns in the chest, popped him in the forehead and went right in on the single leg. The text book precision with which Nick completed the takedown was a thing of beauty and re-lifted the boy's spirits temporarily.

"Nice, Nick," Coach MacCallister offered. "Nerby is a shooter, Kevin, you're going to have to watch for that at Conference and likely at State."

"Of course Nerby is a shooter," Nick thought. That's why Hermanns and Nick were the perfect practice partners at this point. Hermanns had the upper body strength and skill to replicate Spegidos while both of the Castles were shooters like Nerby. Had Kevin forgotten this important point?

"What's your next move, Nick? You've got your two but don't expect that to win you the match."

His coach seemed unusually chipper tonight, relaxed and nearly giddy. "I'll bet that he isn't swimming in girl problems," Nick pondered, thinking back to his uncomfortable lunch. He was pretty sure that his coach had a waiting list of wonderful women vying for his time.

"Fifteen seconds," Ron called, "what are you going to do?"

Both wrestlers perked up with Nick fighting to gain some leverage or, at a minimum, hip position while Kevin looked for an escape route.

Out of the corner of his eye, Nick saw a large form coming up the stairs. Yet, he kept his attention on the mat, ensuring that these remaining seconds of the first period would find him retaining control.

"Time!" Ron called.

As Nick looked to Coach MacCallister to see who would get to choose for second period, he noticed that the young man was over talking to the person who had just ascended the stairs. It was the big man Nick recognized from a few weeks earlier as the coach's roommate.

The boy opened his mouth to ask for the coin toss but instantly clammed up as he saw his coach suddenly break down, apparently getting weak and falling forward into his friend.

None of the wrestlers said a word as Sean quickly came over. His face had turned to an ashen gray and his eyes were getting puffy.

"I've got to go … I'm sorry," was all MacCallister said as he handed Ron the coin and his whistle and, half dazed, stumbled down the stairs with his buddy.

Nick couldn't be sure what was wrong but he felt fairly certain that it was more serious than issues involving wrestling or girls.

Chapter 84

Sean sat on Otis' extra futon in a mental haze. His own phone had been disconnected sometime in the past 24 hours and Otis had been kind enough to lend his phone for Sean to call Amy.

"Dad died sometime early this morning," Amy had conveyed through a stream of tears. "I'm taking care of all of the funeral arrangements. It will be on Friday. Are you coming home?"

In the emotional moment, Sean had said "yes", even though he had no clue how to possibly make it happen. He had no money for a plane ticket and doubted whether he could even pull together enough money for gas if someone were to lend him a car as Kelly had suggested may be an option.

To compound matters, he was feeling that he was on thin ice at work. Missing two extra days due to car travel would surely put him in dire straits. He and Kreitzer had been at odds since day one. Tyler had given him an earful about how stretched he had been when Sean missed the VC tournament. Could he possibly keep his job if he missed another? What impact would it have on the team if they were wrestling with only one real coach this late in the season?

His mind turned back to his dad and his eyes glossed over. He wished that he had been able to engage his father in a conversation like that of the previous day while he had been home over Christmas. Certainly it would have made a difference to both of them to have had better closure in person.

For so many years this news would have had no effect on him. Today it was crippling.

Not having the energy to deal with his hopeless situation or even the stamina to walk back to his room, he lay down on the futon, closed his eyes, and drifted off to sleep.

Chapter 85

Sean."

The low voice was pesky, coming from somewhere too close to Sean's head.

"Sean," the voice repeated.

He opened one eye to see Kelly's large face and frame crouching near him.

"What time is it?" MacCallister asked, feeling terribly groggy.

"It's shortly after midnight," his roommate replied. "You need to go back to your own bed so Otis can get some sleep."

As the disoriented young man stumbled from the futon, Kelly handed him a thin rectangular packet.

"What's this?" Sean asked, trying to focus as they walked into the hallway.

"You need to go home and be with your family," Kelly replied, stopping as they got to the door of their room.

"You get some sleep," the big man continued. "I'm going downstairs to watch ESPN with Darrel."

Sean grabbed Kelly's arm as his eyes adjusted to the light and he studied the thin cardboard pieces in his hand – airline tickets.

"How?" Sean asked pondering his dirt-poor roommate and the expense he had just incurred.

"Get some sleep," Kelly repeated, turning away and walking toward the stairs. "We can talk tomorrow."

Suddenly feeling jubilant, yet still painfully tired, Sean did as he was told, entering the dark room and heading straight for his bunk.

With his focus on getting to bed, Sean failed to notice the large empty space across the room where Kelly's TV had stood for the past three years.

Chapter 86

Nick turned off the television and started his evening stretching, feeling both excited and nervous. It had now been over a month since he had begun hunting Spegidos. For more than four weeks, every night after practice, he had stayed with Ron, Hermanns and Coach MacCallister, preparing himself for the match of his life against the state's most celebrated and dangerous grappler.

Several times each week, including tonight, Nick completed his homework and went right to work reviewing Spegidos matches. He had accumulated more than 20 of them from over the past three years. He was having trouble finding a weakness, any weakness.

As Nick watched match after match, the champion tore through his opponents. Most didn't make it through the first period. With the exception of the match with Ron from the two boys' sophomore year, Spegidos was always the victor. Yet, Spegidos from two years ago was a completely different competitor from Spegidos today. In the match he lost to Ron, the boy had come out conservatively. This was something that simply didn't happen after the boy became unstoppable. Every match, he was now coming out and completely over-powering and out-wrestling his opponents from the beginning whistle. He was relentless, never giving the opposing wrestler a chance to breathe, much less think.

The boy's eyes scanned the room, falling on the newly framed picture of Nick with Coach MacCallister that his mom had taken at the end of the Capital Tournament. He made a mental note to bring the reprint for his coach. He had forgotten it several consecutive days now and it was in danger of being covered by papers in his room as it sat on his desk. Sharing the picture was the least the boy could do to thank Coach MacCallister for bringing Nick to the verge of fulfilling his mission.

The quest had given Nick value far beyond the wrestling mat. For the first time in their lives, he and his brother had a solid bond as they worked toward a common goal. Ron was not only a practice partner but had also become a bit of a mentor. The two watched video together night after night, looking for any Spegidos weakness to exploit. Of course, the unfortunate truth was that, if any existed, it was not yet evident.

Further, it kept Nick's mind off of Sandi, enabling him to escape from beating himself up for not having had the courage to ask her out yet. When he trained for Spegidos, wrestling was his sole focus.

He stretched his legs, feeling more flexible than at any other point in his life. He hadn't lost a match in over a month. Yet, he didn't feel that he had peaked. He still had more to give which led to the two remaining questions in his mind: "Could anybody in the state beat Travis Spegidos?" and, if the answer to that question was affirmative, "Was that person Nick Castle?"

There was only one small tournament and one more dual before the conference tournament. Nick anxiously awaited the chance to resoundingly answer both questions for the world.

Chapter 87

Sean stumbled into his room on the brink of exhaustion. The past two days had been an emotional whirlwind as well as a sleepless marathon as he and Amy laid their father to rest and tried to get as much estate settlement done as possible in their short time together.

Although he raced straight from the funeral reception to the airport and made it to his Friday evening flight in time, his connection was cancelled due to what the airline called "weather issues," a convenient excuse Sean suspected was covering up the real reason of not filling all seats on the Friday night flight.

Lacking both luggage and funds for a hotel room, Sean slept in his suit on the painfully uncomfortable chairs near the gate of his re-booked 4:30 a.m. connection. He suffered additional mishap as the man sleeping on the chairs near him upset a can of soda, drenching Sean's suit coat which he had folded as a pillow.

The connecting flight itself had been uneventful but returned Sean home in barely enough time to catch the early shuttle back to campus so that he could change clothes before work. As he tossed the crumpled mess that was his only suit into his laundry hamper, he was glad he didn't have pending interviews that would require the suit's immediate use.

On the verge of physical collapse, he headed toward Riverside to catch the bus to the day's tournament.

Chapter 88

Nick heard the muffled shouts through the coaches' office door and wondered what all of the commotion could possibly be about. While much of the three-way tirade between the coaches was indiscernible, he was able to make out the words "drinking" and "alcoholic" in Kreitzer's nasal, high-pitched tone.

The boy paused, wondering if he should find some place to kill ten minutes before getting dressed for the morning's practice.

"No," he thought, shaking the option from his mind. His championship match this past weekend had been too close for comfort as he had edged the state's third-ranked wrestler by a mere two points. He had a week left before the conference tournament and needed every extra moment available to prepare.

He pulled open the locker room door with its usual loud creak, which brought the shouting to an immediate halt.

"Whatever the issue is, it must be significant for everyone to clam up like that," Nick thought, hurrying to his locker to change.

It only took three minutes to change into his workout clothes. He had just finished tying his first shoe when he heard the door creak again.

Tensely, he continued on, tying his second shoe and waiting for whoever had entered to make his way past the first row of lockers to Nick's section. The boy froze as Assistant Principal Kreitzer emerged.

Nick looked up, but broke eye contact right away. Most days, the man was a bit shifty but on this particular morning, he was downright creepy.

"What can you tell me about your little friend's problem?" the man asked, moving to a position which blocked the boy's escape route.

"What?" the confused boy answered back.

"Drinking problem," the man continued. "You two are together every day, thick as thieves. Don't tell me you don't know. Has he got you drinking too?"

Nick's mind raced back to his entrance into the locker room and the shouting. Did one of the coaches have a drinking problem? The goose bumps rose on his back momentarily. The only one Kreitzer could possibly be talking about was Coach MacCallister, the coach Nick spent the most time with.

"Coach MacCallister?" the boy clarified, trying to figure out exactly what the line of questioning was about.

"Has MacCallister been purchasing alcohol for you?" the man asked.

Nick was shocked.

"No, of course not," he remarked, again trying to avoid the man's eerie gaze.

"Does he buy for Oscar?"

"Oscar?" Nick repeated.

"Don't play dumb, Castle," the man commanded. "We've only got a few days until the conference tournament. MacCallister is an alki and Oscar just got busted with booze. Did MacCallister buy alcohol for Oscar?"

Nick felt himself turning green. He wasn't completely surprised that Oscar had gotten caught drinking but he was dumbfounded that anyone would suspect Coach MacCallister of buying.

"No," Nick shot back, more forcefully this time. "Absolutely not."

The man shook his head.

"Don't fall in with troublemakers, Nick," the man stated. "They'll only make you a part of their problems."

Not knowing quite how to respond, Nick only nodded a reply as he brushed past the man on his way up to practice.

Chapter 89

Sean was angry as he peered around the locker room, waiting for Nick to arrive. He counted his blessings that he wasn't drinking or he would have likely done something, or at the very least said something that he would have regretted, as Kreitzer tore into him with a verbal tirade.

"Two more weeks," he thought. "Twelve more days to bite my lip and not pummel that arrogant jerk."

The conversation had begun by focusing on Oscar's missing uniform. The boy was supposed to return it before the big dual with South. Unfortunately, when Oscar didn't show, Sean had asked about getting a janitor with a lock cutter to retrieve it. The assistant principal's instructions to Sean had been, "Get the uniform yourself or get a new job."

Beyond fed-up with the man's power-trips, it had taken all of Sean's willpower to refrain from exploding as the man then launched into a speech about how this whole incident with a wrestler drinking could have been avoided if Sean hadn't been such a poor role model.

Kreitzer's words, "incompentent drunk," were still echoing in Sean's ears when he heard the locker room door open and saw Nick emerge with a look of sorrow on his face.

"No luck?" Sean asked.

"I couldn't find him anywhere," the boy replied.

With weigh-in beginning in twenty minutes, Sean looked to the 25-pound weight in his hand, suddenly wishing he could smack Kreitzer in the melon with it but knowing its intended use.

"You'd better leave," he told the boy.

"Why?" Nick asked.

"I don't want to be a bad influence on you," the coach replied.

"Just don't give me any bad advice," Nick smiled.

"In that case," Sean said softly, "don't ever break a padlock using a 25-pound weight and, more importantly …"

The man brought the weight down once, cracking the lock in a single blow.

"… do as I say, not as I do."

Chapter 90

Respect your opponent!"

The words echoed in Nick's brain as he bridged, transferring the weight to his neck and eventually his left shoulder as he struggled to keep his shoulder blades from touching the mat.

This should have been a clean, quick win for a highly ranked grappler like the younger Castle. Facing an opponent with a seven and sixteen record, a freshman at that, Nick should have gone right to work to put the boy out.

Had Nick misjudged this boy? It certainly seemed that way for the moment as the South wrestler inched his way up Nick's torso, attempting to put his weight on Nick's chest before Nick could conclude the journey to his belly and base.

One slip-up was all it had taken. Nick had gotten lax for a moment, not expecting the kid to be as strong or agile as he was. The result had been an off-balance takedown ending with Nick being taken straight to his back.

"Coach's kid," Nick thought, irritated. He knew that his opponent was Coach Nestor's son weeks in advance. The kid had probably grown up with mat burns and cauliflower ears. Why hadn't Nick thought to treat the match as he would treat a match against one of the state's elite?

"From now on, I will," he thought, answering his own question as he completed rolling through. He had a long way to go to make up for the rocky start and less than five minutes to do it in.

"Three points green," the ref bellowed as Nick began to work his way up to his base. Once he got on his hands and knees, he would have more control and be able to start his recovery. He wouldn't underestimate this opponent the remainder of the match. Regardless of who was put on the mat against him, there wasn't a match the rest of the season that he could afford to lose.

"Respect your opponent!" was on his mind the entire next five minutes as he regained his composure and turned the tables, leaving the mat as a fourteen to six victor.

Chapter 91

Weasel!"

It was the only word that came to mind as Cole Tyler sat quietly in the coaches' office and listened patiently to his visitor.

"You have to keep the best interests of the school in mind. Luckily, those coincide with the best interests of the team, in the long term," Kreitzer's voice droned on.

What was it about this man that annoyed him so much? A better question may be, "Is there anything about Kreitzer that didn't annoy Tyler?"

"If we want to bring this team back to its former status, it is going to take funding to get new uniforms and mats. It is hard to argue that a team with juvenile delinquents on it and people with questionable morals coaching it deserves those dollars more than other well-respected teams in this school …"

Most of the seemingly endless stream of words just disappeared into empty space. Cole couldn't imagine what political game he was being pulled into to appease this man's ego. Still, Kreitzer was the assistant principal so Cole sat there, staring at him and nodding his head, thinking "weasel, weasel, weasel, weasel …"

It was no wonder the Riverside program had struggled given the political environment it faced. It wasn't a place where one could stay devoted, and it wasn't a place that Tyler could remain much longer.

The head coach couldn't decide whether it was the choice he was being asked to support or the messenger that was turning his stomach. Perhaps it was both?

The program needed to be funded, decisions needed to be made, butts needed to be saved, and Cole was feeling more and more like a pawn in some deceitful plot.

Chapter 92

Nick sprinted with everything he had, one apparent goal in mind. Ron was nipping at his heels and Hermanns, as always, was ahead of both of them. Nick was committed to changing that.

For Nick, it was the last morning practice before the conference tournament. For those who continued to struggle on the mat, it could be the last practice of their season or even the last of their career. Riverside's "Big Three" were running like there was no tomorrow to ensure they were still in the hunt at this time the following week, day one of the state tournament.

Nick let up briefly as he neared a corner but then accelerated through the turn. How long had he been running full throttle? His body was so well tuned at this point that it didn't seem to matter. His sinewy legs felt like they could perform at top velocity for hours like a biker in the Tour de France.

Kevin was only a few yards ahead. He seemed to realize that he was being chased and had no intention of yielding his position. Down the stairs he bounded, careful to neither lose his footing nor lose a step to his pursuer … he was successful in only the first of the two actions.

Down the hall, all three ran, each with a sense of urgency bordering on insanity. All seemed decisive in their choice to give it all, tearing down the corridor as if something much grander were at stake.

Reaching the final stairway, Nick made his move, leaping up the first four stairs in a single bound and galloping up the remainder of the flight using every last inch of his long legs to his advantage. By the time they reached the top, Nick had pulled even with the 145-pounder with Ron still close enough to dive-tackle either of them.

Running all-out down the final stretch, Nick lengthened his stride, pushing himself with each subsequent step until he passed Coach MacCallister with his stopwatch, the young man exclaiming, "A new team record time, Nick first, Kevin, Ron … unbelievable!"

Nobody else would emerge for another twenty seconds, giving Sean time to turn his attention and talk the three up some more.

"Amazing, guys! How did you find that gear?"

Panting too hard to verbalize, a single thought was running through Nick's mind: "If anyone in this state has a chance of beating Spegidos, THAT is how he would run."

Chapter 93

Fired.

Sean was angry. As the wind whistled by his ears, he felt that sense of anger that can only be accompanied by a sense of treachery. He had been betrayed and it was driving him to a place where he didn't want to go.

How many webs had been woven around the proceeding moments? Unfortunately, Sean had not pieced together the vague signs until it was too late.

Coach Kreitzer had run practice late, something he had never before done in a morning practice. Then, supposedly to ensure that the wrestlers could all get to class on time, he held Sean back from showering so that they could all get ready first. By the time Sean had finished his shower and gotten dressed, the team had dispersed, leaving the two coaches alone. It was at this point that the school's principal, Mr. Skinner, had emerged. After a brief conversation, he fired Sean.

Sean had sat there in disbelief as the man laid out the complaint. Most of the accusations came from Kreitzer. Had that double-crossing coward not slinked from the room as the big boss entered, Sean would have laid him out. Instead, he could only stare numbly as the man told him that he was a danger to the team, a bad example, had willfully destroyed school property and thus, could no longer be permitted to be part of the coaching staff.

Sean, of course, had defended himself where he could. The charge of him being a danger to the team stemmed from his supposed injury of Nick's shoulder two months earlier. As embarrassed as he was over that incident, all he could do was apologize and point out that it was a one-time accident.

The bad influence charge related to alcohol abuse. Sean mentioned that he was in AA, had been sober for over a month and a half and, despite Kreitzer's accusations, he had never purchased alcohol for any of the wrestlers.

The allegation about destroying school property angered him as much as the other two combined. Kreitzer had obviously been running out of ammunition when he forced Sean into that situation. Yet, by doing as he was ordered, he led to his own undoing.

By the time the principal had gotten to the end-game, Sean was too angry to even look at him.

"Assistant Principal Kreitzer is one of my most trusted colleagues," the man stated. "He has gone out and secured a restraining order against you that prevents you from having any kind of contact with anyone on this team. It is effective as of right now, and you will suffer the legal consequences if you are caught violating it."

A restraining order? Like some dangerous criminal? He couldn't believe that he would not even be allowed to say "goodbye" to the members of the team he had grown so close to.

Later, Sean did not remember much else. He recalled feeling dizzy as he grabbed his coat and remembered hearing the man say that he would still be paid half for his final week of unused service but would forego his end-of-season payout. In a haze, he staggered out of the office and out of the school for the final time.

Sean felt like he had been punched in the face and stomach at the same time. His head was spinning and he was breathless. It was like he was reliving being attacked by Kevin Lakes all over again. But this time, the brutal punishment pained his soul rather than his body. Not only was he losing his income, the firing was sure to be a black mark as he looked for his next job. And, worst of all, he wouldn't fulfill his commitment to the team and coaching Nick to a state title.

Out the door, he saw a man cleaning cigarette butts out of an ashtray in the faculty smoking area. Given Sean's lack of employment opportunities and this most recent failure, he wondered if he may be embarking on a similar career in the near future and if anyone would even take a chance on him for this kind of labor. He cringed as the darkness falling over his mind made him fear becoming a burden to his friends and society.

As the bitter February wind stung his face, his thoughts turned back to the wrestling team and how coaching had become the one thing in his life which brought him joy and a sense of purpose. Without it, he concluded that perhaps it would be best for everyone if he were to simply disappear.

Planning for that disappearance would consume him the remainder of his walk.

Chapter 94

Nick accompanied his brother through the commons. As the two met up with the school's elite, Nick noticed them looking at him differently. For so many years, he had been largely invisible. At best, he had been "Ron Castle's little brother" to them.

Today, it all seemed different. They knew of his recent prowess on the mat, his high state ranking, and his likelihood of bringing another state title back to Riverside. He had finally turned the corner, earning their genuine attention and respect.

As the brothers stood, chatting with the captain of the cheerleading team, Nick's attention was drawn to blonde hair bouncing across the far side of the commons on the way to the choir room. Sandi's appearance distracted him such that he was completely unmindful of what the beautiful cheerleader was saying to him.

"I've got to go. I'll see you around, Nick."

His own name made him snap back to the conversation, realizing how rude he was probably being.

"Yeah," he said, blushing slightly. "I'll talk to you soon."

As soon as she left, Ron punched him in the arm.

"You dog," the older boy chided.

"What?" Nick asked, trying to get his head around his brother's strike.

"Girls like Brenda don't talk to you every day …" Ron continued.

As Nick nodded in agreement, his brother finished the thought that Nick himself had been having.

"… and if you don't ask that Davis girl out sometime soon, I'm going to punch you in the head."

Had he been that conspicuous as he was watching Sandi? If Ron had deduced Nick's feelings, did everyone else know he liked her too? Unconcerned about his brother's threat, Nick made his own mental note that his time for waiting was now over and the time for action had arrived.

Chapter 95

Sean crept into the Beta Beta Beta house, hoping that nobody would notice him. He didn't know how he was going to explain losing his job to his fraternity brothers, especially the treasurer who was looking for an already-late rent check. It seemed like the word "Loser" should be tattooed across his forehead.

As he slipped up the back stairs, his mind continued to spin. What should he do? Where could he go to hide from the mountain of debt that seemed to get closer to suffocating him every day? How could he get his head fixed without money or insurance?

A noise in the third-floor hallway made him stop before entering. He quickly peeked around the corner and noticed Randy Hordelman, looking painfully hung over, shuffling down the corridor.

Most days, the sight of the mischievous alumnus would have been exciting to Sean. This day, he immediately ducked back out of sight in the stairwell and waited, hoping the man would disappear into a bedroom or restroom. Yet continuing Sean's recent luck, neither was meant to be.

Randy almost collided with Sean as he tried to enter the stairway.

"Whoa, shooter!" the surprised man commented, still looking as if his mind was a bit hazy and grabbing Sean's shoulders for support.

"Hey Randy, I was just going back to bed," Sean threw in, trying to get past the man and into his room. The thought of sleeping for a while seemed like a wonderful option and may give his tired mind a chance to escape from the nightmare that had become his life.

"You need a haircut and a shave. And how are you going to get a job dressed like that?" Randy asked, not letting go.

"What?"

Sean immediately began getting hot. How could Randy possibly know that he had been fired? Would the high school have called to broadcast the news to the house? Why would they do that? He felt his fist clench and desperately wanted to hit something or someone.

"Isn't your interview this morning?"

Sean looked at the smiling man, and continued to get more agitated.

"Don't start with me, Randy, I'm not in the mood," he growled, abruptly pulling himself free and marching toward his room.

"Serious," Randy insisted, following a few steps behind. "The Career Center called yesterday. I left the message for you on the kitchen whiteboard. Didn't you see it?"

"You're messing with me and I'm going to punch you in the melon if you don't give me some space," Sean retaliated, arriving at his door and pushing it open. "There are no Engineering interviews on campus today; and even if there were, I didn't apply so I don't have an interview."

"Yes, you do," Kelly's voice came from inside the room. "Doris called from the Career Center this morning and said you're supposed to be interviewing for a Project Manager position. It was awfully nice of her to track you down on the house phone since our phone was disconnected."

Sean looked at the two men. Randy appeared to be sincere and he had no reason to not trust Kelly.

"What time is this supposed interview?"

"9:30," Kelly replied, pointing to the clock which read 9:27.

"So I'm going to be late," Sean commented, heading toward his closet and realizing that his suit was still crumpled up in a pile from after his father's funeral.

"No worries," thought the young man. "I'll show up late, look like trash, and be completely unprepared for whatever this thing is. In the end, it won't matter because I didn't sign up for any interview and it's all just a waste of time."

He didn't know at the time that he was only partially right about the entire situation.

Chapter 96

Nick paced around the basement, angry and anxious.

He had already made the call twice, getting nothing but a very happy voice on Sandi's family's answering machine. As his 9:00 cut-off loomed, he picked up the phone to dial one last time.

Why couldn't Coach MacCallister have been at practice tonight? Nick fumed as he tensely held the receiver in his hand. He was pretty sure that the assistant coach had no problems on the dating front and would have been a wonderful source for advice as Nick prepared to make the call. Was the man sick? Had he been in some kind of accident? Nick had asked Coach Kreitzer but the assistant principal had just brushed Nick off, responding only that he didn't know what MacCallister might be up to.

Adding to the boy's frustration was that he had finally remembered to bring Coach MacCallister's picture from the Capital Tournament which was now in danger of getting lost under a mound of stuff in Nick's locker.

Nick gazed over at the clock – 8:56. He only needed to connect before 9:00. After that, it wasn't rude if the conversation lasted a while.

He thought back to Dino and Cheri. It was the weekend of the conference tournament last year when the big guy had been killed. Cheri never knew how much Dino liked her ... at least she never heard it from Dino himself.

8:57.

Nick started dialing again and the sick feeling jumped around in his stomach as his nerves took over. He dialed all but the final number and paused, considering whether or not he should just hang up and save himself the potential embarrassment.

Why was this so hard? Nick wrestled with heavyweights at practice and had called out the premier wrestler in the state. Why should he be the least bit intimidated by a small blonde who couldn't weigh a hundred pounds soaking wet?

His finger trembled as he hit the last number, a seven. Perhaps it would be lucky for him this time?

This call was the beginning of the end. He couldn't turn back if this didn't pan out. Sandi would know that he liked her and would have to choose whether or not she liked him back enough to go out on a date with him. If she did say "yes," would it further damage his strained friendship with Oscar? If she said "no," would it damage his confidence going into the following day's conference tournament? All he knew for sure was that if he didn't at least give his best effort in this, it would haunt him the entire weekend, likely carrying over onto the mat.

His head was spinning as he heard the first ring.

"Please don't answer," he thought as his nerves got the better of him. Then, he quickly reprimanded himself. What if he brought that kind of attitude to active competition? Would he ever win a match? The night before the conference tournament was no time to start doubting himself in any facet of his life. He slapped himself in the face with his free hand for even allowing such a thought to enter his mind.

As the phone rang a second time, he started to get more comfortable. She wasn't home. He could put this off for another day. But ... should he leave a message on the answering machine this time?

During his first two attempts, he hadn't left a name, a number, anything. He had just hung up when he realized that nobody was going to answer. He certainly couldn't ask her out over the answering machine. That would be wrong, wouldn't it? What if her parents listened to the message first? Would that be embarrassing?

There were too many things going through his mind as the third ring sounded. One more and he would have to decide whether or not leaving a message was appropriate. Maybe he could just leave his name, number and nothing else?

Click.

Nick froze as someone picked up the phone on the other end. His bowels did an unexpected dance, making him suddenly wish that he had gone to the bathroom a tenth time instead of just nine during the two hours he had prepared. This was his moment. "Go Nick Go!" he thought.

"Hello?"

The voice was that of a woman, not Sandi. Nick was all at once relieved and disheartened as it was only prolonging his agony.

"Hello ..." Nick stammered. "Is ... Sandi there?"

His heart was pounding so loud that he doubted whether or not he would be able to hear the answer. This was it. There was no turning back now.

"No," the woman replied, causing Nick's heart to suddenly fall to his ankles. "She and her dad went to her grandmother's for the weekend. May I take a message?"

Should he leave a message? That would mean, if Sandi chose to call Nick back, she could do so at any time, whether he was ready or not. Worse yet, what if she didn't call him back? Should Nick call her after a few days to follow up or was it just an indication that she didn't want to talk to him? What if the woman didn't give the message to Sandi, and Nick had to endure endless days of no contact? Why did his mind always have to spin through such dreadful options?

"Yes," he said finally. "Will you please tell her that Nick called? Nick Castle?" He gave her his number and waited for her response.

"I sure will, Nick," the woman replied after a moment. Her voice sounded happy but who was he to judge what that meant? Moms always liked Nick; it was their daughters that seemed to need more convincing.

"OK ... thanks." Nick said. He hung up the phone and held his head for a minute. The phone call had gone all right, no need to dissect every last word. Perhaps now he would be able to get a decent night's sleep before having to get up early to board the bus for the conference tournament. As he headed upstairs to go to bed, his undivided attention returned to wrestling.

Chapter 97

During his sixteen and a half years, Nick had never been drunk. Thus, the day after the conference tournament was the closest thing he had experienced to a hangover after a major high.

Saturday night had found him unstoppable, winning the conference championship by a major decision. He had not even trailed in a match the entire tournament. To add to his elation, Ron had eked his way into the state tournament with a third-place finish, and five other Riverside wrestlers would be loading their gear on the bus on Thursday to seek their fortunes at state. While it wasn't a full return to Riverside's glory years, it was the best state line-up they had seen since Nick was in grade school. Nick was at the top of his game. Everything that happened on the mat showed him that he was ready to challenge Spegidos.

As well as he had wrestled while being coached by Coach Tyler and Kreitzer, Nick was sure he could handle anything or anyone once Coach MacCallister returned. He had missed the man but was determined to not let his coach's untimely unexplained absence draw his focus.

To the boy's surprise and credit, Coach Tyler had even commented that Nick's leadership had contributed to the team's success, possibly the first compliment the man had ever bestowed on him. The boy felt infallible.

Then, Sunday had seen everything come crashing down. Nick woke early to check the other conference results, feverishly paging through the Sports section of *The Herald* until he found the one he wanted. It hit him like a punch to the gut. Travis Spegidos had won his conference championship at the 135-pound weight class. Nick had failed to bring him up to 140, seemingly rendering all of the boy's extra preparation a grand waste of time.

He had slogged through his paper route with a chip on his shoulder, suddenly dwelling on everything negative in his life: his lack of dates, the animosity between him and Oscar, and most importantly his abandonment by Coach MacCallister.

He had to take control. He knew he wouldn't be able to reach Sandi and had no desire to trade barbs with Oscar. Thus, his focus beginning mid-morning was to reach Coach MacCallister and find out why he had deserted him.

Since the only number Nick had for the coach had been disconnected, he took some extra time to round up the fraternity chapter house's main number. This led to a second issue in that the phone rang on and on with nobody bothering to pick it up.

By Sunday evening, the frustration got to him and he drove to the university to find his answer. Pounding on the door, the long-awaited reply to his question made him feel totally betrayed.

Some guy named Darrel had answered the door as he walked out with a suitcase. The young man wasn't especially pleasant nor did he seem very bright. He mentioned that he hadn't seen Coach MacCallister since Friday and that some guys figured that he had gone on a major alcohol binge. Yet, it was the man's last comment that struck Nick like a hard slap in the face.

"I don't know what Sean's so shook up about. I'd go out and celebrate if my boss had fired me."

Nick felt the wind leave his lungs as he tried to make sense of it all. The only thing that was absolutely clear was that somebody had fired his coach and nobody had summoned the courage or decency to tell him.

He staggered away from the fraternity house and back into the night.

Chapter 98

When he was growing up, nobody was ever there to stand up for him."

Coach MacCallister's roommate's words from a month earlier echoed through Nick's mind as he sat in the dimly-lit hallway, leaning back against his locker. Had he made the right choice? His guts were tied in knots as the question haunted him with the big man's words being the only affirmation.

Everyone else who had earned a berth in the state tournament was at the optional Monday-morning practice. Yet, for the first time ever, Nick was missing. He wrung his hands and wrinkled his nose as he thought through his early morning altercation.

* * *

Nick was as petrified as he had ever been when he had confronted Coach Tyler.

"Did you think I wouldn't find out?!" Nick had charged, his words filled with frustration.

"We were going to tell you today, Nick," the coach replied. His voice was stern yet calm, as if he understood Nick's outrage.

"The choice to let Coach MacCallister go was not one that was made lightly. The school's administration felt that he was a danger to the team and needed to be removed."

"The school administration? You mean Mr. Kreitzer?!" the boy pressed.

"You've heard the accusation that he was purchasing alcohol for minors," the coach continued.

There was an odd tone in Coach Tyler's voice as Nick suddenly realized that the man had dodged the question. The man never shied away from anything, it made Nick curious.

"You mean Mr. Kreitzer?" Nick repeated, pressing the issue.

"Mr. Kreitzer, what?" stated a voice behind him.

Nick jumped and spun as the assistant principal entered through the door behind him.

"You fired Coach MacCallister!" Nick ranted, starting his battle on a second front.

"The man is a menace and he shouldn't be allowed around high school children," Kreitzer countered.

"Menace? Children? What planet have you been on? Coach MacCallister has always been there for this team. It never mattered how tired he was, he was always here to open the doors early for me so that I could get an early start on morning drills."

"He was tired because he was probably still drunk. The man is an outrage."

"At least he cared."

"I care, Nick. I care about this team which is why I won't let someone like that near it or any of its members. He's a bad influence, he ..."

"He is my coach!!!" Nick interrupted. "He is the one who spoke up for me!!! He is the one who trained me!!! For two years, when nobody else was on my side, HE was the one who believed in me!!! I want him to coach me at the state tournament!!!"

"Nick ... listen to me ..." Kreitzer seized the opening. "I want to coach a state champion, that's why I took this thankless job. I'm going to be your coach, just like at the conference tournament."

"No, you won't!!!!" Nick yelled. "I have a coach!!! I have ONE coach!!! He's the one I wrestle for and his name is Sean MacCallister!!!"

The boy gritted his teeth as he looked his assistant principal in the eye and continued.

"If I'm going to bring a state title back to Riverside, Coach MacCallister needs to be there."

Kreitzer half-laughed as he tried to argue with the student, "You just plowed your way through the conference tournament, impressing everybody and earning the top seed in the state tournament and you're saying now you can't wrestle without MacCallister, who wasn't even there?"

"You're not listening," the boy said grimly. "I'm not saying I CAN'T wrestle without him. I'm saying I WON'T."

With that, not knowing whether the threat would do a bit of good for his coach or not, the boy brushed past his assistant principal and went to find a dark hallway to gather his thoughts and re-group.

* * *

Half an hour later, Nick was still trembling as he sat alone, eyes closed in the hallway. If nobody had ever stood up for Coach MacCallister in the past, somebody certainly had now. But would it be enough? Could Nick truly stand by his threat if the school's leadership refused to reinstate his coach? Could he turn his back on his state wrestling title, his life's ambition?

He opened his eyes, wishing that the nightmare would come to an end.

Chapter 99

Ron sat in the doctor's office listening, more relieved than surprised at the news. The key assertion was that he had torn a muscle in December but that it had healed well as all of the MRI results except one showed his back to be in perfect health. The final scan showed an area the doctor thought was a normal variation but he wanted to check it again in a few months to make sure it was stable. There was certainly no result that indicated he shouldn't wrestle at the state tournament.

He stared contemplatively out the window as he waited for the doctor's final approval to leave. He had spent way too much time in doctors' offices the past two years. He was ready to move on. Yet, having a few minutes to himself was a nice change from his usual rigorous schedule.

He pondered Nick's situation. He knew how much Coach MacCallister meant to his brother but didn't truly believe that Nick would sit out the state tournament, regardless of what kind of idealistic crusade he was on. A sane person didn't spend an entire lifetime dreaming of winning a state title and then go on strike while seeded first.

Ron cringed a little when he thought back to Nick's request that Ron and Hermanns threaten to walk off as well. As much as he would have liked to do something to burn Mr. Kreitzer, he couldn't allow himself to throw away his last chance. Even with Ron's poor position going into the state tournament, he needed to continue his quest.

It encouraged Ron that his brother had taken Coach Tyler up on his offer to continue practicing. The boy hadn't let up at all when it came to mat-time intensity which helped Ron maintain his own energy level. He just needed to keep it up through three more practices.

He pulled on his jacket as he got ready to leave. He had already seen the list of wrestlers at 135 and had heard the skeptics questioning whether Ron was good enough to even place.

Getting to his feet, an odd question dawned on him, "Which Castle brother was fighting for the more significant lost cause?"

Chapter 100

Nick felt a little better as he took Hermanns down. He needed a release to burn off some anger and this afternoon's practice had been just what the doctor ordered.

He thought of Kreitzer as he began working to turn the 145-pounder. The smug man had already ridiculed Nick for his threatened boycott, stating that the kid didn't have the guts to follow through ... although the man hadn't used the word "guts."

"You'll be on the bus tomorrow," the man had informed him. "You're not stupid enough to give up this chance."

"So you've re-hired Coach MacCallister?" Nick had shot back, using the added opening to break through the stubborn man. As the assistant principal tried to walk away without acknowledging, the boy added, "If you really want to coach a state champion, you know what it's gonna take."

"Dig your own grave, Castle," the man had sneered. "You need this much more than I do. Besides, you don't want to see your buddy in jail for violating his restraining order, do you?"

Nick rolled Hermanns to his back with Kreitzer's words still reverberating in his brain, not fully knowing what to make of the last phrase. The ease by which he was winning the battle of the state's top ranked 140-pounder against the state's top ranked 145-pounder didn't resonate with Nick at all. Today, the bigger battle to him was clearly the one taking place off the mat.

With only a day to go, he was getting deeply concerned that it was a battle that only offered one outcome ... "Lose."

Chapter 101

Nick sat quietly in the cafeteria, trying to get his head back in the game. He looked around to see if Sandi would possibly join him but the girl was nowhere to be seen. It was probably just as well. She had returned his phone call two nights earlier while he was out but he had been semi-avoiding her as too many other stresses were weighing on him. The last thing the boy needed was to add her possible rejection to the list.

He was sure that his nervousness showed in the trembling of his hands. He felt "on edge" as he fidgeted with his salad. Oscar had abandoned him so he was conspicuously alone.

It was no surprise that the ejected wrestler was avoiding Nick. The two had exchanged words the prior night as Nick urged Oscar to come forward and let the school administrators know that their coach hadn't bought any alcohol for him. Stubbornly, the boy had refused, stating, "I'm going to exercise my right to stay silent on this one. If I say that it wasn't MacCallister, they'll try to get me to name my buyer. I'm not going there."

Nick bristled with the memory as he looked over at a neighboring table of sophomores and caught one looking at him before the boy quickly turned away. With nobody else at the table, Nick felt like the center of attention, the role he dreaded more than any other.

He felt angry. Why did he have to be in this situation? What was with these stupid politics that got his coach kicked out? Why couldn't the arrogant jerks just bring Coach MacCallister back so that Nick could wrestle with good conscience?

The "why's" didn't matter. Unless something miraculously changed within the next few hours, Nick would have to make the devastating choice. He could either stay loyal to his coach and mentor or pursue his dream of winning the state title.

He was sure that everyone was looking at him. There had to be somewhere else he could sit, somewhere that he could just be alone with his thoughts, a place where nobody else could stare at him. Nick shot a quick glare over toward the sophomore table as he picked up his salad plate.

"Are you leaving, Nick?"

The boy nearly jumped at the sound of his name, partially due to being so on edge and partially due to the voice attached to the question.

He turned to see Sandi's beautiful smile.

"I was going to find someplace else to eat," he replied, watching her raise an eyebrow that begged the next question and made him continue. "I just need a place where I can clear my head. It's too loud in here."

Sandi nodded slowly, clearly thinking of a solution.

"You could come back to the choir room with me," she suggested, causing Nick to cringe. He didn't know the choir crowd very well. All the suggestion sounded like to him was a change of setting where he would be even more conspicuous and out of place.

"Sometimes when I want to get some studying done, Mr. Kenwood lets me use one of the practice rooms that the choir uses for its quartet and sectional rehearsals. It will be quiet there."

Nick felt an adrenaline surge and wanted to kiss her. But for a change, it was not just because of how beautiful she was or her girl-next-door sweetness. This time, he also wanted to kiss her for offering the perfect location for his escape.

* * *

The two juniors entered the small room. Nick had not been surprised when Mr. Kenwood had given approval for them to use the site. Who could say "no" to Sandi? Yet, he did feel that the man eyed him a bit suspiciously during the conversation.

Sandi flipped on the light to reveal a bare-bones setup with a piano, a music stand and not much else. Nick quickly set his salad on the music stand and motioned for Sandi to take the piano bench, the only seat in the place. She smiled shyly at him and, for a moment, his mind disengaged from his wrestling dilemma.

It was very peaceful. Nick could hear someone practicing violin in the band room next door. For a moment, it felt like background music in a movie. He took a large forkful of turkey and spinach and enjoyed the serenity.

"Is something on your mind?" Sandi asked, disrupting Nick's tranquility.

For whatever reason, Nick felt calm about it now. He took a deep breath and a drink of water before slowly launching into the story about Coach MacCallister being fired, Nick's declaration that he wouldn't wrestle at state without Sean, and the friction that the combined situations was causing. He was happy that she didn't seem to judge him for what others were calling his misguided idealism.

The two sat quietly for some time afterward, enjoying their lunches and the violin and letting Nick's story hang in the air.

Finally, Sandi summarized the situation, "So what you're saying is that you're considering giving up your friends on the wrestling team and the state title you've dreamed of since you were a little boy in exchange for keeping your integrity and being loyal to your coach who the other coaches eradicated."

He didn't know how she had taken his five-minute story and condensed it into a single sentence, but he had to nod in recognition that she was correct.

"The only thing that I'm wondering, having never met Coach MacCallister, is what kind of person he is. Would he do the same for you?"

Nick had never quite thought of analyzing the situation from that angle. So why was it that the boy immediately came to the conclusion that, if the situation were reversed, Coach MacCallister would stand by Nick above all else?

Chapter 102

Sean looked out the window of the bus and watched the sky scrapers get closer and closer until he was in their midst. It had been an exhausting few days during which he had completely altered his life. The young man's thoughts drifted back to Friday. He had run into Julee Novak on his way to the career services office. She didn't seem to notice his dreadful appearance and, unexpectedly, even gave him a "good luck" kiss which provided a nice spark as he went to sort out the interview mess.

From there, things had gotten even more strange and complicated.

* * *

Sean was more uncomfortable and self-conscious than ever as he sat in the career services office in a stained and wrinkled suit and shirt. Showing up for an interview for a position that he wasn't qualified for and hadn't applied for was more of a move to not burn bridges with the Career Center than it was an honest attempt to enter into his career.

He had asked to talk to Doris, the center's administrator, but of course she was gone and would not be returning for an hour. Thus, he had no option but to wait for the recruiter.

He looked around at the waiting room's empty seats. The only other person present was a young woman with a pinched face waiting to interview for an accounting internship. She had taken one look at him when she walked into the room and opted to keep her distance.

In his haste to make it to the appointment and not be too late, Sean had skipped shaving. Pondering his appearance, he tried to remember when his last haircut had been ... certainly close to a month earlier.

In all, it didn't matter. Sean only needed a few moments to explain to the recruiter and the career services staff that he hadn't signed up for the interview. It would allow him to leave in peace and still stay in the good graces of the Career Center should a position open in the future for which he was qualified.

"Project Manager," he read the job description's title out loud, causing the young accountant to jump. Was he really that scary or was she naturally skittish?

"Eight years experience required, master's degree desired," he continued reading politely, hoping to help calm her. He received a partial nod for his efforts.

A man emerged from the interview room hallway, dressed to the nine's. If it were possible to look over-groomed for a meeting, this man would be a prime example. He looked to Sean, then to the accounting candidate, and then back to Sean with a puzzled, frustrated look on his face before disappearing behind the half-wall to where the administrative assistant sat.   There was low indiscernible mumbling and the man's head peeked out again for a brief moment.   Barely audible was the man's exasperated voice commenting, "You have got to be kidding me."

A period of two to three seconds passed with no movement before the recruiter re-emerged with a very bright smile, heading straight for Sean.   The change in the man's temperament caught Sean completely off guard as the man approached with his right hand extended.

"Sean, I'm Dave Talbott," the man stated loudly, grabbing Sean's hand with an iron grip before Sean could even get to his feet. "Let's grab a conference room and talk."

"I ..." Sean started before being instantly cut off.

"Can I get you something to drink? Coffee? Water?"

"No, I'm fine," Sean replied, trying to gauge what was making the man behave so oddly. Who did this man think Sean was?

They continued back to the interview room with Mr. Talbott making small talk and preventing Sean from saying much of anything with any meaning as he did his best to answer the man's "get to know you" questions. Sean tried to find a time to change the subject and not be rude so that he could be on his way, but the recruiter didn't leave an opportunity.

"Recruiter?" Sean wondered as the man rambled on. "Why don't they just call them 'rejecters;' it would certainly be a more accurate description."

Arriving in the interview room, Sean finally got his chance to come clean.

"I apologize for my appearance, but I really didn't know about this interview until half an hour ago. I didn't sign up for it and didn't take any time to prepare; so I can save you some time, if you don't mind just letting me go."

The man looked a bit taken aback by MacCallister's blunt statement before changing to a wry smile.

"You think I'm here to interview you?" the man asked, displaying a perfect set of pearly whites.

Sean froze, only managing a "yes" in response. If this wasn't going to be an interview, what possibly could it be?

"I don't think you understand, Mr. MacCallister," he replied. "I'm not here to interview you. I'm here to offer you a job."

Speechless, the young man sat and stared at the recruiter for a moment.

"When you didn't apply, we simply told the Career Center to bring you over anyway. They weren't able to give us specifics on which offers extended by other companies may have gone to you, so we took the liberty of taking the top offer given to an Engineering student according to their records and increased it by five percent. We think that you'll find our profit-sharing plan and other benefits to be in line with or above those offered by most other companies."

Not wanting to tip his hand, Sean only asked the key question that loomed in his mind.

"I appreciate your interest," he stated, "but I'm wondering why you would hire an undergraduate student for a Project Manager position."

"Larry Darkins is the new General Manager for our business unit. His top priority for filling this position is to find someone who," the man made quotation marks in the air with his fingers, "'gets the job done' and 'genuinely cares about the organization.' Based on his meeting with you last year, he feels that you fit both criteria."

"Larry Darkins," Sean thought. The name sounded vaguely familiar, but he couldn't place it for the life of him.

"He's right of course," Sean replied coolly. "I'm curious as to what were some of his prime examples that led him to conclude this?"

Dave studied him with a suspicious look. "He said that you picked him up last year when he was on campus recruiting accountants. You got him to his appointments on time and found someone to pull his rental car out of a snow drift. The garage manager refused payment for the towing and repair stating that 'towing is free for friends of MacCallister.' Your name also came up during interviews that day as being a top Physics tutor who is able to explain the subject matter to business majors who don't understand the mechanics of what makes things run."

The light bulb went on for Sean, remembering back a year earlier when he picked up a snow-covered man out near the airport. All he really remembered about the guy was that he needed better winter clothing and that he owned a classic Mustang.

"We need engineers who can bridge the gap with the business minds in our company. Larry feels that you will do that. The only issue is that we need someone who can start mid-semester."

"You tell Larry that I'm looking forward to seeing him again and checking out his Mustang," Sean said. "If you can show me the written offer, I should be able to make my decision by the end of the weekend."

* * *

Sean wearily stared out the window of the shuttle bus as it pulled up in front of a very nice hotel 700 miles from home. He was still reflecting on the series of events that his acceptance of the offer had set off. He had scurried to get approval to leave school early, negotiated with professors to let him submit papers from afar in lieu of taking exams, and gotten on an airplane to do his first company visit and meeting with management, all within six days of first laying eyes on Dave Talbott.

The flurry of activity had enabled him to keep from dwelling on the political nightmare he had just gone through at Riverside but it had not made him forget about his wrestlers. He only wished that he could contact them without legal consequences.

On their way out of town, he had requested that Otis take him on a round-about way to the airport, passing by Riverside.

"Good luck, Nick," he had whispered as they drove by the school, temporarily pacifying his final regret about leaving.

Chapter 103

The Riverside High School parking lot stood in near darkness as the small band of wrestlers loaded their duffle bags, one-by-one onto the small bus. Few words were spoken as the boys' respective minds focused on their physical destination, 200 miles away and the prize each sought on top of the state tournament's podium.

Chapter 104

NICK!!!!!!"

Sean sat straight up in bed, covered in sweat, his heart racing as he woke from the dream.

Sean blinked a few times in the darkness of the hotel room as he tried to figure out where he was although it didn't seem nearly as important as contacting Nick. Had he left the boy in a lurch by leaving town? Certainly Nick knew about the restraining order and that Sean couldn't contact anyone on the team ... or did he? Would Kreitzer have just told Nick that Sean quit? How would Nick wrestle at the state tournament if he felt that he had been abandoned?

"I've got to get in touch with Nick," he said aloud, not having any idea how he would do so. The team would already be holed up in a hotel, getting a good night's rest before their first weigh-in.

Sean held his head, wishing that his mind could be the fresh, problem-solving machine it had been the prior year.

He turned on the bedside lamp and squinted as his eyes grew accustomed to the light. He picked up the phone, quickly cobbling together a plan which would need to include Kelly. Even if Sean wasn't allowed to contact members of the team directly, he could sure contact them via the big man. He only hoped that doing so could deliver the message of encouragement and support to bridge the gap between a jaded performance and a state title.

Chapter 105

Ron sat on the warm-up mat stretching his hamstrings. He knew that his mind should be on his opponent but too many distractions floated in and out.

If he won this match, he would be one of sixteen wrestlers still in the running for the state title. The odds-makers, if they paid attention to high school wrestling, would have likely already locked Spegidos in as the state champion. Who would bet against that? Yet, for all intents and purposes, any one of the sixteen who made it out of this round still had a shot.

His mind drifted back to his opponent. Ron had never seen this kid wrestle. He didn't even recognize the sophomore's picture in the program. The kid was obviously an up-and-comer. He hailed from the southern edge of the state. Ron shook his head. Regardless of the boy's talent level, Ron most certainly had more experience. He would stick with his traditional plan: technique first, conditioning second, and muscle third. He would be aggressive, yet patient. There was no need to give up points being sloppy.

He suddenly became aware of a dull ache in his back. Had that been there a while or was it just the looming match bringing all minor aches and pains to the forefront? The inconclusive MRI from his doctor's visit earlier in the week briefly passed in and out of his mind.

Again, his focus coasted from where it should be, this time landing on his brother. Ron could hardly believe that Nick would give up his top seed in the tournament. While he agreed that it was ridiculous that Coach MacCallister had been fired, he would find other ways to rebel that allowed him to still wrestle.

"I've still got next year," Nick had commented a day earlier as the two had said their final "goodbyes" in the Riverside wrestling locker room. The younger boy had taken on a stern stubborn look in his eyes that Ron had never seen before.

"But nothing is guaranteed," Ron shot back. "You could get injured, you could get sick ..."

"Nothing is guaranteed this year either except that, if I step on the mat and wrestle when I vowed that I wouldn't unless the school fixed this stupid mess, I'm letting everyone down. I will let down Coach MacCallister by giving up my fight for him. I will lose face as a leader of this team by backing away from my principles. And I will give up my own integrity, knowing that I'll never be able to look in the mirror again without thinking about how I made a pledge and then went back on my word."

Ron had thought that he had seen a mist forming over his brother's eyes but the boy was too quick, grabbing Ron in a big bear hug and whispering, "This is your tournament, big brother," before quickly turning and walking briskly toward the locker room door.

"I've still got another year," he had shouted over his shoulder as he kicked the door open and raced out into the hall.

"I DON'T have another year," Ron thought, the phrase quickly bringing him back to reality. "It is 10:00 a.m. now. At best, I have another 34 hours until my high school wrestling career ends."

The thought sent a chill up the boy's spine.

"Up-and-comer or not, this kid's going to have to come to grips with being in the consolation bracket very soon."

With a look of intensity to match his brother's from the day before, Ron grabbed his head gear and walked purposely toward his mat.

Chapter 106

Ron arched his back with every remaining ounce of energy he had. From his position, he couldn't see the scorer's table but he was fairly certain that someone with a towel would be coming out soon to tap the ref. He only needed to hold his position and thus, his seven to six lead for another 15 to 20 seconds.

The old joke about the Russian Pretzel Hold crossed his mind although he was in too much pain to smile. His opponent had been successful in trying to get leverage by pulling both of Ron's arms between Ron's legs, looking to find a way to turn him for back points. Ron had responded by hooking his inner knee around the boy's leg and pushing his own chest into the mat, as flat as possible. It wasn't a position that one could hold for an extended period of time but it did slow the kid from moving toward Ron's upper body and turning him.

Ron flexed every necessary muscle that he could. Having made it to the quarterfinals, he was set on ensuring that his journey didn't stop there, even though his lower back was starting to feel the effects of the gruelling tournament. Having come this far, he only needed to hold on for another dozen seconds to ensure that he placed in the tournament. Never mind that this opponent had beaten him at the Capital Tournament, Ron hadn't under-estimated the boy this time around and was about to reap the rewards, if he could only hold on.

The kid was getting desperate. He pushed Ron forward, hoping to break his arch and get the turn and nearfall points. Ron realized that there was a danger in going over. In desperation, he braced himself with the only body part that remained – his face. Pushing his own forehead and right cheek as hard as he could into the mat, Ron slid on sweat for an inch or two before his skin dried and adhered.

Another inch, "Ow, that hurt!!!" Yet, Ron planted his face even more firmly.

Another inch, maybe two ... if Ron had blurted out the profanities that were running through his head, he surely would be disqualified. The mat burned the entire right side of his face, nearly pulling his clenched eye open.

"How much longer could this possibly last?" he thought, biting his lip to keep from yelling. "How much longer can I possibly hold on?"

His first question was answered by the referee's whistle, negating the need to answer the second. Ron slumped to the mat while his exhausted opponent sat back, feeling the funk of disappointment.

It was a hard-fought victory, one that would show itself across Ron's face for weeks to come, but it was a victory nonetheless.

Stiff and sore, Ron slowly made his way to his feet and to center mat to have his arm raised.

Chapter 107

Nick hung up the hotel room phone and swallowed hard, tightening his stomach muscles to suppress the sick feeling that was doing its best to take over his mid-section. He clenched his fists and exhaled in a huff, similar to what he did in getting ready for a match.

The boy had watched his brother's semifinal win in relative obscurity, sitting with his hood up with his parents perched high in the stands. Now, for whatever reason, Ron was insisting that he needed Nick to be in his corner for the championship match.

"Focus," Nick thought as he tried to control his nerves.

Front and center at mat-side for the state championship was not a place for someone who shunned attention on his best day. Combined with Nick's unorthodox choice to relinquish his number one seed rather than wrestle for a team that had betrayed his coach was enough to push him over the edge … and that was even before considering what his brother was about to be walking into at the center of the mat.

The specter of Travis Spegidos hung in the air. Nick pondered for the millionth time whether or not anyone in the state was capable of beating the returning champion. He reflected on the past six weeks of his own training. Every bit of extra preparation – extended practices, dissection of Spegidos' matches, pushing himself far beyond what he had believed was possible – Ron had been with him every step of the way.

Nick grabbed his jacket, hat and gloves and ran out the door. He needed to go for a run to clear his mind and somehow get through the next 24 hours.

Backing out was not an option. He had given his word to Ron that he would do whatever he could to help him bring home the title … and there was no way that he would allow himself to fail his brother.

Chapter 108

Sean stared blankly at the message, neatly written on a page of the hotel's stationery, not sure of what it meant.

His mind was oatmeal after an especially rigorous "welcome to the company" day. He had signed the official acceptance of the company's offer right away at breakfast with Larry Darkins and had a few tense moments as he was asked to tell the story of how he had gotten his scar in addition to explaining some incidents from his heavy-partying years that turned up on his background check.

"I have faith in you, Sean," Larry had commented. "I've taken some heat about entrusting this role to someone with limited experience. You need to promise me you'll keep your nose clean; no more bar fights, and no more run-ins with the law."

Looking the man in the eye, Sean could only utter two words, "I promise."

From breakfast, he had been whisked over to corporate headquarters to meet the executives, the engineers, the project team, and seemingly everyone else under the sun.

By the end of the working lunch, he had already spent three hours getting to know the technology but was feeling like he had an uphill climb to learn enough to develop it. His main thoughts were focused on getting to know the team and gain their trust. He didn't know whether it was a step forward or backward when he joined them for dinner and was the only one to not drink an alcoholic beverage.

Several times during the day, he had wondered about the Riverside wrestlers. He knew the state tournament's first-day schedule well enough to get distracted by these thoughts around the time the quarterfinals and later the semifinals began. Thoughts of his boys' potential success made him eager to get back to the hotel to hear whether or not Kelly had been successful in contacting Nick to give the wrestler the encouragement he assumed would be lacking with Kreitzer at mat-side.

It had been over 16 hours from the time Larry Darkins had picked him up in the morning until his new boss dropped him off at night. He was amazed that the whole chain of events had not brought on a migraine.

During the entire walk from the car to the elevator and to his room, all he could think about was how he could possibly finish his degree at night if he was going to be expected to work until 9:00 every evening. Yet, he knew that he would find a way. Sean MacCallister always found a way.

Opening the door to his room, he had found the note, hand delivered by the concierge.

Message from Kelly:
Nick Castle defaulted his first two matches. I searched all day but couldn't find the kid. I ended up driving home.

What did it mean? Had Nick gotten injured? Had Sean failed him? Had he just bitten off more than he could chew on this new job as well? Would he fail the company too?

The young man's hands began trembling and he dropped the paper … a moment before the migraine hit.

Chapter 109

Nick's whole body shook as he trotted briskly across the parking lot. The violent wind cut at him from every angle, forcing him to pull his jacket collar over his face almost as much for physical protection as for concealing his identity as he approached the state tournament.

The boy had ditched his letterman's jacket for the weekend and had instead chosen to wear his canvas wrestling jacket under a lighter fall coat. Wanting to avoid being recognized at all costs, he feared that wearing the letterman's jacket, which had always been a source of pride, would have resulted in people pointing and surmising that the big "R" on his chest stood for "Reject."

Nick's first close-up glance at his older brother in the past two days made him cringe. Ron was standing in the lobby as promised, dressed in sweats. The right side of the wrestler's face looked like it had been dragged behind a car.

"Thanks for coming," Ron commented, leading his younger brother past security and toward the warm-up area.

The finals would begin at 7:00. The brothers' one-on-one time the remainder of the afternoon would be spent warming up and strategizing with a single focus in mind – beat Spegidos.

Chapter 110

Ron sat quietly on the warm-up mat, stretching his quadriceps. His hood was up, hiding his eyes as he stared vacantly out at the 125-pound championship match. He had mentioned to Coach Tyler that he needed some time alone to prepare. The man had gone straight to the team and informed them that if anyone got within fifty feet of the potential state champion, that person would not see the following dawn.

Ten feet away, his brother paced around, seemingly as nervous as Ron himself. Nick was the extra guard and would also be acting as Ron's assistant coach during this contest.

It was fortuitous that Hermanns had also made it to the finals. The boy had reminded Coach Tyler of his promise that, should he make it to the state championship, Mr. Hermanns could join him at mat-side as the assistant coach. Ron immediately used the opening to get Nick into his corner, arguing that, if anyone in the state had studied Spegidos enough to find a weakness, it had been Nick.

Although neither finalist would admit it out loud, they both relished the opportunity to stick it to their Assistant Principal for his treatment of Coach MacCallister. Neither would allow the man the satisfaction of taking any kind of credit for their success.

Not surprisingly, Kreitzer had been livid, demanding that the second chair was rightfully his. Ron had never seen Coach Tyler look more menacing than at the moment when he informed Kreitzer that, should the Assistant Principal come anywhere near Tyler's wrestlers during the championships, he would be physically removed by the head coach himself.

The head coach then revealed that he had received an offer to coach at the university level again the following year. It was exactly where he needed to be … far from Riverside politics. He tendered his resignation effective upon the conclusion of the 145-pound final.

This, of course, brought Ron to the match at hand. Within the next 15 minutes, he would once again step onto the mat opposite Travis Spegidos. Nobody expected Ron to win. In fact, nobody expected that he would last through the opening period, considering the nature of his first two losses this year to the same opponent.

Did that mean anything? Ron thought about the previous contests. In only four instances this past year had a wrestler even lasted the entire match with Spegidos. He dominated his opponents with superior strength, but more than that, had the best technique of anyone that Ron had ever seen step on the mat. Yet, they would start their match, as all matches began, tied at zero.

The 125-pound match entered its third period and Ron changed position to stretch his back. He had completely changed his wrestling style in late December. "Undue strain," his doctor cautioned him, "could put you at risk of losing the use of your legs forever. You should stop wrestling."

Unable to bear losing his life's dream, Ron had informed the doctor that he would consider the man's advice, but reminded him that he was eighteen and could make his own decisions. Nobody, including his parents, needed to know the risks.

Rather than quit, he chose only to wrestle defensively during January and February, avoiding lifting and undue spinal stress. He hadn't gone back to his traditional, more aggressive style until the state tournament.

As the 125-pound match ended, Ron began to rise, promising himself that he would be a state champion by night's end. Then, realizing how empty the words in his head sounded, he bit his lip and swallowed hard, knowing what he had to do to make the promise real.

Jumping up, he crossed to Nick in five quick strides. Pulling his brother toward him, he grabbed him by the back of the neck and held their foreheads together. Then, closing his eyes, he stated the words aloud.

"Tonight I will be a state champion. I promise you," he said.

He could feel his brother's discomfort as the easily-embarrassed boy snorted, "uh, huh," and tried to pull away.

Grasping him tightly for a final moment, he continued with the part that he dreaded.

"I promise I'll win the state championship tonight …" he reiterated. Then, swallowing hard, he continued, "… or I'll die trying."

He was prepared to wrestle this match as if it were the final match of his life. Nobody knew at the time that this was exactly what the match would be.

Chapter 111

Nick sat on the edge of his chair as the chills continued to run down his spine. How could he be so nervous when his brother seemed so calm?

There was no doubt that Spegidos was the best wrestler in the state. In the past two years, he had racked up an impressive 65 wins with zero losses. He had appropriately been named the state's "Mr. Wrestling" prior to the championship round beginning, a designation voted-on by the coaches.

Nick watched in awe as his older brother strode to center mat, took a knee, and fastened his green ankle band. He sensed absolutely no fear in his sibling, despite indications that the thousands of spectators filling the stands viewed the dark-haired boy as a piece of raw meat about to be devoured by the Spegidos lion.

Something had changed in Ron but there was an overwhelming sense of something familiar. He was going off to battle in the only venue that had ever mattered to him. With all that had happened in the boy's life these past two years, just the fact that he had walked to the center of the mat was miracle enough. That he had done so exuding such confidence seemed more like an insane man's cry for help.

Yet, what had affected Nick the most did not have much to do with the match itself. It had more to do with unfinished business, something out in the shadows. In an event unprecedented in Nick's sixteen and a half years, before walking out to face his opponent, Ron had grabbed his younger brother and pulled him close, startling the younger boy.

As the words left his brother's mouth, promising to be a state champion, Nick felt like he and Ron were, for the first time, fully intertwined. Due to all of Nick's studying of Spegidos, he felt like this match was a team effort.

Having no idea what he may be able to contribute, he focused on the mat, ignoring all of the spectators he was sure were pointing at him and making comments. He even caught Spegidos' eye as the boy glared at him while he walked slowly, methodically out to center mat, like an animal stalking its prey.

"Let him look," Nick thought. "Let them all look."

Whatever remarks were being thrown about behind Nick's back didn't register.   He heard only two words: "Ready ... wrestle."

Chapter 112

The first period wasn't what the crowd expected. Had Ron been watching the spectators, paying attention to anything other than his opponent, he would have seen many people walking toward the concession stands.

This would be a short match. Spegidos would pin Ron in the first period. Everyone in the audience knew this. Everyone in the audience was wrong.

Nick's heart was pounding as he sat in the assistant coach's chair beside Coach Tyler. Everything calm and measured about Spegidos disappeared the instant the match started. He attacked with the vigor of a rabid wolf, immediately moving in, muscling Ron's upper body, and going for the throw, the kill.

He had started so many matches this way, always with the same result. He clearly intended for this one to be no different, focused mainly on chasing the "fastest pin" record for a state title match. This being the case, there was a brief look of shock on his face when he realized that Ron was no longer in his grasp. In a show of uncommon quickness, Ron had ducked under, pushing Spegidos' arms in the air and penetrating his unprotected legs.

Time stood still and the crowd gasped as Ron Castle lifted his opponent into the air and took him to the mat, straight to his back. "Two points green," instructed the ref.

Before his opponent could react, Ron had locked his arm, keeping him from turning. Spegidos was caught facing the lights. All it would take was one slap of the mat for the contest to be over.

It was in roughly this position that the two boys would stay for the remainder of the first period. Each grunt from Spegidos caused Ron to re-focus and adjust his weight. Knowing that it was unlikely that he could pin the stronger boy, he put all of the weight that he could on his opponent's chest, in hopes of breaking him down. Finally, after nearly two minutes of minor adjustments and counter-adjustments by the two competitors, the foghorn sounded, allowing the two athletes to separate and the referee to announce, "Three points green."

Chapter 113

The referee flipped the coin, resulting in the green side up. As Ron deferred his choice, he cringed for a moment, before shaking off the possibility that he may not make it to the third period to make his decision.

Spegidos chose "neutral" but came out much more cautiously for the second period. Ron's memory flipped through all of the Spegidos matches he had watched in recent months. In the first period, as planned, he had taken advantage of his opponent's total lack of respect for him, using it to his advantage and refusing to be intimidated by the champion's inhuman aggression. This period, he would need to change his strategy as Spegidos became more cautious.

The two boys moved toward each other and Ron heard his opponent panting a bit. Staying off of one's shoulder blades for the better part of a period took significant effort, which helped to even the playing field for the older Castle.

Despite Ron's attempted defense, he found the stronger boy tying up with him. The thought that he didn't have a clean shot was going through his mind as he felt his neck pulled toward the mat as Spegidos completed the duck-under, passing below Ron's right arm and arriving behind him, pulling him to the mat.

"Two points red," the ref bellowed.

Spegidos immediately put a leg in but Ron successfully eluded giving the boy reasonable hip position. Then, as suddenly as Spegidos had struck, Ron countered, rolling through and crashing all of his weight into his opponent's thigh causing his nemesis to lose his grip and his control.

"Reversal, two points green," was the call as Ron came out on top, fighting to keep Spegidos on his back. While he wasn't as fortunate in hooking an arm as he had been in the first period, he did manage to keep the champion from turning to his belly for several seconds before the stronger teen was able to power himself over to the safety of a chest-down position, avoiding giving up any points.

Though he was getting winded, Ron knew he could not let up, even with a seven to two lead. He inserted a leg and tried his best to work Spegidos' beefy arms to no avail as, eventually, the period ended with no further scoring.

As he dismounted and heard himself panting, a fear suddenly swept over him that taking the match to one of the nation's top wrestlers for two periods was a magician's feat. So much of any wrestling match is spent second to second – anticipating, reacting and creating new openings. He was getting concerned that his hat was out of rabbits and that he needed additional insight for a refill. For the first time ever, Ron looked to his corner for guidance in making his final choice.

* * *

Nick froze as he saw his brother staring at him, searching for an answer. He looked to Coach Tyler but in a moment of inspiration, he suddenly felt his right thumb go up.

At first, Ron's glance told Nick that he was nuts but then he nodded his head as if he understood. For two periods, the older Castle had spent nearly the entire match on top. Spegidos had yet to find a way off the bottom. Even if Ron could ride for an additional half minute, he could continue to wear down his weary competition and leave him with little time to catch up.

Nick felt himself using as many muscles as the two boys donning referee's position at center mat as he sat tensely, hoping that his direction proved to be sound.

The whistle blew, and Spegidos rushed forward. Within seconds, he tried to sit out and proceed to his feet but Ron was a step ahead of him and put him straight to his back again for a moment before he was able to roll through to his stomach. This time, as he moved to his knees and then quickly back to his base, Ron inserted both legs and powered Spegidos' arms out from under him, sending the boy crashing face-first to the mat. With time becoming the greatest factor, Spegidos fought off half nelsons from the left and right as he crawled with Ron on his back to the mat's edge and finally managed to fling both of them out of bounds with just under half a minute remaining.

Nick's stomach was in knots. As he watched Ron race back to center mat, the senior's own panting was more than offset by his opponent's wheezing as the two boys got into position for one last volley. This was already one of the longest contests Spegidos had participated in all year. All Ron needed to do was keep up his attack and not give up the pin and he would realize the dream both Castle brothers had pursued for nearly a decade.

The words, "Ready … wrestle," rang out, unleashing a sight that lasted a mere instant but was forever burned into Nick's mind in slow motion.

From his position at the side of the mat, Nick had not seen the elbow coming any more than his brother had.   It wasn't uncommon for the bottom man to throw an elbow back, trying to throw his rider. What was uncommon was the strength behind this one and the ferocity with which this elbow connected with Ron's left eye and temple, splitting his eyebrow in the process.

Nick felt his feet on the mat an instant before he realized that he had leapt out of his chair. His heart palpitations were masked only by his cry of, "RON!" as he watched his brother seem to hang in the air for a moment and then crumple to the mat, lying completely motionless.

Chapter 114

Ron felt arms pulling him up. Had Spegidos somehow gotten behind him? What was the score?

"Oh please, God, no!" he prayed.

This couldn't be a replay of two years earlier. He tried to resist but his body wouldn't respond. All he could do was stare at the bright blue blur which was the mat and wait for those powerful arms to slam him back to the mat, turn him over and pin him.

Ron's mind feverishly moved through the match. What had happened? He was supposed to be on top. Why wasn't he on top? The last thing he remembered was a numb feeling in both of his forearms, having alternated grabbing each ferociously as he had applied half nelsons and various other moves trying to turn his opponent. Sore arms could not possibly account for this total lack of bodily function. He contemplated his first period takedown, second period roll and the minor strains both had put on his lower back. He hadn't felt any damage but now, in his panic, he began pondering the cumulative effect.

His thoughts spun back to his recent MRI results and the inconclusive one. Then, they reeled even further back to his December appointment when the doctor had cautioned him to consider quitting wrestling.

Was it truly all working out in the worst way? Was he about to lose his bid for the state title and the use of his legs all at once?

"I've got you."

Ron was startled by the voice behind him as it certainly wasn't the one he had expected to hear. The fog continued to clear as he recognized the calm tone.

"I've got you, big brother," Nick's voice continued as the older Castle brother tried to sort out what had happened and why he couldn't seem to open his left eye.

Chapter 115

Nick surprised himself as he pulled all of the elements into place. With Ron safely in his corner, Nick summoned the trainer who was ready with cotton, tape and a number of other materials, which she used to fix the cut over Ron's eye.

"Ron, are you all right?"

Nick's question was met with a bleary gaze and eventually a positive-sounding grunt. He knew that the injury time was ticking away, he just didn't know what could possibly be done to get his brother to a coherent state to finish the 25 seconds remaining on the clock.

It was fortunate for both of the boys that the trainer was already thinking along these lines. She stuffed something in Ron's nose that made his good eye open wide and his other eye, which was quickly turning black and puffing shut, take notice as well. Ron placed both hands on the mat and tried to push himself up as Nick smiled thinking, "he's still got the tenacity to finish."

The smile quickly faded as Ron lost his balance and fell back to his butt. Out of the corner of his eye, Nick noticed the referee crossing toward them. He hoped that they had enough injury time left for Ron to regain his faculties.

"Are you ready to go?" the referee asked Ron.

Nick felt a dash of joy as Ron nodded. Yet, that joy came to an abrupt stop as he heard Coach Tyler's voice behind him tell the ref, "He can't finish the match."

Nick went somewhere beyond livid. This was the final match of his brother's high school career, a chance to live his dream, and a moment to show the entire world that miracles do happen. He felt his hands clench into fists as he turned to face his former coach. This time, he would not give up. He had nothing to lose for fighting and Ron had everything to lose if he did not.

As Nick got to his feet and turned to confront Coach Tyler, he was surprised that the man didn't look at him. He didn't seem to pay attention to Ron either, he only stared out across the mat.

Nick followed the coach's gaze over to the opposing corner where Spegidos seemed to be in pain as his trainer and coach felt the wrestler's left arm.

"He fractured his olecranon on my wrestler's head," Tyler continued, nodding toward Spegidos as he looked the ref in the eye.

The ref seemed to be losing patience.

"He what?"

"His olecranon," the coach continued, "the tip of his elbow, he broke it. He can't wrestle like that. He has to forfeit."

The situation didn't look that bad to Nick. Certainly Spegidos wouldn't forfeit with Ron in the shape he was in. Why would Coach Tyler even suggest such a thing? Why would … ? The answer hit Nick like a ton of bricks as he realized his coach was creating a diversion, distracting the ref to buy Ron some more time.

"He just hit his funny bone," the ref continued. "It's nothing serious, he'll be back."

"Nothing serious?!!!" Coach Tyler began to yell. "He can't even bend the thing. What do you think is going to happen when Castle here gets on top of him and starts twisting on that left arm? He's going to have some permanent damage."

As the two men argued, Nick looked down and saw his brother's focus continue to improve. Ron reached for his brother's hand, grabbed it, and pulled himself to his feet. Losing his balance for an instant, he grabbed his younger sibling and held onto him as his coach and the referee walked over to Spegidos' corner, discussed matters with the West Clay coach, and then returned to Ron, exchanging words all the way.

Finally, the ref looked at Ron.

"Can you wrestle?" he asked.

Ron turned his attention to the referee, staring the man down with a look of grim determination.

"If he can, I can," the wrestler answered.

Chapter 116

Spegidos assumed the bottom position. As Ron went to mount, he noted that his opponent's left elbow was beginning to bruise and swell.

"That thing looks like my face feels," the groggy wrestler thought for a moment. He opted to mount on Spegidos' right side. When the whistle blew, he focused on his rival's right arm.

Ron marveled at how easy it was to break his opponent down. Based on Spegidos' lethargic start, he believed that there may have been a grain of truth to his coach's assertion about the boy's arm. It would be easy to turn the champion. With no left arm to protect against Ron's onslaught, he could make history.

"*Castle Pins State Legend*," the headlines would read. It would be a story the state's wrestling community would talk about forever … and one that would possibly ruin Spegidos.

As the seconds ticked away, it was the latter portion that got to Ron. So close to seeing his own legacy turned to nothing, he chose not to diminish that of his opponent. He rode out the match on the strength of a half-baked half nelson.

Chapter 117

Ron reached down and removed his leg band. In his daze, he barely noticed the thundering roar coming from the crowd. Having just wrestled the match of his life, he didn't even consider the fact that it would be his last. He would go to college out east the following year and turn his focus to academics.

As his hand was raised in victory, Castle felt the blood momentarily leave his face. He stood there dumbfounded and embraced the moment unlike any other.

Crossing the mat to acknowledge his opponent's coaches, he turned back and noticed his brother. What if he hadn't grown up with a brother who pushed him so hard? What if Ron hadn't had the competitive nature to be pushed in return? Would tonight have ever happened?

An uncommon urge raced over the boy. As the world watched, he raced across the mat and jumped into Nick's arms. His little brother held him extra high for everyone to see.

The past was gone and the future looked bright as for six minutes, on a bitterly cold February night, Ron Castle defied the odds and proved himself to be the best.

Epilogue

We're ready for him."

Sean took one last look around the hospital waiting room, feeling a bit overwhelmed by how many faces were looking back at him. The same faces would spend the next several hours waiting for word on the outcome of his experimental procedure.

At his core, he was feeling surprisingly resigned, open to both the best and worst case scenarios that had been described to him – the elimination of his post-concussion symptoms or death.

It was an odd time for Sean to think about Nick. He still wondered why the boy hadn't wrestled at the state tournament but had already made a steadfast promise to ask Nick in person after the restraining order ended. Seeing and supporting Nick gave Sean added incentive to survive the surgery.

He had put out a seemingly innocent call weeks earlier, seeing if anyone would be willing to visit him during his recovery. He was shocked by the number of people who had travelled, some nearly a thousand miles, to be there for him today.

Kelly had led a convoy of half the Beta Beta Beta house. The big man had given up precious time in front of his new big screen TV, purchased by Sean, to ensure that his friend felt supported.

Amy and her boyfriend, a handful of Sean's new co-workers and several other friends appeared out of nowhere. Julee Novak had shown up a week early for an extended visit. It was her soft hand that Sean held until the hospital staff wheeled him from the room.

For someone who had always feared dying alone, the overflowing crowd gave him added serenity.

Sean closed his eyes and let his other senses take over: smelling the sterile hospital air and hearing the sounds of hospital staff in the hall and the drone of televisions as they passed patient rooms on the way to the operating room.

Whether or not the procedure would provide the desired results, the thing that was clear to the young man was that he had already built a very solid family.

"I'm going to count backward from ten," the anaesthetist said. Sean took a quick look around at the people who were about to open up his head.

He thought of tomorrow; the rest of his life started tomorrow. "Thank you for my life," he prayed silently as he closed his eyes, breathed deeply and went to sleep.

He looked at the name and took a quick look around before stretching on his tip toes to run his fingers over the engraved, "Ron Castle – 135" which now embossed the Riverside wrestling room wall. Sweat from his afternoon workout ran down his arm as he admired the only name added to the "Ring of Champions" this year, a location reserved for those who had done the improbable and succeeded in their quest for a state title.

Yet, his brother had not only done the improbable. Many would say he had done the impossible. Going from a wheelchair one year to beating one of the most storied wrestlers in the state's history the next, the older Castle certainly deserved to have his name on the wall of the wrestling room where Nick's wasn't ... nor possibly ever would be.

He reflected for a moment on other amazing wrestlers who had not made it to the ring due to not quite reeling in the state title. Dino in particular came to mind. While Nick considered this a travesty, school administration had refused to budge, stating that the line between "state champion" and "non-state-champion" was very clear. The politics gave the boy a headache.

After several weeks of stare-downs with Mr. Kreitzer in the halls, Nick and the man had finally exchanged words in a most unpleasant manner, a parlay which ended with the man remarking, "You just try to get back onto my wrestling team next year. You won't even make it past the first week."

The thought of wrestling anywhere other than Riverside stung him as he strolled across the mat, breathing deeply to fill his lungs with musty Riverside wrestling room air. His eyes began to mist a little as he thought of all of the memories this room held for him, his home away from home the past two years.

Maybe things would change. It was always possible that Kreitzer would leave after all of the heat the man had taken over his baseless allegations which had led to Coach MacCallister being fired. The man's threats certainly hadn't stopped Nick's quest. He had gone undefeated through Freestyle season and had already started to add well-toned muscle due to his weight-lifting routine.

As he again thought forward to the next year's state tournament, he promised himself that he would be there ... and knew he wouldn't be alone. An unsigned postcard had arrived a few weeks earlier postmarked from a city far away. Based on its message, there was no doubt in Nick's mind who it was from.

Win the state tournament next year. Integrity: no excuses, no compromises. I promise I will be there.

He stared at Ron's name again. As he had promised over a year earlier, there was a state championship plaque sitting on the mantle at the Castle house. The boy cringed for a moment, hoping that he had not given up the prime opportunity to add one of his own.

"It's of no consequence," he thought. His refusal to give up doing what was right by his coach this year in no way meant that he was giving up his dream of becoming a state champion.

He took one final look at his brother's name, turned out the lights and watched the room fall into a calm darkness as he slipped out the door.

The afternoon's workout had left him in desperate need of a shower. Today, cleaning up would be especially crucial … he had a date to get to.

He headed down the hall with well-earned confidence in his walk, continuing his journey to be the best.